THE OBSIDIAN SISTERHOOD

2

A TANGLE OF OBSIDIAN

LYDIA M. HAWKE

**Published by Michem Publishing,
Canada**

This is a work of fiction. Names, characters, places, and incidents either are the sole product of the author's imagination or are used fictitiously, and any resemblance to actual persons, living or dead, business establishments, events, or locales is entirely coincidental.

A Tangle of Obsidian

June 3, 2025
Copyright © 2025 by Linda Poitevin

Cover design by Deranged Doctor Design
Interior design by AuthorTree

ISBN: 978-1-989457-36-8
MICHEM PUBLISHING

Dedicated to the warrior in all women of every age.
May we never stop fighting.

CHAPTER 1

"Fuck," I muttered, staring at the tree stump in the center of the clearing. It sat twenty feet from where I crouched, unadorned with so much as a single strand of spiderweb.

Again.

I lifted my hand from the half-frozen earth before me and uncurled my icy, aching fingers from around the stone in my grip. The polished black square sat unmoving on my palm, just as a stone should. Except this one was supposed to do more. It *had* done more. So much more. I'd seen it cocoon and destroy men in the past, and I'd wanted it to do the same to the tree stump now.

Not because the stump deserved such treatment, but because I needed to know that *I* was in control rather than the stone. That I could stop its awful power before it—before I—killed again. Because for better or worse, I had become the stone's keeper, and its wielder, at least until we found the being who had brought it to Earth along with five others of equally terrifying power. The alien being that the Obsidian Sisterhood had named Methuselah.

Although, if what Sister Margaret had heard about the alien was true, I might remain the stone's keeper beyond that, but that—that was a future worry. With a lot of other worries between now and then. A lot. Such as getting to Quebec City, and finding the Ursuline nuns who had last had Methuselah in their care, and keeping Phoenix, Talia, and Sister Margaret alive until we did. Keeping them safe.

None of which I was feeling particularly confident about in view of my continued failure to master the one weapon we had against Mage magick. My gaze went back to the unblemished stump.

"Fuck," I said again.

I closed my fingers around the stone again and pushed stiffly to my feet. The November sun had long since disappeared, taking the last of its faint warmth with it. Leafless maples and oaks sat in silence amid deepening shadows, and I shivered, tucking the stone back into my front jeans pocket. I'd lost track of how long I'd been out here again, but it had been long enough that my fingers hovered somewhere between painful and numb. My hips didn't feel much better, and I wouldn't be surprised to hear them creak when I started back toward the little cottage a few dozen feet away.

For the moment, however, I remained where I was, flexing and curling my stiff fingers, not yet ready to join the others. Light spilled from one of the cottage windows—the bedroom I shared with Phoenix—into the gathering dark. As far as safe houses went, the place Talia had found for us wasn't fancy, but it was enough for four women needing to lie low while they healed after narrowly escaping capture and/or death at the hands of various Mages. Well, three women, because despite the injuries I'd sustained in my own fight, the stone had taken care of any healing I'd needed. Which was a whole other problem as far as I was concerned, but I digressed.

Location-wise, the cottage sat an hour outside the city of Kingston, which meant that we could still get supplies, but we were isolated enough to satisfy Talia—who remained the vigilant cop despite having taken an extended leave of absence so she could look after us.

Her words, not mine, because the *looking after us* part was debatable, in my opinion, given the pins and plates holding her wrist together after our fight with Eldon Rusk and his mountain-monster in the woods that night. But she'd been right about us being safe here. A woman from the local mosque, one of the Obsidian Sisterhood that Sister Margaret was part of, delivered our groceries once a week. We'd gone into town for medical appointments needed by Phoenix and Talia, and no one had followed any of us for the entire time we'd been here.

All seven weeks of it.

Seven weeks of trying and failing to tap into the stone's powers, all while knowing that if the Mages weren't out there looking for us, it meant they were looking for Methuselah. Which was actually worse. Much worse.

I scowled, thinking back to that night and the consortium of Mages that Rusk had claimed he belonged to. Mages in general were bad enough, but an entire, organized consortium? The idea was terrifying. Especially if Rusk had been telling the truth about them already having the other five stones. Because that meant that if they got to Methuselah before we did, before *I* did ...

I drew a steadying breath. One step at a time. Talia saw the orthopedic surgeon tomorrow morning—hopefully for the last time—and Phoenix had one more appointment with the eye surgeon in the afternoon, and then we'd be on our way to Quebec City and the Ursuline nuns. Given that the alien had disappeared from their care eight months ago, it wasn't a lot to go on, but it was a place to start. And it was more than the Mages had.

We hoped.

My head jerked around at the sound of a twig snapping. With my heart lodged in my throat and the stone, useless as it was these days, back in my hand, I scanned the darkening trees for long seconds, but there was nothing there, nothing in the clearing, nothing around Talia's SUV where it sat in the pool of light from the window, covered in fallen leaves. I held my breath and listened harder, but only a rustle of wind stirring the treetops punctuated the silence. The same silence that had sat over us for the last seven weeks and weighed more heavily on me with each passing day.

Just as our inertia did.

Compressing my lips against the omnipresent irritation that had taken up residence beside that heaviness, I returned the stone to its pocket—again—and headed around the cottage to the sagging covered porch clinging to its front. I looked down the long, narrow driveway that wound through barren trees to a road that wasn't much wider, saw nothing there, either, and with a sigh, climbed the stairs and pushed open the door.

A rush of warm, humid air washed over me as I stepped inside. Sister Margaret, wearing her usual apron over a plain navy skirt and white blouse, with her habitual pale blue veil in place over her short hair, looked up from stirring a steaming pot at the stove, a product of today's grocery delivery.

"Soup," she said cheerfully, as though I'd asked. "Vegetable lentil. With spinach."

The irritability I'd tried to leave outside sauntered in to join me. Good, simple, nutritious food. True to her training at St. Paul's under Mother Annunciata's frugal hand, the nun had proved herself a master of producing it, even though her right arm had been in a cast until yesterday, and I knew I should be more grateful. Cooking was what the nun knew how to do, she was better at it than the rest of us, and it wasn't her fault that me and my grumpy ass would have sold her to the Mages in a heartbeat in exchange for a hamburger.

I wouldn't have, of course. Not really.

But maybe.

I salivated at the idea of meat—real, actual meat—then swallowed my irritation and forced a smile. "That sounds delicious," I lied.

I looked over to where Talia sat on one of the kitchen chairs, awkwardly tugging her boots from her feet with her one good hand. Unlike Sister Margaret, she'd had her cast removed after only a week, when the orthopedic surgeon had pinned her wrist instead—and then warned her of all kinds of dire outcomes should she use it too much before the pins were removed again. For the most part, thankfully, she had chosen to listen. Also thankfully, the pins were scheduled to come out tomorrow, because even though she'd followed the instructions, she hadn't been happy about it, and her irritability was not helping with my own.

I caught her eye now and motioned at her boots in silent inquiry. The Toronto police detective, who'd put herself on the line to protect Phoenix, taken a leave of absence to follow me to Kingston, and then stayed to babysit us, shook her head. We'd come to an unspoken agreement not to discuss our various injuries after our battle against Rusk. Essentially, it worked like this: each of us trusted the other to ask for help if she needed it, and each of us trusted the other to give it.

If we could.

I thought about my failed efforts to use the stone and wondered if she'd seen. How much she'd seen. I hadn't heard her—or maybe I had. Maybe that was the twig I'd heard snap.

"You went out?" I asked.

Talia set her boots beside the wall beneath the coat hooks, alongside those of Sister Margaret and Phoenix. "You were busy," she said. "I didn't want to disturb you."

So she *had* watched. Wonderful. I shrugged out of my coat and hung it on one of the hooks, then slipped my boots off and lined them up with the others. Somehow, knowing that someone else had witnessed my failure to harness the stone's power made the problem seem more … foreboding? Serious?

Insurmountable.

But if there was any judgment in Talia's brown eyes, I couldn't see it. Not when she avoided my gaze the way she did. I frowned, suddenly aware of the aura of tension surrounding her, visible in the deeper than usual lines around her mouth and the tightness of the dark skin over her cheekbones, as if she feared giving something away.

I inhaled through flared nostrils, and Talia's gaze flashed to mine. She gave a tiny, almost imperceptible shake of her head. *Not now*, it said. Slowly, I released my breath again as Sister Margaret looked around from her soup making and called for Phoenix to come and set the table. Talia headed toward the bathroom, ostensibly to wash for dinner, as the young woman came out of the room she and I shared at the far end of the open living area. Neither had far to travel.

The website listing had called the cottage "rustic," but "adequate" would have been a more accurate descriptor. The walls, floor, and ceiling were all bare plywood, and apart from one table lamp in the living room, the electrical fixtures were equally bare. There was a two-piece bathroom (the shower was outdoors and involved too many spiderwebs for any of us, so we sponge bathed in the kitchen sink), a combined kitchen-living space with furnishings that had seen far better days, and two small bedrooms. One of the bedrooms had a set of bunk beds with thin mattresses—that was the one Phoenix and I shared—and one had a sagging, queen-size bed that touched all four walls and required Sister Margaret to climb over its foot board to get into it.

Talia and her not-quite-legal sidearm slept on the lumpy couch.

I gave Phoenix a distracted half-smile as she and I sidled past one another behind the couch—Phoenix on her way to the shelf of dishes above the small kitchen counter, I on my path to find out what Talia was hiding. I stepped into the bathroom behind the detective and closed the door. Our gazes met in the reflection in the mirror above the sink where she washed her hands.

"What's happened?" I asked.

She didn't prevaricate any more than I had. "The ice," she said. "The edges are broken along the shoreline. Like something's been walking there."

My breath hitched a little in my chest, and I swallowed a flutter of panic as my brain immediately conjured up the worst-case scenario. *Mages. The Mages found us.* But I dug my fingernails into my palms and put the brakes on my wannabe runaway thoughts. *More information first,* I told myself. *If Talia thought it was Mages, she would have led with that.*

"Animals?" I suggested hopefully.

"Not likely. I jumped up and down on it and couldn't break it." Her reflection's expression was grim as she turned off the tap and reached for the threadbare hand towel hanging beside the sink. "I found footprints, too. From something big enough to leave indentations in the frozen ground."

Ice shot through my veins. She didn't mean … she couldn't mean …

"How big?" I asked.

She heaved another sigh. "Huge," she admitted. "Mountain sized."

She did mean.

The goliath had found us. The monster that had

ripped apart the motel with its bare granite paws and taken Phoenix, the one that had tossed Talia aside like a hurricane tossed a twig—it had found us. The panic I'd been trying to hold back exploded through my chest. A hundred disparate thoughts followed suit in my brain.

I haven't mastered the stone yet. Sweet Mary, I can't even access it right now. Maybe I've been trying too hard. Maybe I haven't been trying hard enough. Maybe it was never the stone at all. Maybe the Mages' own magick just backfired and—

"Pack your bag," I said. "We're leaving. Now."

CHAPTER 2

I didn't wait for Talia's response. Instead, as I strode to the room I shared with Phoenix, I bellowed over my shoulder at Sister Margaret, telling her to turn off the stove, leave everything, and pack her things. By the time Talia followed me scant seconds later, I'd already hauled a duffel bag out from under the bottom bunk, opened the top dresser drawer, and started transferring Phoenix's few belongings from drawer to bag. Four pairs of underwear, three pairs of socks, a spare bra, two pairs of jeans, three T-shirts, and her hormone pills. I shoved the drawer closed and moved on to the one beneath it. My hand closed over my own jeans, and then Talia's warm hand closed over mine.

"Stop," she said, holding me still. "*Think.* If it wanted to hurt us, it already would have. It's been watching, Monica. That's all. Just watching."

She was the only person alive who called me Monica—just Monica, without the *Sister* title that I still laid claim to despite having been thrown out of the church some twenty-seven years before. Not that I was counting. And not that it mattered in the least at the moment, because *goliath.*

"That's—just—" I jerked free of her hold and waved the jeans at her in astonishment. Disbelief. Affront. All of the above. I caught a glimpse of Phoenix's concerned face over the cop's shoulder and tried to rein in my rising ire.

"A living mountain has *just* been watching us," I repeated, lowering my voice from a near shout to just loud, "and that makes the situation better *how*, exactly?"

Talia sighed. "I agree it's concerning, but—" She held up her good hand to ward off my anger. "*But*," she said, "if we panic, we'll just get ourselves into trouble. More trouble. There are signs that the goliath has been out there for at least a few days, maybe longer, and—"

The rest of what she said faded into gibberish in my head as I stared at her in both horror and astonishment. Horror because *fucking monster watching us,* and astonishment because—

"How," I grated between my teeth, "in the *hell*"—I drew myself up to my full five feet four inches—"can you be so calm? They've *found* us, Talia. The Mages have *found* us, and—"

"And we'll leave tomorrow," she said, "as soon as—"

I didn't let her finish. Cop or not, she obviously didn't understand just how much danger we were in, and I wouldn't—couldn't—let her take the lead on this. Dimly, I noted that Phoenix, never a fan of conflict, had departed again.

"We'll leave *now,*" I snapped, "because if that—that *thing*—really is here, and the Mages know where we are—"

"Even if they do," she interrupted in the ultra-reasonable tone of voice she pulled out when she thought I needed to be talked off a ledge, "we're far more likely to see something coming for us in the daylight than we are in the dark, regardless of whether it's the goliath or a Mage. Besides, what would you have us do? Drive around all night waiting for the train station to open? And what about our appointments? I can't keep these damned pins in forever"—she waved her arm at me—"and Phoenix needs to see the ophthalmologist before we go haring off to another province in search of Methuselah."

Closing my eyes, I gritted my teeth together tightly enough to make them—and my jaw—ache. I *would* have had us drive around all night, to be honest. But the reminder of the injuries that Talia and Phoenix were still recovering from made me pause long enough for my cooler self to finally prevail, and to admit that okay, maybe I *should* let her take the lead on this, because I was obviously in no state of mind to be doing so myself right now.

In fact, I was so on edge at the mere idea of the goliath that I felt like I was going to crawl out of my skin. Like I—

I frowned at myself. And at the thought, because *wait*. That wasn't quite it. There was more to it than that. It was more like—

My eyes snapped open, and I stared down at the jeans I still clutched in my right hand. More precisely, at the hand doing the clutching. Even more precisely, at the faint ripple that traveled between the tendons on the back of the hand and up my wrist and forearm, disappearing into the sleeve of my—

Oh, hell.

"Monica?" Talia's voice held a new tone, an edge of alertness. "What is it?"

My gaze lifted to hers, then went past it to the door. "Get Phoenix and Sister Margaret," I said, dropping the jeans back into the open drawer I'd taken them from. "Get your boots and coats on. Grab whatever you—"

A scream cut me off. For a heart-destroying instant, I thought it was Phoenix, and my entire world teetered on the precipice of agony. Talia, however, spun around to face not the bedroom door to the rest of the cottage, but the window behind her, the one overlooking the car and the clearing beyond. The scream came again.

Raw, hoarse, anguished—and unmistakably that of a monster that was built like a mountain. The goliath was coming for us. And where there was a goliath, there were—

"Mages!" Phoenix shouted from the kitchen she'd returned to. "They're here!"

TALIA HAD HER GUN IN HAND AND WAS HALFWAY ACROSS the tiny living room when I caught up to her and pulled her to a stop.

"Not you," I said. "Me."

"But the stone—" She shot a quick glance at Phoenix and Sister Margaret, seeming to remember that they didn't know about my impasse where the stone was concerned. Yet. Her soft, worried brown eyes returned to meet mine and, tightening her lips, she shook her head. "You can't face them alone."

"We don't have time to argue, Talia. Take Sister Margaret and Phoenix out the back window to the car," I said, "then come for me at the front."

"Monica, you can't—"

"I can," I said, "because I have to. Now go. I'll hold them off as long as I can."

The goliath outside screamed again and, without waiting for her agreement, I headed for the front door. A pale, wide-eyed Phoenix stepped between me and it. "Sister Monica?" she whispered.

She sought reassurance, I knew, but I had neither time nor inclination to give it. I might not have access to the stone's powers, I was learning, but it sure as hell still had access to me, and right now, it wanted to be out on the porch.

I stepped around Phoenix and reached for the knob. "I'll be fine," I said. "Do as Talia says."

"But, Sister—"

My earlier irritation flared, but before I could give voice to it—and traumatize poor Phoenix more than she already had been—a rock crashed through the window beside the door, sending a shower of glass across the floor and narrowly missing her.

"Phoenix!" Talia yelled, and without further hesitation, the young woman bolted toward her and—I hoped—safety.

I, on the other hand, wrenched open the door and headed in exactly the opposite direction.

Cold shocked through me as my bare feet hit the porch floor. Too late, I realized that I had no boots, no coat, and nothing in the way of a weapon—apart from the stone that had found its way into my hand again, for whatever that was worth. Within seconds, I regretted my hasty exit and lack of forethought. A ring of figures faced me, their forms barely visible in the light from the door behind me, their faces lost in shadow. Or were those hoods over their heads?

It didn't matter, because whatever they'd come for, they weren't going to get it.

The one closest to the porch spoke up. "Give us the girl," he said, his muffled voice answering my question. "The one who knows how to find him."

More than one of my questions, actually, because now I knew both what they wanted and that they were wearing hoods. Or maybe masks. Either way, they didn't want their faces seen, and that made a whole host of other questions pop into my head, because ... weird. None of the other Mages I'd faced had tried to hide from me. Those Mages had been confident to the point of arrogance, certain that they would be leaving the fight still standing, and that I wouldn't.

These ones, though? These ones were different. These ones—

One of the figures—there were six altogether that I could see—shuffled its feet, boots scraping against the frozen earth.

They were nervous. These ones were nervous.

Stone still gripped in my hand, I crossed my arms, hoping I looked challenging rather than half-frozen. Darkness had brought a sharp drop in temperature, and the wind had picked up. It danced across the clearing between me and the figures, carrying a whirl of dry leaves with it and slicing through my pullover.

"Give her to us," the man insisted, "and we'll go. No one has to get hurt."

"No," I grated. I would have liked to add more, such as a hearty *fuck you*, but I'd clenched my teeth so hard in my efforts not to shiver—a sure sign of weak old lady if ever there was one—that I couldn't pry them apart. I dug the fingers of my free hand into the opposite bicep, and the ones clutching the stone into my ribcage, using the pain to distract myself from the ache seeping into my feet from the cold of the porch floor.

More feet shuffled against the earth. Five pairs of them, judging from the shifting in the shadowy forms. Only the apparent ringleader held his ground. My gaze narrowed. Maybe word was getting around about what the weak old lady could do if you pissed her off enough? Sweet Mary Magdalene, I hoped so, because such a reputation was literally the only thing between me and—

A deep, guttural cry split the night and echoed through the woods, and my heart hit the porch beside my frozen toes. Or, I supposed, they might not be nervous at all about the old lady, but were instead waiting for their monster to join them.

"F-f-fuck," I mumbled from between chattering teeth. I focused on the stone in my grasp, because it had called to me in the cottage, and perhaps in a time of need …

But there was nothing. No heat. No heaviness. Not so much as a frisson of energy between me and it. The stone was just that, a stone, and nothing more. Which meant I was on my own—and seriously screwed if I didn't come up with a weapon right now.

I shoved the inert lump back into its pocket—useless or not, it was still mine to protect—and cast a quick look around me. My gaze settled on a snow shovel propped beside the door, half a dozen steps away. A momentary flashback to my first fight with a Mage blindsided me—the arrival of the skeletal woman, the man who wanted the stone she carried, the broomstick I'd picked up to fight him off, the crowbar he'd carried …

I swallowed hard. This was different, I told myself. I knew what to expect this time.

A little voice in my head laughed with an edge of hysteria, because oh, it was different, all right. This time there were six of them—with a monster on its way.

And a plan, I told the voice as I fought back the paralysis and reached for the shovel. *We have a plan.*

All I had to do was stay alive until Talia and the others—

The first boot hit the porch as my fingers closed around the shovel handle. Whirling, I swung my makeshift weapon low and hard, aiming for the legs that would make an easier target than a head, tempting though the latter was. The impact jolted through my hands and up my arms, sending a shaft of remembered pain into the shoulder that had taken the impact of the crowbar on the shelter lawn a lifetime ago. I absorbed it like the phantom it was, stepped across the screaming

Mage whose knee I'd probably broken, and raised the shovel high.

Two more forms came out of the shadows at me, and in the dim light from the fixture above the door behind me, I saw a baseball bat in one's hands. So we were back to beating up the old lady? Awesome. Also, what the hell was with the no-magick thing? I hadn't seen so much as a glimmer from any of—

In the woods, the monster roared again, and my innards turned to liquid.

Never mind. That was magick enough.

The baseball bat headed for my face, and instinctively, I twisted away. My hooded opponent adjusted his swing to compensate, and the bat hit my ribcage just below my shoulder blade. I staggered, caught myself, and returned the favor. The edge of my shovel's broad, metal blade bit into a fleshy upper arm. The Mage shrieked and dropped his weapon, and the one coming up onto the porch behind him scooped it up and ran at me.

"Aidan, leave it!" a young woman's voice cried out from the driveway. "Can't you hear it? The goliath is coming—we have to get out of here!"

Half of my brain wanted to focus on her words—they weren't using magick and they weren't with the goliath? What in the actual hell?

The other half noted that the bat-bearer named Aidan was coming in to take another shot at me.

"Not"—he grunted in response to the woman as he swung and missed—"without"—another swing and miss—"what we came for!"

He took a third swing, but this time I was ready for him. I'd buried the agony of a broken rib—or maybe two—and found my footing, my balance, and the center that came with decades of training. Holding the shovel across me in both hands, I blocked the incoming blow, twisted my own weapon around his, and tore the bat away. It clattered to the porch floorboards and rolled under the railing, and I delivered a quick uppercut with the shovel's D-handle to Aidan's chin. The Mage dropped like a sack of potatoes.

"Aidan!" the woman screamed.

Age be damned, I thought with grim satisfaction. I still had what it took to hold my—

From the corner of my eye, I saw someone vault over the rail to my left with another baseball bat in hand—or maybe it was the same one I'd just gotten rid of. It didn't much matter as it connected with my right wrist, shattering bones there. More bones than I wanted to think about. More than I *could* think about through the haze of agony that dropped me to my knees. Out of sheer instinct—partly due to my years of martial arts training but mostly to self-preservation—I threw myself flat and rolled to the side. A second blow landed where I'd been a scant millisecond before. I didn't give him a third chance.

Landing on my back, I brought my knees up toward my chest and lashed out with both feet and all the strength I could summon at the shadow between me and the porch light. Bone snapped once more—his rather than mine this time—and with a bellow, he fell toward me. I rolled again, narrowly avoiding being crushed as I came up short against the porch railing. And then—then I just stopped, held immobile by pain and shock and cold while the two men whose legs I'd broken lay whimpering, and the young woman who'd cried out for Aidan sobbed over his unconscious form a few feet away, and the stone ...

The stone did nothing. It didn't demand my touch. It didn't turn warm against my skin through the thin lining of its pocket. It just sat there, between my hip bone and the cold, hard porch floor and—

And shit, I thought with a small blink of surprise, my lashes catching on the rough wood beneath my face. It really had been just me against six Mages. I turned my head and rested my cheek against the porch as I surveyed the scattered, fallen bodies. Well. Six minus the ones I'd somehow managed to take down, which left—

Another monstrous scream pierced the night woods. Without thinking, I levered myself upright—or tried to. Searing pain shot through my smashed wrist as it gave out under me, and then through my ribcage as I thudded onto the porch again.

"Sweet Mary Magdalene," I wheezed. But I had no time to catch my breath, because that scream had been closer—a lot closer—and it reminded me that it wasn't just me against the remaining Mages, it was me against the remaining Mages and an entire mountain. I pushed upright again, carefully this time, and then staggered to my feet.

It wouldn't be easy—and I hoped to hell and back that the stone would at least lend me its healing powers again, even if it was otherwise inert—but I had to hold on. I had to hold the monster back. Because Talia and the others were relying on—

The sound of an engine cut my thoughts short. I'd no sooner identified it when headlights slashed crazily across the dark forest, and then Talia's SUV roared around the corner of the cottage. Two hooded figures dived out of its way, and it slewed to a stop at the bottom of the stairs as Talia leaned across the passenger seat and thrust open the door.

"Get in!" she yelled, but the monster's voice drowned out hers, and then it was there.

It stood in the driveway in front of Talia's car, its massive, doglike head thrown back as it bellowed at the night sky. Framed in the headlights with its shadow looming against the trees beyond, it looked even bigger than I remembered. And infinitely more dangerous.

The young woman on the porch shrieked at the Mage named Aidan to wake up, terror lacing her voice. The two other men on the porch struggled to their feet and half hopped, half fell down the stairs and sprawled on the ground. The remaining two shadows that had dived out of Talia's way abandoned the injured altogether and crashed through the underbrush along the driveway, racing toward a van parked halfway to the road.

"Monica!" Talia yelled again. "Get in the damned vehicle!"

I blinked at her, and then at the men sprawled between me and her, and then at her again—and then at the towering monster. My brain tried to make sense of it all. Especially the part where the Mages that had attacked us were just as terrified of the goliath as I was. Maybe more so.

"For fucksake, Monica!"

Later, I told my half-frozen, reeling mind. *I'll figure it out later.*

Gathering what little remained of my ability to function, I hobbled as fast as I could past Aidan and the young woman—what was she, twenty at most?—evaded the grasping hands of one of the fallen men, and fell into the passenger seat of the SUV.

I was still trying to catch hold of the door handle to pull the door shut behind me when Talia hit the gas and aimed the vehicle at the goliath. At the last second, she veered around it, dropping the tires on my side into the shallow ditch and wrestling the steering wheel to keep the rest of the SUV from following. The passenger door I'd been trying to capture glanced off a sapling and slammed shut, narrowly missing my hand—and then, abruptly, our flight to safety ended.

The goliath took two enormous bounds past our fleeing vehicle and was in front of us again. This time, it filled the narrow space between the woods and the Mages' van, and there was no way around either of them.

Talia slammed on the brakes. "Fuck," she whispered into the heavy silence that filled the SUV.

"Jesus fuck," Phoenix whispered in agreement from the back seat as the goliath raised its two massive paws into the air, swung them in an arc …

And sent the van crashing into the trees with so much force that a smaller one snapped like a twig and began its descent toward us. Before I'd even processed the new danger, Talia had already reacted. With both hands gripping the wheel, she took her foot from the brake, hit the gas pedal, and aimed the SUV at the sliver of driveway still visible. The goliath's scream followed us as we shot past it, bouncing wildly over ruts and between the edges of the driveway.

This time, however, the monster itself did not give chase.

Chapter 3

No one spoke on the trip into Kingston. In the glow from the dashboard and the occasional passing vehicle, Talia shot concerned glances at me every so often, usually when I shifted my weight—at all—and a little hiss of air escaped me. But she didn't ask, and I didn't volunteer.

Unspoken agreement.

It would have hurt too much to turn and look at Phoenix and Sister Margaret in the back seat, so I told myself that it was enough to know that they were there. That they were safe. That I'd held the Mages off long enough for Talia to get them to the vehicle.

A thousand disjointed thoughts ricocheted through my brain. A thousand questions. Because what the hell? The Mages had shown no evidence of magick at all—not so much as a sparkle—and they'd been so young. Too young. Were they even Mages at all? Or even disciples? The more I thought about it, the less likely it seemed. Their behavior had been more like the street gangs in the Toronto neighborhood where the shelter had been.

Except they'd come looking for Phoenix, which meant that they'd known at least something. And the goliath— they'd known about the goliath, too, and they'd been afraid of it, as if—

As if what? As if it had been out of their control, or it had been after them. *Had* it been after them? But no, it had been watching us long before they'd arrived on the scene. Unless … had it saved us? But why? And on whose orders? Someone had to have sent it, because surely to Mary Magdalene the thing wasn't able to think for itself. Surely.

And if someone had sent the goliath, then someone had known where we were and had known that the Mages —if that's what they were—had been coming. And if they weren't Mages, who were they?

It continued this way inside my head all the way to Kingston, except in the moments when the physical pain intervened. Pain and the whatever was going on inside my body as the stone worked its own magick. That part of the stone's power, at least, still worked. Which I was both grateful for, as it healed me, and pissed about, because the stone could have prevented most of my injuries from even happening if it had just goddamn cooperated with me.

By the time we pulled up at the first stoplight on the edge of town, however, I had settled on mostly grateful—at least for the moment. The pain in my wrist had subsided dramatically, as had the every-breath-I-took knife in my ribcage. I still hurt, but in an achy, beat-up way rather than a wanting-to-curl-up-and-die way. I was, however, frozen to the bone. My feet felt like blocks of ice despite the heat blowing on them, and as Talia pulled up in front of a bank in a small strip mall, shivers wracked my body from head to toe.

Talia put the gear shift into park, then shrugged out of the hoodie she wore over her blouse and placed it over me, telling me to shut up when I tried to object. Leaving the engine running, she took both my bank card and her own to the machine to withdraw as much cash from both our accounts as the system would let her. We would do the same again in the morning, she'd said, and then we wouldn't use either card again. Whatever we had left after we bought our train tickets to Quebec City—with cash— would be all that we had for the four of us.

I hoped to hell we were going in the right direction.

While Talia was gone, I moved my ribcage experimentally, found that I could do so, and twisted around in my seat to look back at a silent Phoenix and Sister Margaret.

"You guys okay?" I asked.

Sister Margaret summoned a tired smile that didn't reach her hollow eyes. "More worried about you than anything. You're healing?"

I gave a terse nod, and her shoulders relaxed a fraction. I turned my gaze to Phoenix. "And you?" I asked. "Are you okay?"

"It saved us, you know," she whispered.

"What?"

"The goliath. It could have killed us, but it didn't. It saved us."

I stared at her, a slow anger born of fear building in my core. It didn't matter that the same thought had crossed my own mind. This was different. This was sympathy for a creature that may not have damaged us this time but hadn't hesitated to do so in past—and would very likely try to do so again in the future. And it wasn't the first time Phoenix had tried to defend the beast that had torn apart the motel and almost killed her.

Except it hadn't. It had left her beside a tree in the woods for me to find, only to reappear later, when I'd destroyed Eldon Rusk in that clearing. Talia had reached to take the journal from the billionaire just as he'd exploded, but the sweep of a huge, granite arm had saved her, and—

I thrust the image away, reminding myself that the goliath's sweeping gesture had knocked her against a tree and shattered her wrist so badly that she'd needed surgery to repair it. That it had intended to harm, not help. And that letting Phoenix think otherwise was downright dangerous.

"No," I told her, curling my hands into fists against a

desire to snap at her. "No, it did not save us. It spied on us and probably brought the Mages to us, and—"

"It knocked aside their van," Phoenix's voice was stubborn, "so we could get past them."

"And if Talia hadn't been as fast as she was to react, we could have been next. *Talia* saved us, Phoenix, not that thing."

The shadows in the back seat weren't enough to hide the flash of annoyance in Phoenix's eyes. Tight-lipped, the young woman flipped the hood of her hoodie up over her head, crossed her arms, and slumped against the door, staring out the window. I wrestled with my own irritation, but before I could give voice to the *whatever* that sat on the tip of my tongue, Sister Margaret caught my eye and gave a small shake of her head.

Let it go, the shake said, and my irritation surged anew. I knew she was right, but—

A tiny furrow appeared between the nun's eyebrows. She flicked a glance at the young woman in the seat beside her, then returned her gaze to me. Her quizzical, concerned, watchful gaze that made me feel like there were needles beneath my skin.

"Are you all right?" she asked.

I didn't think she was referring to my physical health, and suspected that she would have asked a different question—a far more pointed one—if it had been just the two of us in the car. Something like, *What the hell is going on with you?*

Or maybe that was my own question. Because this went far beyond exhaustion or pain or the trauma of the evening's events. Something in me wasn't right. No, scratch that. Something was really, really wrong, and it had been for a while. Because this level of irritation? With Phoenix, of all people? The sweet, tough-as-nails, soft-as-marshmallow young woman who had survived so much already, whom I'd silently vowed to protect as I hadn't been able to protect Josephine?

My heart twisted in my chest as I looked at Phoenix, curled into the corner of the back seat, and Sister Margaret, waiting for an answer I didn't have.

Because what in the hell *was* going on?

WE SPENT THE NIGHT IN THE VEHICLE IN A SPRAWLING parking lot in front of a big-box retailer. Talia parked in a pool of light beneath one of those high-intensity, towering lamps that turned night to almost day. Tersely—because everything felt terse between us right now—she and I agreed to take turns keeping watch, but in truth, neither of us slept.

Neither did we speak, not even when the deep, even breathing of Sister Margaret and Phoenix told me that they'd fallen asleep in the back seat.

Our silence wasn't so much because of our unspoken agreement as it was just … I wasn't sure, to be honest. Sheer overwhelm? Recrimination on my part and apprehensive accusation on hers? All of the above, probably. And who could blame either of us?

Talia had failed to listen to me about leaving; I had failed, period.

Even when I had most needed it, I still hadn't been able to access the stone, and now our situation had become far more tenuous, far more fragile. If Talia hadn't gotten Sister Margaret and Phoenix out the bedroom window and into the vehicle, if she hadn't pulled up in front of the porch to rescue me when she had, if the mountain hadn't tossed aside our attackers' van the way it had—

I shuddered at the fractured snippets of memories piling up in my brain. Another vehicle turned into the parking lot and drove slowly past the storefront, and I felt Talia tense beside me. The vehicle—a tiny two-seater that I suspected a Mage wouldn't be caught dead driving—continued out the other side of the lot.

The woman in the seat beside me relaxed again, and I returned to my thoughts. This time, however, I focused on a more immediate issue, because the question that Sister Margaret had raised had been spinning like a dervish in the back of my brain and refused to go away. And my annoyance with Phoenix was inextricably tangled with it. Even thinking about being irritated made me … irritated. What *was* going on with me?

And when had it started?

I tried to think back. I'd been mightily annoyed with Talia earlier, too, before the Mages had put in their appearance, but I'd had reason to be … hadn't I? Or had that been another overreaction on my part?

I was so immersed in my thoughts that when Talia spoke beside me, I jumped.

"Are you okay?"

Shit. Now she was questioning my mental state, too? Before I could answer—or, more accurately, unclench my jaw enough *to* answer—she clarified her question with another.

"You're sure you're not hurt?"

My jaw—and shoulders—relaxed a fraction.

"I'm sure."

"They hit you pretty hard."

"Yes."

"You were down, Monica."

"Yes."

A handful of seconds slipped by.

"Is that what happened when you were attacked the first time? At the shelter?" She shifted in her seat, turning toward me. I knew because I could feel the intensity of her gaze boring into the back of my skull.

My mouth twisted as I stared out the window into the artificially lit night. Apart from the fact that the stone hadn't worked this time and there had been no exploding Mages?

I nodded.

"How?" she asked. "How does it happen? How are you able to heal like this?"

I tipped my head left, then right, then left again. There was a satisfying *crack* at the base of my skull, followed by a slight easing of the ache that had begun to form there. I might heal well, but that didn't mean that the attack wouldn't leave its mark on me. I glanced down at my no longer broken wrist that had turned black and blue. And purple.

Several marks, actually.

I shifted my weight on the seat and turned to face Talia. "I'm not sure," I said. "But remember when I showed you the stone for the first time, and its webs looked like they were joined with my skin?"

She nodded warily.

"I think they've done more. I think—" I broke off and steeled myself for the admission, because thinking it was one thing, but speaking it aloud was quite another. Speaking it aloud would make it—

"What?" my friend prompted. "You think what?"

"I think the webs have become … part of me. I think the stone has. I think it's everywhere inside me, Talia, and I'm afraid—" I broke off and swallowed hard as the physical and emotional and mental signs I'd been experiencing all converged in my mind. "I'm afraid it's taking over."

There was a swift, indrawn hiss of air from her side, and I closed my eyes. Speaking my fear aloud had made it more real, more immediate, and infinitely more terrifying. I had no idea how to even begin absorbing the idea—or to contemplate its consequences.

A warm hand covered my clenched fist on my lap. It squeezed gently.

"One thing at a time," Talia said quietly. "If Methuselah is the owner of the stone as Sister Margaret says, he'll know what to do. We just have to find him."

It was on the tip of my tongue to remind her that that would be easier said than done, but I bit back the words and let my head drop back against the headrest. I didn't need to remind her of something she already knew. Just for now, just for tonight, I thought, maybe it was okay to let go of tomorrow. To borrow a friend's confidence and accept her reassurance when I could find none of my own.

Because perhaps Detective Talia Dawson was better at this *looking after us* thing than I'd given her credit for.

CHAPTER 4

IN THE MORNING, TALIA FOUND A SERVICE STATION WITH AN exterior access restroom where my appearance would draw as little attention as possible. She parked in front of the restroom door and went inside the station to fetch the key for me, emerging a few minutes later with a bulging plastic bag and a cardboard drink tray that had four disposable cups tucked into it.

Before getting back into her seat, she went around to the rear of the car and opened the trunk. Sounds of rummaging reached through the silence—I wanted to think everyone in the car was quiet because it was early, but I knew I was lying to myself—and then the trunk lid slammed shut again. A second later, Talia opened the driver's side door, reached over her seat to hand the bag to Phoenix, and slid in behind the steering wheel.

She handed me the restroom key and dropped a pair of boots in my lap.

"You'll probably swim in them," she said, "but they'll at least keep your feet warm. I'm sorry I didn't think of them last night."

I murmured my thanks and looked over my shoulder at Phoenix, who was poking through the plastic bag's contents. She hadn't spoken a word to me in the hour she'd been awake, and she didn't look up when I cleared my throat.

I tried again. "Phoenix? Did you need the restroom?"

She didn't reply, but the still-hooded head shook. My hand on the door handle, I hesitated. I hated that we weren't speaking, and I hated that I was to blame, and—

Talia reached out to touch my arm. She shook her head in a *leave it* gesture, the same way Sister Margaret had done the night before. I didn't like it any more now than I had then, but neither did I trust the surge of annoyance that responded in me. I didn't trust it, and I refused to own it.

That was not me, I reminded myself. Whatever it was, it was *not* me.

I gritted my teeth and opened the car door. Boots in one hand, and the key and Phoenix's duffel bag—the only one to have made it out of the cottage—in the other, I hobbled across the freezing pavement to the restroom.

I'D HAD TO MAKE DO WITH SPONGE BATHS BEFORE, BUT I'D never had to endure one that involved the rough brown paper towels that so many public restrooms favored. Or the slimy pink soap that accompanied it. It was … unpleasant, to say the least, especially when the ice-cold water that came from the tap had a tendency to make the soap thicken and stick to me, rather than rinsing it off.

Still, by the time I'd washed and changed into one of Phoenix's hoodies—making a note to myself to thank her later for her presence of mind in grabbing the duffle bag that also contained her hormone pills—I felt a great deal cleaner. And, dare I say it, more in control.

Until I met my reflection's gaze in the hazy mirror above the sink and saw a tiny wisp of white float across my left iris. Horror gripped me, its fingers wrapping around my throat and cutting off my breath. For an instant, hysteria threatened to join it. And then …

Then I rested my hands against the edge of the counter and leaned on them, letting my head drop between my shoulders as I closed my eyes. So I'd been right. The stone's webs really were taking over. I mean, I'd suspected as much—hell, deep down, I was pretty sure I'd *known*—but seeing it like that, *seeing* the wisp of a strand in my eyeball—

I shuddered, a deep, bone-rattling shudder that began at my toes and ended by trying to make my hair stand on end. Shit, I thought, tightening my grip on the counter's edge until my knuckles protested and my forearms ached. Shit, shit, *shit.*

Under Talia's direction, we took every precaution to minimize our chance of being followed. We'd long since dumped our phones, so we couldn't be traced by them, and now that we had cash, we wouldn't use our bank cards again except in the most dire emergency. We abandoned Talia's car in a park-and-ride lot on the outskirts of the city and took a bus from there to the train station, where Talia gave fake names for each of us and paid cash for tickets on the first train to Quebec City, leaving at nine.

I'd felt it incumbent upon me to suggest that we wait until after her appointment with the surgeon—and Phoenix's with the ophthalmologist—but she'd gruffly vetoed the idea, Phoenix had agreed with her, and I hadn't argued. Niceties such as self-care were going to have to take a back seat for a while in favor of self-preservation.

I sat with Sister Margaret on the Kingston-to-Montreal leg. I had to ask Phoenix to move first, because she had already planted herself in the seat next to the nun, who had fast become her favorite person in our little group. Or perhaps the one that caused her the least anxiety.

My heart ached a little at that. Once, I had been the person Phoenix had turned to, but—well, my temper and I weren't exactly reassuring to anyone these days. Besides, the most important thing was that she had someone, I told myself. It didn't matter who.

I wished I could believe me.

Regardless, when I asked to trade places with her, her agreement was only a little grudging, and with a minimum of reshuffling, I was quickly seated beside the nun while Phoenix ignored Talia a few rows away. I might as well have saved all of us the trouble, because I didn't get the answers from the nun that I had hoped to.

As soon as the train was underway and the general noise level increased enough to cover a quiet conversation, Sister Margaret heaved a great sigh and reached to cover my hand on the armrest between us with her own. Thin, timeworn fingers squeezed mine and held tight. My surprised gaze flew up to meet her sad one.

"I wish I had the answers, Sister Monica," she said. "I really do."

"I haven't even asked anything yet."

The sadness in her eyes deepened, and the lines at the corners of her mouth drew tight. "You don't have to. I can see what's happening—how you've changed. I suspect it's the stone, but I don't know why or how."

I digested this while the intercom overhead issued instructions in case of an emergency, first in English and then in French, most of the words too faint to be heard. When the voice finished, and I was no clearer on what to do than I'd been before it had begun speaking, I turned my attention back to the nun at my side.

"So this has never happened before? Nothing like it happened to you when you had the stone?"

"I never—" she began, then stopped and tried again. "I didn't—"

"It never bonded with you," I said, remembering her story of finding the stone on a dead, cocooned disciple and not being able to bring herself to use it, not even when she'd been held captive and slowly starved. "You never gave it the chance."

"No." Her gaze slid away, as if from the memory, and she shook her head. "No, I didn't. And if this"—she gestured at me—"has happened before, the only record of it would have been in the archive. Or perhaps in the journal that Sister Anne Louise gave you."

Both of which had gone up in flames. The archive along with half of St. Paul's when the Mages had located it, and the journal a few hours later in the woods, when Eldon Rusk, the billionaire Mage, had tried to take it. Both things gone before I got any of the answers we so desperately needed about where Methuselah might be.

I subsided into my seat. Navigating this situation at all felt impossible. Navigating it blindly the way we were *was* impossible.

What would we find when we got to Quebec City? Would we make it there, or would the Mages try to stop us again, and this time succeed? Were the Ursulines who had cared for Methuselah even still alive? No one had heard from them since Methuselah's disappearance six months— I paused and did some mental math, adding in the last seven weeks—make that almost eight months before. If they *were* alive, they were ancient by all accounts, and Sister Margaret had already warned us not to expect much in the way of help from them.

And then there was my biggest question of all and my

greatest fear: How much of me would I have left when we got there?

Sister Margaret gave my hand another squeeze, then withdrew hers to her lap.

"Why was I never recruited to the Sisterhood?" I asked.

"Pardon?"

"Sister Anne Louise said that I left the monastery before I could be recruited, but she didn't—" I broke off, not wanting to remind Sister Margaret of the reason that the old nun at St. Paul's had run out of time for explanations. I shifted to a different tack. "But that's all I know. What happened? I mean, sisters Ernestine and Ruth and Helen and—"

"You were too visible."

I stared. "I beg your pardon?"

"The Obsidian Sisterhood has always relied on invisibility for its safety. Those who remain still depend on that invisibility. You, Sister Monica, were never invisible."

I wondered whether I should be offended, but after a moment decided that Sister Margaret hadn't meant her words that way. And that she was absolutely right. Standing up to Mother Annunciata and the Archbishop the way I had, leaving the church, being excommunicated ... none of those were things that let one fade into the background. But I'd had my reasons, and I would do it all over again if I had to. Only sooner.

In time, perhaps, to have saved my sister Josephine.

CHAPTER 5

"What the fuck do you mean, we've been upgraded?"

I winced at the snarl in my voice even before Talia's left eyebrow shot up and Sister Margaret and Phoenix exchanged a look. To say I was on edge would be a massive understatement, but my spidey senses weren't just tingling, they were up in arms. Because upgraded from economy to business class, the railway's version of first class? I'd traveled by rail often enough in this country to know that kind of upgrade didn't randomly happen all by itself.

And Sister Margaret hadn't said, *"I upgraded us,"* she'd said, *"We've been upgraded."* Those were two entirely different things and begged the question of who had been behind the upgrade. And why? And—

I realized my companions were staring at me. They were likely waiting for an apology for that last outburst, and rightfully so, because we were *all* on edge, but I was the only one taking it out on the others. I pinched the bridge of my nose and closed my eyes. Whatever my problem was, I needed to tone down my … well, my everything, if I was honest. Or this would be the longest five-and-a-half-hour layover in history.

I squeezed my eyes tighter. Five and a half hours. Five and a half fucking—

I gritted my teeth. There I went again. But being stuck all afternoon in the Montreal train station had *not* been part of the plan. We'd booked our tickets with the shortest possible connection—fifty-five minutes—but there had been delays along the track, and now we got to hang out like proverbial sitting ducks in the second-busiest train station in the country for the better part of the day. And *we'd been upgraded*, and—

"You done?" Talia's voice inquired dryly. "Can Sister Margaret finish, now?"

I pressed my lips together against another snarl and dropped my hand to my side. I met Sister Margaret's wary gaze.

"Sorry," I muttered. "Go ahead."

The nun cleared her throat. "Economy class on the earlier train was sold out," she said, "but they offered to bump us up to business. I—I thought it would be all right."

"They offered," I echoed. "And that didn't seem strange to you? Did they upgrade anyone else?"

Sister Margaret gave a helpless shrug. "I have no idea. I went to the counter, gave our names—the ones Talia used to book our tickets in Kingston—and they said they could bump us. Should I have said no?"

Yes, I thought. And no. And how the hell should I know?

"It means that we leave at sixteen-forty instead of eighteen twenty-five," Sister Margaret continued, speaking now to Talia and still sounding apologetic. "Earlier is better, right?"

My scowl deepened as I tried to do the math around the transportation industry's use of the damned twenty-four-hour clock. A barrage of suspicions made the task impossible, because I was still stuck on the *upgrade* idea.

Trains don't upgrade you. Airlines might, but trains—

"Four-forty," Talia supplied the answer my brain couldn't come up with, "instead of six twenty-five. It only saves us a couple of hours, but isn't that what you wanted?"

Yes, because it meant fewer hours of proverbial sitting-duckness here in the train station, and no, because it still didn't explain the upgrade. The only explanation I could muster involved Mages with the kinds of connections that could track my bank card, tail my car, find me in a monastery that was supposed to be an Obsidian Sisterhood safe house, send a mountain monster to save us from what might well have been a rival faction, and—

And hell, I didn't even know what else they were capable of, and wasn't that enough?

"I don't like it," I muttered. "Being upgraded like that. It's not—"

"Maybe it's because Sister Margaret is a nun," Phoenix broke in, making a head-to-toe gesture toward Sister Margaret. "I mean, it's not like a full habit or anything, but that thing you wear on your head is still pretty obvious."

Sister Margaret put a hand up to her veil with an expression of relief. "That must have been it," she said. "I've certainly encountered favorable treatment in past because of that. People tend to be nicer to us—just in case we hold sway with ... you know." She pointed skyward, and Phoenix snorted.

She was right. I'd experienced the same, even after I'd left behind the habit of St. Paul's and simply introduced myself as Sister Monica, but the admission didn't help with the headache that was forming between my brows. Although neither, I suspected, did my continued scowl.

"*Or*," I muttered, "someone gave them our names and told them to watch for us."

Phoenix's eyes rolled. "Fake names, remember?" she asked dismissively.

Talia, on the other hand, looked pensive. She quirked an eyebrow at me.

"What do you want to do?" she asked. "We have to get to Quebec City somehow."

I stared at the floor between us. I had no answer,

because I knew she was right. Quebec City was our only lead right now. Our only plan, if you could call any of this a plan at all.

As if sensing victory, Phoenix did a little happy dance beside Sister Margaret. "Yes!" she exclaimed. "They feed us in business class, right? And we get drinks? God knows we could all use a—"

"No," I said. "No alcohol. We need to stay alert."

Although for the first time in my life, I was leaning heavily in the direction of intoxication at the moment. At least it might help me sleep for a while.

Phoenix rolled her eyes in a way that my generation would never have dared and her own had mastered. "Not even wine with dinner?"

I was about to double down on my veto when Sister Margaret put a gentle hand on my arm. I raised my gaze from it to meet her brown eyes, which were as gentle as her hand.

"Monica," she said, and the single word—my name alone without the usual *Sister* title she applied—held a world of meaning that stopped me in my tracks. Perhaps if she'd said it harshly, I might have been able to stand against it, but she didn't. Instead, her voice was as gentle as her eyes, damn it, and it was my undoing.

In a flash, I pictured myself as my companions must see me. Wild-eyed, spiky-haired, disheveled, and so tightly wound that I was surprised I wasn't visibly vibrating.

My arm trembled beneath Sister Margaret's touch.

Okay, so maybe I *was* visibly vibrating.

So very, very tightly wound.

"Monica," said Sister Margaret again. "We're okay. We got away from the goliath. We're here. We're on our way to the Ursulines. I know"—she held up her free hand in a *let me finish* gesture as I opened my mouth, and I snapped my teeth shut again—"I know the Mages might be following us, but if they were going to attack, do you really think they'd go to this trouble just so they could do it on a train?"

Well, when she put it that way …

The nun gave my arm a gentle squeeze and smiled reassuringly. "We don't know what we'll find in Quebec City, but for now, for just this minute, we're safe. All right?"

I wanted to believe her. As the Mother of All was my witness, I wanted to. So badly. But I could not. I couldn't access the stone anymore, let alone control it, and we had no idea what was waiting for us in Quebec City, if the Mages would let us get that far, or if we would find any trace of Methuselah there. At worst, we were on a wild goose chase that might—and probably would—culminate in more people dying; at best, we would find the elusive alien, and people would still die.

Still …

Still.

As much as I didn't believe Sister Margaret's assurances, her belief, her faith, at least I had a lifetime of pretending behind me that would let me feign otherwise. I'd managed to remain a nun for more than twenty years; surely I could pretend calm for a few short hours.

I drew a deep breath and let my shoulders drop away from where they'd climbed up beside my ears. Covering Sister Margaret's hand on my arm with my own, I returned her squeeze.

"You're right," I agreed, lying through my teeth. "We are safe for now. And you're right, too, Phoenix. Wine with dinner would be nice."

Sister Margaret's smile widened into relief, and Phoenix punched the air with a delighted whoop of "Yes!" before turning to head toward the lounge set aside for business class travelers. Our nun companion fell in behind her, and Talia and I brought up the rear.

"Trains don't give upgrades, Talia," I said quietly, falling into step beside the cop.

She didn't reply, and silence dogged us for a few dozen steps as we wended our way through a crowd gathered around a center kiosk and crossed the gleaming tile floor to the lounge into which Sister Margaret and an enthusiastic Phoenix had already disappeared. Then, as Talia reached for the handle on the stylistically frosted glass door, her brown gaze met mine.

"I know," she said, and my shoulders climbed back up to my ears.

So much for calm.

CHAPTER 6

We spent four hours and twenty minutes in the lounge, all of which were entirely uneventful. Sister Margaret fell asleep in one of the leather club chairs and snored softly, drawing amused glances from most nearby fellow travelers and making one well-appointed man scowl, grumble under his breath, and move to the far corner of the room. Phoenix glared daggers at his departing back, but she refrained from comment when Talia caught her eye and gave a warning shake of her head.

I didn't comment, either, but still uncomfortable with the whole *upgrade* idea, I shifted in my seat to keep the man in my line of vision in case he turned out to be a problem of the Mage variety.

He didn't, and a short while later, when a Toronto-bound train was announced, he left altogether, unknowingly accompanied by Phoenix's middle finger and Talia's poorly hidden smile while Sister Margaret snored on.

At one point near the end of our long, drawn-out wait, Talia and Phoenix went in search of food and returned with an assortment of sandwiches—smoked meat, goat cheese with roasted peppers and bacon, and grilled chicken. Sister Margaret woke up long enough to devour hers—I was pretty sure she was still recovering from her near-starvation at the hands of the Mage disciple before she'd escaped and brought me the stone, because the woman could put away food like there was no tomorrow—and then promptly went back to sleep.

Phoenix and Talia ate their own sandwiches at a more sedate pace, and I stuffed mine into my coat pocket for later, even though Phoenix reminded me that they would be feeding us again on the train. My stomach was tied in so many knots, I didn't think I'd eat that meal, either.

At four thirty-three p.m., our train to Quebec City was called. We were almost there.

THERE WERE FIVE TRAIN CARS WAITING ON THE TRACK: three economy and two business class. Ours was the last one in the line. It was also less than half full. Talia glanced over her shoulder as she made her way down the aisle, looking for row number eleven. Our gazes met for a fraction of an instant past Phoenix and Sister Margaret, who were sandwiched between us, but it was enough to tell me that I wasn't the only one feeling paranoid these days.

It was kind of nice to have company.

I scanned the passengers straggling in behind us, but there was nothing out of the ordinary, nothing amiss. No one looked our way, everyone traveled with luggage of some kind or another, and it appeared that Sister Margaret's prediction that we would be safe on the trip might hold true.

I could but hope.

We found our row halfway down the aisle. Talia snagged the two seats on the left that faced one another, letting Sister Margaret and Phoenix take the side-by-side ones on the opposite side of the aisle. As soon as I sat down with a full view of one end of the train car, I saw the advantage of Talia's strategic choice.

"Good one," I murmured, as she settled into the seat

opposite me and watched the other end of the car with casual disinterest.

She ignored me, but one side of her mouth curved a little. It was indeed nice to have company.

As soon as the train was underway, the differences between economy and business class became apparent. In economy, passengers had to pay for anything they wanted in the way of snacks or drinks—as we would have done if we hadn't had the bag of things Talia had bought at the service station. In business class, however, we were served complimentary drinks a few minutes out of the Montreal station—our choice of tea, coffee, or other beverage, either alcoholic or non-alcoholic—along with little packets of snacks. Phoenix ordered a glass of white wine, discovered that she had to produce government ID to confirm her age, admitted she didn't have it with her, and ended up with a cola instead.

I'd wanted to speak up on her behalf, but Talia kicked me in the ankle and shook her head, then leaned across to murmur something about drawing undue attention. I'd subsided while the attendant poured Phoenix's cola, then tried to catch the young woman's eye to give her a sympathetic smile. She studiously ignored me, however, and after a few seconds, I gave up.

We'd no sooner consumed the snacks (I slid my packet onto Phoenix's drop-down tray, but she ignored that as well) when the attendant returned with a bin of hot, wrapped towelettes for washing our hands before the meal was served. We all dutifully did so, then sat back in our seats to await the next wonder of our upgraded travel.

Across the aisle, Phoenix stared out the window. Beside her, Sister Margaret had closed her eyes, head nodding as she dozed. I felt a twinge of envy at her seeming ability to nod off on demand. That woman could sleep like no one I'd ever met.

Talia nudged the sole of my foot with her boot toe, and I looked across at her.

"They weren't Mages, were they?" she asked. "At the cottage, I mean. They weren't Mages."

So she'd noticed the lack of magick, too.

"No," I replied. "I don't think they were."

"What the hell, Monica."

I lifted one shoulder in a shrug. "I have no idea. Disciples, maybe?"

"Acting on their own? You think?"

"I'd rather that than the alternative."

"Someone sending them, you mean," she said. I nodded, and she glowered. "So not only do we have that consortium Rusk told you about, but we could also have other factions in play as well? It was bad enough when they were all working together."

I snorted. "You of all people should know that power-mongers don't work together, Talia. At least, not for long. They're more likely to tear one another apart in their attempts to get to the top."

Her expression turned bleak. "If that's the case ..."

"We're screwed?" I suggested, as the meal cart rolled to a stop beside me. "Yeah. I know."

WE HAD A CHOICE BETWEEN A BEEF RAGOUT OVER RICE OR poached halibut with asparagus and roasted potatoes for dinner. My stomach churned at the thought of both options, but Talia brushed aside my attempt to decline the meal. She smiled at the attendant, informed him that I would take the halibut, and after he'd given Sister Margaret and Phoenix their trays and moved on, she pointed at the foil-wrapped meal before me.

"It will be easier on your stomach than the beef," she said, "and you need to eat something. Like it or not, we need you, Monica. Preferably upright and functioning."

I opened my mouth to tell her that I was fine, but she forestalled my words by leaning forward to pluck the foil wrap from the divided ceramic plate. Then she unwrapped the napkin from around my cutlery, set the knife aside on the tray, and held napkin and fork out to me.

"Eat," she said softly, her tone managing to sound pleasant and send shivers down my spine all at once, "or I will feed you myself, do you understand?"

Wordlessly, because I had no doubt she would make every attempt to carry out the threat, I reached to take the fork and napkin from her. She held onto them for a moment, waiting for me to meet her gaze. I did so reluctantly, and with no small amount of quiet fury at being ordered around like this.

Her quiet words took the irritated wind from my sails.

"We need you," she repeated. "Whatever this is, we can't do it without you. So … please. Eat your damned dinner."

Seeming confident that she'd won the argument, she released her hold on the items and turned her attention to her own meal. I tried to summon renewed annoyance at her highhandedness, but—

I sighed. But the truth was, she *had* won. And she was right. I couldn't even remember the last time I'd eaten. The sandwich she'd given me in Montreal was still in my coat pocket in the overhead baggage compartment, and last night's attack on the cottage had precluded any of us from eating the soup that Sister Margaret had made. I poked at the fish with the fork, picked up a morsel of it, and carried it to my mouth. I would eat enough—as Talia had said—to keep me functional. And to keep her happy.

But the detective wasn't done with me yet, and when the beverage cart passed by again a few minutes later, she ordered us each a glass of white wine to go with the meal. I accepted mine with tightened lips but no comment, not wanting to cause a scene and already planning to pass it to Phoenix as soon as the attendant had passed. Talia beat me to the idea, however, handing her own glass across the aisle to Sister Margaret and pointing to the young woman by the window.

For a moment, I thought Phoenix would refuse the offering, but Sister Margaret nudged her in the ribs with an elbow, and she accepted the wine with a mumble of thanks. I knew it was petty of me, but I was glad that it wasn't just me she was cold-shouldering right now.

With a last, lingering look down the Mage- and magick-free aisle, I took a long swig of wine and then picked up my fork and ate my damned dinner.

CHAPTER 7

I SAW HIM AS I RETURNED FROM THE RESTROOM.

We were about twenty minutes out of Charny, the train's next-to-last stop a little more than half an hour before Quebec City, and I'd managed not only to eat the dinner Talia had insisted I have, but with the help of the wine she'd ordered for me—because wine always made me sleepy—to also catch about a half-hour of sleep. Between food and nap, I almost felt like myself again. Rested, alert, and optimistic—albeit mildly so—for the first time in days.

And maybe just a wee bit remorseful about how much of a hard time I'd given the others about the whole train thing—which had turned out to be as incident-free as Talia had assured me it would be. Sister Mary Margaret and Phoenix had obviously enjoyed the extras that had come with our unexpected upgrade to business class, and even Talia had indulged in a glass of wine the last time the cart had passed by. By then, I'd let go of most of my angst and decided that she deserved it. They all did—hell, *we* all did, and later, I would make a point of telling them so. And apologizing.

As for the optimistic part, it had been a hard sell, but I'd managed to convince myself that I was looking forward to Quebec City and finding the Ursulines and some answers. I wasn't expecting them to simply produce Methuselah, but the fact was that he had spent decades with them, and they would have the best idea of where he might go or what he might do. Talia and I had talked about it after dinner (before the wine and overwhelming sleepiness had claimed me), and she had shared with me the kinds of questions she would ask as a cop to help narrow the scope of our search. Because yeah, as far as scope was concerned, *global* wasn't exactly doable.

But if we knew what his favorite pastimes were, she said, and what kinds of things he liked to do, or if he'd ever used transit by himself or had access to money …

Or if he'd retained any powers that we should know about.

That last question had been my suggestion. It had been a tiny niggle of worry in the back of my brain for weeks, but I hadn't wanted to share it because—well. Because I'd known it would have the same effect on my companions as being hit with a baseball bat might. And it had. Poor Talia had gone quiet for long seconds that had dragged into a minute or two before she'd leaned back in her seat again, her expression strained.

"I hadn't thought about that," she'd murmured. "Do you think Sister Margaret—?" She'd glanced across the aisle at the nun who'd fallen asleep against Phoenix's shoulder.

"Doubtful," I'd replied. "The Sisterhood didn't share much in the way of information. The less any one of them knew, the less chance there would be of something getting into the wrong hands."

"Fair," Talia had said. "But yes. Let's ask that question, too."

The possibility continued to weigh heavily on me as I pulled the restroom door closed and headed back down the aisle. The train lurched under my feet, and I stumbled and grabbed for the molded handhold on the side of a nearby seat, startling the occupant. Train and I both steadied, and I met his gaze with a quick, apologetic smile for having disturbed him. He was an older, well-dressed gentleman with a salt-and-pepper mustache, the kind you expected to be at least halfway polite, but he turned back to working on the laptop on his tray without returning—or so much as acknowledging—the smile. I rolled my eyes at his balding head and continued on my way.

Three steps past, I stopped so fast that I stumbled again. I caught myself with another handhold, and then I froze.

Every instinct I possessed shrieked at me to turn and confirm what I thought I'd just seen. Prudence held me still. If I *had* seen what I thought I'd seen, if he'd noticed that I'd seen—

I gripped the hard plastic handhold and smiled down at the elderly woman looking at me in puzzlement. At least, I tried to smile, but judging from the way she shrank away in alarm, I didn't quite succeed. I nodded my head as pleasantly as I could manage, then pried my fingers from their grip and jolted unevenly back to my seat. Talia looked up at my approach, and her narrowed gaze zoomed in on my face.

"You look like you've seen—"

"Stop," I hissed at her. "And for the sake of Mary Magdalene herself, stop frowning at me and *smile*, damn it."

Her features instantly relaxed and rearranged themselves, and she tipped back her head and laughed. Sister Margaret and Phoenix both looked our way. Phoenix opened her mouth to speak but closed it when Sister Margaret lifted a hand in a shushing motion. They subsided into concerned stares, waiting for me and Talia to speak.

Blessed be those who were quick on their mental feet.

Still chuckling, Talia shook her head in feigned amusement and gazed out the window. "What did you see?" she muttered.

"A ring," I said, sitting down with my back to the restroom I'd just left. The hair on the back of my neck prickled a warning, and I knew—just *knew*—that he was staring toward us. "On a man three seats away from the restroom on our side."

"A ring?"

"Like the one Rusk had on."

Her gaze flashed to mine. "I don't remember a ring."

"I'd forgotten about it myself," I said, "until I saw it again just now. He—Rusk—was wearing it when he—I remember seeing it on the hand he was holding the journal with. When you tried to grab it away from him."

"You're sure," she said. "This isn't just ..."

"Paranoia?" I finished. I met her gaze squarely. "I don't know. It might be."

She blew out a long, slow breath. "But it's not."

I shook my head. "No. It's not."

"What do you want to do?"

I had no idea. We could confront him, I supposed. Even without the stone, there was only one of him, and if we had the element of surprise on our side—

But what if we didn't? What if he knew I'd spotted him? Or if there were more of them on board, or—

"Sister Monica!"

The hissed whisper from Sister Margaret across the aisle made the blood freeze in my veins. In the same instant, a presence loomed at my elbow and a throat cleared beside me. I had zero doubt as to its owner. Talia came half out of her seat, her expression dark with warning, but she hesitated when I caught her eye. I gave a tiny shake of my head, and she subsided again. Her hands gripped the armrests on either side of her, giving the distinct—and probably accurate—impression that she was either holding herself down or readying herself for launch, depending on what happened next.

The throat cleared again, more loudly this time. And then came a deep, cultured voice.

"Sister Monica Barrett?" it inquired. "I believe I have a proposition for you."

I DIDN'T TURN TO THE INTERLOPER, FOCUSING INSTEAD ON Talia's face as I digested this new development that was both unexpected and … not.

I'd been afraid of exactly this. A Mage following us onto the train. A confrontation. A battle I could not hope to win without the stone's powers working through me. Dread and dismay unfurled in my belly, and I realized that my breathing had grown shallow. I took a moment to deepen it. To inhale calm and exhale the fear that would only lead to panic.

The man beside me oozed with the sort of arrogant confidence that I detested and had encountered far too often among his ilk. It buffeted against me like a cold, unwelcome wind, trying to diminish me and make me shrink away.

I refused to do either.

The tendrils of spiderwebs that had become a part of me writhed in my belly, seeking the source they couldn't seem to find these days. My fingers twitched toward the stone, but I held them still in my lap. I'd hoped last night, when I'd faced the circle of Mages or whoever they'd been outside the cottage, that need would be enough to waken my connection to it and let me wield its power the way I'd done in the past. I'd learned otherwise. If it hadn't been for—

The goliath flashed into my mind and I shoved the image away. No, not that. If it hadn't been for *Talia*, I would be dead and the interlopers—the disciples, or Mages, or whoever they had been—would have what they'd come for: Phoenix, who had been the only one of us to read the journal that the keeper of the Obsidian Sisterhood's archive had given to me.

Which was what this Mage wanted, too. He'd been following us to Quebec City in the hope that she would lead him to Methuselah, and now that he'd been discovered, he'd had no choice but to out himself lest we give him the slip.

Proposition, my ass.

"Go to hell," I told him.

Silence met my response. From the corner of my eye, I saw his hand, a Swiss watch wrapped around its wrist, curl into a fist. I counted off the seconds—one, two, three ...

I reached six, the hand relaxed again, and the man stepped forward, stopped beside Talia, and turned to face me. He was fully in my field of vision now, and it was pretty hard to ignore him. Or the tight line of a forced smile beneath the salt-and-pepper mustache. Or the icy, controlled calm of piercing gray eyes.

I took my hands from my lap and settled them across my belly, my fingers loosely linked and as near to the edge of my pocket and the stone as I could rest them without being obvious. Just in case, I told myself. Just in case I needed it. Just in case it worked this time.

The sharp gaze followed the movement and rested briefly on the pocket where the stone nestled, as if the man sensed its presence. His smile turned even tighter.

"We're willing to pay," he said. "For any information

the girl has about its"—he nodded at my pocket—"true owner."

My answer remained the same as the one I'd given him scant seconds before.

"Go fuck yourself," I told him. Well, it was essentially the same answer, I thought. Just a little more strongly worded.

In the window seat on the other side of the aisle, Phoenix snorted.

A dangerous light glinted deep in the eyes that regarded me. I refused to flinch from it. My fingers shifted their grip on one another, and I lifted my chin, waiting for his response.

"You could be rich beyond your wildest dreams," he said at last. "Think of the good you could do with the money. You could rebuild your shelter, find more lost sheep to care for."

A streak of pain lanced through my heart, taking my breath away. I unlinked my fingers and clenched my hands so tightly that my nails dug into my palms, and Talia leaned forward to place her own hand on my knee.

Careful, her touch warned. *Don't let him bait you.*

I avoided her eyes, making no promises to her—unspoken or otherwise. I looked up at the man again. At the sleaze masquerading as confidence, at the evil wearing a suit that would have funded the Mary Magdalene House for Women for an entire month before he and his kith had destroyed it in their search for ever more power. He *was* baiting me. Why? It didn't seem like the kind of thing you'd do if you were trying to strike a deal with someone for something you wanted as badly as the Mages wanted Phoenix, and through her, Methuselah.

My spidey senses tingled. Something more was going on here, something that I was missing. But what?

My gaze flicked past the man to the monitor suspended from the ceiling that showed where we were on our route. I didn't have time to figure out Mage motives right now. We had ten minutes before Charny, which meant that I had ten minutes to make sure that we weren't followed past that point. Not to our final destination of Quebec City, and especially not to the Ursulines.

I looked out the window at the lights marking an approaching bridge. Deep in my brain, the beginnings of a plan began to come together. A desperate, impossible plan that was our only chance. Without stopping to think about it too carefully—without daring to—I reached out and flagged the attention of an attendant looking our way.

The Mage scowled at me. "What are you doing?" he asked. "This is between us. If you try anything—"

"I'm telling them about the bomb you're carrying," I said, dropping my voice to be sure it didn't carry past our cozy little group. Yet. "The one under your seat."

"Monica!" Talia almost choked. "You can't make a false—that's a federal offense!"

I ignored her and kept my focus on the Mage.

"You wouldn't," he said.

"Try me."

"You know I can destroy this entire train."

"And you know I can stop you," I bluffed. Lied. Whatever. "Then what? No one has the girl, the consortium is back to square one, and you're dead. Is that the game we're playing?"

He looked toward the attendant making his way toward us. Confidence gave way to bluster, then hesitation, and then the Mage snapped, "Fine. But this isn't over. I know where you're going, and Quebec City isn't big enough to hide in. I'll find you again. *We* will find you, and there will be no more offer."

"Bite me," I retorted.

"Excuse me, is there a problem here?" the attendant's voice broke between us.

The Mage held out for another second, maybe two, and then, with a muttered imprecation that made the hardened city cop across from me blink in mild astonishment, he growled at the attendant, "No. No problem at all, just a misunderstanding. I'm going back to my seat."

He stalked away, and the attendant raised his eyebrows at me.

"All good, ma'am?"

"No," I said. I drew a deep breath and blurted out the rest of my plan that had Talia's eyes growing wider with every word—although she couldn't say she hadn't had warning. "That man—I overheard him on the phone when I went past him. He was telling someone that the bomb is under his seat, and it's set to go off in—" I broke off and made a show of looking up at the ceiling display again, letting my eyes widen in horror. "Oh my god. Three minutes. He said three minutes."

The attendant stared at me, his expression blank with incomprehension. From what I could tell, he'd stopped breathing. So had Talia. I stared at her with my fiercest *trust me* expression, then raised my voice to a panicked pseudo-whisper designed to carry at least as far as the seat in front of us and hopefully further, because if this was going to work, I needed the attendant to act. *Now.* And if I needed to create panic to make that happen, so be it.

Because I could not let the Mage follow us.

"Didn't you hear me?" I hissed at the frozen attendant. "He has a *bomb!*"

CHAPTER 8

I'D NEVER EXPERIENCED PANDEMONIUM ON THIS LEVEL. AT least, not in such a small space.

My voice had carried—or at least the word *bomb* had—to two rows of seats in both directions. A young woman of about Phoenix's age had taken it from there. She'd stood up, yelled, "Bomb! There's a bomb on the train!" and suddenly everyone in the car was in motion. Including the attendant, who was yelling into a radio and trying to push his way back down the aisle toward the front.

We'd taken on more passengers in both Saint-Hyacinthe and Drummondville, and the car was near capacity, so watching the attendant fight through the people already pushing and shoving one another was like watching a salmon throw itself upstream through rapids. But whatever he'd yelled into the radio had already had an effect.

The shriek of train brakes against steel ties pierced the chaos, and a sudden loss of momentum threw several passengers to the floor. I had seconds to make this work.

I grabbed Talia's wrist, my fingers closing over the puckered surgical scar and the plate that remained beneath her skin.

"Listen to me carefully," I said, "and don't argue. We don't have time. They're going to stop the train and send security back here. You can't let that happen. You need to get everyone out of this car and make them uncouple it and get as far away from us as you can."

"I can't—they won't listen to me."

"Make them listen. Use your badge, if you must, but

—" I broke off, distracted by a tiny black filament that drifted past my nose. Landing on my sleeve, it promptly ignited. I yelped and slapped out the flames. What the—

Someone screamed—more than one someone—and I looked up to see other filaments falling from the ceiling, each of them flaring into a tiny fire as soon as it touched anything. Seat backs, clothing, hair. I froze for the time it took me to blink at them—because what fresh hell was this?—then seized Talia's other hand and leaned forward until scant inches separated our noses.

"*Make them listen,*" I growled, willing her to do the same.

She ducked one filament, stomped on another that landed beside her foot, and pulled her hands from mine. "Be careful," she said.

We both stood, each with our assigned tasks. Hers, to funnel a panicked mob down a narrow aisle now alight with small fires and through an equally narrow door to safety; mine, to deal with a Mage with or without the stone's help.

I wasn't sure I liked either of our odds.

"Wait—what about you?" she asked.

"I'll find you in Quebec City. Go to the Ursulines. Look after Sister Margaret and Phoenix for me."

Talia hesitated for the space of a heartbeat, then pulled me to her for a quick hug. "Don't let it win," she whispered in my ear.

My brain snagged on the *it*, but she'd already pushed me away again and turned to flick falling filaments away from Sister Margaret and Phoenix. I caught the young woman's panicked, confused gaze over Sister Margaret's head. The desire to reassure her, to explain … to say goodbye … almost overwhelmed me, but—*we don't have time*, I reminded myself.

I turned away from her, away from the hurt and

betrayal I knew I would see when she realized I was leaving her, and steadfastly, stubbornly forced my way against the push of passengers, blocking the Mage from following the others. From following Phoenix.

It was time to take on a Mage.

Another one.

Hail Mary Magdalene … come and fight with me.

HE STOOD ALONE BY THE TIME I REACHED HIM, HIS LEGS spread wide to counter the shuddering lurch of the train in its final throes of making an emergency stop and his hands loosely clasped in front of him. Behind me, at the other end of the car, I heard shouting as the car finally stopped moving. The voices of at least two men plus Talia. I couldn't hear their words, but all were equally heated. Talia's, however, held an authoritative edge that cut across theirs.

Make them listen, I urged her. The doors hissed shut, and the voices disappeared.

I stopped half a dozen feet from the Mage and lifted my gaze to his. I already knew this would not be a battle of magick—at least not on my part. I could feel the stone's inertness in my pocket. Its lack of … interest? Caring? It seemed absurd to attribute emotions to an inanimate object like that, but I didn't know what else to call it. All I knew was that I couldn't let the Mage leave the train to follow the others, and that I was on my own.

Which was why I'd already cataloged all the items I'd seen between leaving my seat and arriving here. The bits and pieces that had been abandoned in the chaos of panic.

Six rows back, on the window seat to the left, a reusable water bottle; two rows after that, same side on the aisle seat, an open laptop still playing the cat videos its owner had been watching; same row, opposite side, a baseball cap with a company logo on the front.

And just ahead of me, in the next row as if placed there deliberately within reach of my right hand, a knitted winter scarf. In bright rainbow colors, no less. How very apropos.

The car jerked beneath my feet, and a shriek of metal filtered in from behind the sliding door far behind me. I reached for the handhold on my left to steady myself. Talia's task was almost complete. In a moment—

Another shriek. Another lurch. And then stillness but for the long, insistent blasts of the train horn that grew fainter as it left us behind.

"Right," the Mage said. "It's time to see what you're really made of, Sister Monica Barrett." He smiled and dropped his hands to his sides, clenching them into fists. "Remember," he added, as crimson fluid trickled from between his fingers and puddled on the carpet at his feet, "it didn't have to be like this. We really would have made you rich."

"I take it back," I responded, flexing and curling my own hands, visualizing what came next, breathing intention into the flow of moves that I would make.

Breathing.

Gray eyes narrowed on me. The puddle of crimson began to bubble. I made a mental note not to touch it when I went for him.

"Take what back?" he asked suspiciously.

"You shouldn't go fuck yourself," I said. "You should go fuck your entire consortium—and *then* yourself."

A mask of pure fury descended over the Mage's face,

and loathing laced his eyes. Neither were any match for my own. Even as he turned his hands over and lifted them sharply as if to pull the puddle he'd made upward, I was already moving. Already striking.

I scooped up the scarf from the seat as I stepped past it, stretched it taut between my hands as I ran toward the Mage, leapt over the crimson *whatever* that he'd been conjuring, and struck him full in the chest with all the strength I possessed in my five-foot-four-inch frame. All the anger I'd held in since that first day on the lawn of the Mary Magdalene House for Women.

The Mage uttered a surprised squawk and sprawled backward onto the floor, his arms flailing wide as I landed on top of him. Without pausing to catch my breath, I pulled myself upright to kneel over him, one knee planted in his diaphragm so he couldn't catch his breath either, the other on his left arm, which was partially wedged beneath a seat. Then, before he could recover, I grabbed his other hand and tied the scarf around it.

He was fighting me now. His face was a dark, mottled purple that didn't bode well for his heart, but I had no intention of waiting to see whether nature would take its course. I leapt lightly to my feet, checking over my shoulder to be sure I still avoided the crimson puddle behind me—was that a *face* moving in it?—and the Mage did likewise.

Although maybe in a more blundering fashion.

I waited until he was upright and swinging at me, then used his own force against him. I caught hold of his incoming wrist and twisted down and back until he squealed and gave up trying to resist. He turned until his back was to me and dropped to his knees. Swiftly, I wrapped the scarf around the second wrist, binding it to the first behind his back. Then, for good measure, because

I wasn't taking any chances and because the scarf had stretched to almost three times its original length with all my pulling and knot-tying, I wrapped it around his torso twice, pinning his upper arms to his sides and securing it with yet another knot. Whenever I'd seen a Mage gather magick, it had involved a lot of finger wiggling and hand waving. With luck, that meant no hands, no magick.

Something behind me wailed in disappointment, and I looked back to see a malformed head melting back into the puddle of whatever the hell the Mage had tried to conjure. My breath snagged in my throat for an instant, and then my prisoner pulled free of me and floundered to his feet. Calmly, I watched him half-run, half-limp to the exit door behind him.

Serenely, I stood up, too.

Sedately, I followed him.

I was almost done.

CHAPTER 9

By the time I caught up to him, the Mage had fumbled the door open and fallen off the little platform at the back of the car onto the train bridge. His arms still pinned to his sides by the scarf, he lay half on his side, half on his belly in the shadow of the car. The lights along the bridge weren't bright enough to illuminate his face, but I didn't need them to know what his expression would reveal.

Fury, absolutely. Fear, perhaps. But both of those would be overwhelmed by the three primary emotions endemic to those who thought themselves superior, who were certain they couldn't be bested, who refused to accept that they had been.

Hatred. Disbelief. Denial.

This privileged, entitled man would die knowing that he, a powerful Mage, had been bested by me, an old woman. I realized I was smiling at the idea and, horrified, wiped the curve from my lips.

What the hell, Monica.

A tiny vibration in my pocket distracted me. Was that the stone? Was it … *purring?* With happiness? Distaste rippled through me, and I suddenly remembered Talia's parting words.

"Don't let it win," she'd whispered in my ear. I hadn't understood then what she'd meant, but now … now, I wondered. I wondered about the ever-present irritation that seethed just below my surface, the growing distance between me and the young woman I loved more than I'd

loved anyone since Josephine, my inability to control the power before—or to reach it now, as if …

"If someone who practices dark magick touches a stone, it binds to them the way yours did to you," Sister Margaret had said when she'd told me about the stone she'd thrown to me that fateful day on the lawn of the women's shelter. *"It feeds off of the darkness."*

She'd assured me that I wasn't at risk of that happening—only the Mages—but in the same breath, she'd also admitted that the Obsidian Sisterhood didn't really understand how it worked. *Fuck*, I thought, shivering in the below-freezing wind that swept over the bridge as I blinked down at my captive. And then I thought it again.

Fuck.

What if the nun had been wrong? What if the stone *did* feed off the darkness in me, too? Was *I* the one who thought the Mage in front of me now needed to die, or was that *its* idea?

The very fact that I asked myself that question was answer enough. Ice that had nothing to do with the outside temperature slid through my veins. Dear sweet Mother of All, I'd been going to kill a man—not using the stone in self-defense as I'd done before, but with my own hands. In cold blood.

And even if it hadn't been my idea, I'd been about to let the stone make me do it.

If that wasn't letting it win, I didn't know what was.

At my feet, the Mage struggled to sit up, but with his arms bound tight to his sides, he looked like a fish flopping on the bridge deck.

Fuck.

Far down the track, safely on terra firma, the train had stopped again. Its lighted windows were filled with faces pressed against the glass, too far away to make out their features. Flashlights bobbed alongside it but didn't come our way. They'd be waiting for backup, of course. Reinforcements to do a sweep of the train car and, when they found no bomb, to arrest the crazy old woman who'd broken who knew how many federal laws with her wild story.

I was going to have a lot of explaining to do, and that explaining might—*might*—be made easier if I could send the cops after a mysterious man who'd disappeared into the night. Especially since the train's interior was scorched from whatever those evil little firefly things had been, and I still bore the marks of last night's Mage encounter at the cottage.

One day, however, I would really, really like to have an actual plan to follow instead of having to create one on the fly like this.

I yanked my captive to his feet, anger lending strength to my effort. Well, anger and probably the damned stone, but I was wise to it now, and I wouldn't let it get the upper hand again. My roughness, though? That, I would happily own.

"Start walking," I growled, yanking on his arm to turn him around and giving him a shake when he stumbled. I'd tell the cops that I'd tied him up and he'd escaped, I thought, planning for my own capture once the cavalry arrived, because I had no intention of untying him and giving him access to his magick again. Who knew? Maybe I'd get really lucky and he'd fall down in the weeds somewhere and not be able to get back up.

I might not be able to kill him in cold blood, but I'd happily let nature take its course.

"You're letting me go?" The Mage looked over his shoulder at me. "Why in God's name would you do that?"

Clamping down on a surge of fury that I didn't recognize as my own—and ignoring the reference to the deity he and his ilk had appropriated as *their* own—I ground out, "Because I'm not you, and I won't let you or your cohorts" —or the stone, for that matter—"turn me into you. Start. Walking."

He didn't move. "You know I'll just come after you again."

"And *you* know what I'm capable of if you do," I said. Bluffed, lied, whatever. I mean, theoretically, the stone could work for me again, right? One day. I gave him another shake, adding, "Do not mistake my reluctance for inability. If I see you again—"

The rest of my threat died in my throat when the Mage stepped back abruptly, pulling me off balance. I released the arm I'd been holding and recovered. Too late, I realized that while I'd been talking myself out of taking drastic measures against him, he'd somehow managed to free his hands from the scarf I'd tied them with. Hands that were now spread wide, with blue fire stretching and surging between his fingertips. Swiftly, before I could stop him—or even think *how* to stop him—he brought his hands closer and rolled them around one another. The fire became a sphere, and with another quick movement, he launched it at me.

I threw myself to the side, fast enough to duck the fireball but not fast enough that I didn't feel its passing heat. And sweet Mary, there was a lot of heat. Air hissed from me as the pain in my cheek registered, but again, there was no time to dwell. The blue sphere had hit the train car behind me and spread to envelop it. Heat battered my back as I dragged myself to my feet—and the Mage was already forming another ball of blue.

My fingers twitched toward my pocket, but I stopped them. After my latest realizations, I trusted the stone less than ever. No, I was going to do this the old-fashioned way —and if I was right about my opponent, he would be too cocky to see it coming. Even after losing our train battle.

The Mage readied himself for another pitch. I didn't wait for it. I launched myself at him, tackling him around the waist and carrying him toward the ground with my momentum … just as the train car behind me exploded. The force of the explosion picked both of us up before we'd hit the bridge deck and hurled us over the railing.

When they say that time slows down in your last moments, they're not kidding. I knew that I fell for only seconds, but even as the black water below rushed toward me, I felt the wind ruffle my hair, still marveled at the height of the flames shooting upward from the twisted remains of the train car, still wondered if the bridge would survive the explosion.

Then I wondered what the authorities would think about the crazy old lady on the train now as I watched burning chunks of metal drop past me to land in the water with angry hisses as flames turned to steam. And then—

Pain slammed through me as the water hit me like a brick wall and, in an instant, time suddenly moved at lightning speed. Black closed over my head, and bitter cold sank through to my core. The shock made me gasp, and I inhaled water rather than air. Panic set in. Grimly, I fought it off—along with the urge to suck again for air. I was still descending through the water, and the cold was making my brain glitch. There were rules for surviving winter water, but I had never been a strong swimmer to begin with, and I could remember none of them. Was I supposed to leave my boots on, or try to take them off? What about my coat? Would that drag me down if I kept it on?

My feet touched the gravel bed at the bottom of the river. For a second, I didn't register the feel of it, then sheer survival instinct kicked in, and I pushed off again, pointing myself toward the flickering orange and blue and yellow light that marked the surface above.

The Mage was there when I broke the surface. There, then gone, then there again. His eyes were wild, the whites of them glinting in the firelight. His thrashing was even wilder. He wasn't going to make it if he kept it up.

"Stop it!" I yelled at him, treading water a few feet away, but if he heard me, he gave no indication. He went under a third time. *Fuck*, I thought. Then fuck, fuck, *fuck*. Because I couldn't just let him die.

Well, I could, but—no.

I mean, yes, I'd killed before, but not on purpose. Never on purpose, because I was not that person. And more importantly, I was *not* the stone.

"Don't let it win."

The Mage's head reappeared again, but it wasn't as high this time. He was tiring fast. I was, too. If I was going to get to him, it needed to be now. Grimly, I struck out toward him in my best dog paddle. Arms and legs made of frozen lead made progress difficult.

I got within arm's length. The Mage faced away from me, and I lunged for the back of his collar as he slipped again beneath the surface. I may not have been a great swimmer, but I knew enough to tow him from behind, where he couldn't get hold of me and take us both—

Shit.

He'd reached back over his head, strong fingers had clamped over my wrist and, despite my intentions, I was going under with him.

I released my hold on his collar and pried at his hand, but my fingers had lost all feeling and most of their strength, and I was no match for what was fast turning into his literal death grip. I'd managed to fill my lungs with air before the water closed over my head this time, and I held it there now, cradling it within me like the life-giving force that it was, searching for calm within its presence. The Mage had taken no breath, however, and without the buoyancy, he was sinking fast.

The need to free myself clawed at my throat and wound like gossamer steel through my veins. *Wait*, I told it. *We just need to hold on until he can't.*

Even in the fight against panic, the wording of my thought was not lost on me.

We. I'd thought of the stone and me as *we.*

It occurred to me that my mind was beginning to cloud, not just from a lack of oxygen but from the cold, too. The latter had lost its initial bitter sharpness and turned insidious, sneaking into the places in my core that I wouldn't normally notice. My kidneys, my intestines, my liver …

Soon, one by one, they would begin going offline.

Hail Mary Magdalene, full of grace, come and sit with me.

A faint boom thudded against my eardrums, and the orange glow above us brightened. Another explosion, I registered distantly. The light from it blossomed through the water and illuminated the Mage clinging to me. He floated no more than two feet away, his face still and his eyes wide and empty and staring at something awful that only he could see. He was gone.

Hail Mary Magdalene, sister to us all, come and pray for me.

With the last of my strength, the last of my coherence, I reached for the hand holding my wrist and disengaged the last bond holding him to this earth. He floated down and away, caught in the river's current.

I followed.

Chapter 10

I woke cocooned in soft warmth. It was bliss.

For about two-point-five seconds.

Then the horror of recent events flashed back to me. I remembered the train bridge and falling into the river and the panicked Mage who had grabbed hold of my wrist. I remembered watching him thrashing in the water, his eyes widening as he slowly sank to the bottom. I remembered him drowning … and thinking that I would drown, too, and freeing myself from his death grip. I remembered the current carrying him away and depositing me on the shallow, rocky shore, and being so cold that I hadn't been able to feel my arms or legs, and—

And I should be dead, not feeling all warm and cozy, wrapped up in …

I cracked an eye open to see where I was, but there was only white, as if a sheet had been pulled over my head or—

Or, hold on. I recognized this. I grimaced and then blew at a wisp of web that was tickling my nose. Because that's what it was. Spiderweb. I was cocooned the way I'd been in the woods when Rusk had called the spiders. Only this time, it was winter, and there were no spiders, and Talia wasn't here to remove the webs, which meant that I was on my own and that the webs had come from—

Fucking hell.

In a microsecond, I went from warm and cozy to ice-cold and terrified as Sister Margaret's story of the disciple flashed back to me. He'd touched the stone, she'd said, and it had bound to the darkness in him and cocooned him.

He'd died alone at the side of a field and been half-eaten by some kind of animal, probably a coyote, and—

I squeezed my eyes tight against the hazy light coming through the webs encasing me, because dear sweet Mary Magdalene, there might not be spiders at this time of year, but there were sure as hell still coyotes, maybe even wolves, around here, and—

Another thought flashed in to join that one, and fresh horror filled me. Sister Margaret said that she'd found the disciple's remains and seen the terror frozen on what remained of his face. I hadn't thought it through then, but I did now. *What if he'd still been alive when the animals found him?*

I surged up into a sitting position and clawed at the cocoon surrounding me. I'd cleared my head enough to see the trees to my right and the tall grasses surrounding me before my hands stilled and my abject panic eased enough for me to note that this was nothing like what had happened at Rusk's hands. That those webs had held me like steel bands, and it had taken Talia's and my combined efforts to tear them away from my body. That this was … different.

The webs themselves were different.

As if they'd formed around me not to hold me captive, but to protect me.

And now, like fine, filmy fabric that shredded at a touch, they fell away because they'd done their job.

Huh.

Also *huh* at the fact that the cocoon had worked. I'd survived. I had no earthly idea where I was, and I was rapidly chilling again now that I'd lost its protection, but I had survived. And the Mage hadn't.

Momentary horror threatened to derail my calm(ish) analysis of my situation as an image of the drowned Mage floated—yes, I know, bad choice of words—into my mind's eye. Sweet Mary Magdalene, what an awful way to die. I braced for a shudder but instead felt a warm slither of something wrapping around my insides, like a physical manifestation of contentment. As if something—I stopped myself.

Right. It was time to start calling a spade a spade here, because that wasn't just *something*, it was the stone. And not just the stone, but the stone expressing pleasure at the Mage's demise.

"Don't let it win," Talia whispered again in my ear.

That made me shudder.

But this wasn't the time or the place for panicking over the connection—I refused to call it a bond—that had formed between me and the object I carried. I needed to set priorities here, and the first of those was simple survival, followed by getting my butt to Quebec City to meet the others.

I set my jaw and went to work clearing the remainder of my cocoon from my legs, my ankles, my feet. Then I turned my attention to my top half but paused with my hand resting on my shoulder. I hadn't stopped to put on a coat before I'd thrown the Mage from the train car, and I had no idea how far I was going to have to walk to find help. Whatever I might think of the stone—and I considered my feelings about it to be justifiably mixed—the cocoon had done its job of keeping me warm. My jeans and Talia's boots were wet but adequate for the weather as long as it didn't change, but my shirt alone?

That would not do.

I lowered my hand again and used it to push myself up and off the ground. Then, standing amid dried, brittle grass and leafless scrub brush, I wrapped the cocoon remnants around me like a cloak and took stock of my circumstances. The river flowed past about twenty feet away, the rush of water tumbling over rocks the only sound I could hear. I remembered it depositing me on the shore, so I must have crawled away from the water to the edge of the trees before the stone's webs had cocooned me.

The long span of train bridge that sat to my right said that I'd miraculously—or perhaps magically, I thought, wrapping my hands tighter into the cocoon—floated only a hundred yards or so downstream. I'd never been in this part of the country before, however, so that didn't tell me much. I frowned, trying to get my directions sorted out based on the few clues I could pull together.

First, I noted, the sun's pale orb peeped out from behind slate-gray clouds across from me; second, I knew that Quebec City sat on the shore of the Saint Lawrence River and was northeast of Montreal; and third, in all like-lihood, this river flowed toward the Saint Lawrence, which meant that it had carried *me* north.

Ergo, I thought with no small flare of triumph, the sun was in the west, and I was on the east side of the water. And since the train had been heading east over the river, too, I was going in the right direction.

Or I would be, once I figured out *how*, I amended as my triumph fizzled out.

Because apart from knowing what side of the river I stood on, I had nothing. I had no idea how far I was from Charny and its train station, or how far Quebec City was beyond that, or if either of them would be within walking distance. Especially in wet boots and the tattered remains of a cocoon.

On the other hand, with the cloud-shrouded sun sinking ever closer to the treeline, I didn't have much choice other than to try, because I wasn't exactly equipped for spending the night out here. Shivering, I drew the tatters of cocoon tighter around me. *Another night*, I amended, because I had no idea how long I'd been lying out here, either.

As for where to start my walk … I grimaced over my shoulder at the solid wall of trees behind me. I didn't relish going back to the train bridge, but I supposed that following a railway track I knew would eventually lead me to Saint-Foy made more sense than trying to forge a path through an unknown forest I would likely get lost in. And after I got there?

Well, one overwhelming problem at a time, right?

With a deep sigh drawn all the way up from wet toes that squelched inside wetter socks and boots, I picked my way around boulders and across rocks and headed back upstream toward the train bridge.

I'D MADE IT LESS THAN FIFTY METERS WHEN A MAN'S LOUD shout had me diving to the ground, heart pounding.

My first thought was that the Mages had somehow found me, but when I gathered my wits (and nerve) enough to peep up over the river grasses, it was to find a hive of activity on and below the section of bridge that had been screened from my view before.

The part with the twisted, skeletal remains of a train car still sitting on it. My breath snagged in my throat as I took in the devastation. Dear sweet Mary, I'd survived *that*? How? I swallowed hard.

Chunks of wooden railway ties littered the shoreline between me and what was left of that section of bridge, and three figures walking along the rails beside the wrecked car gingerly hopped over what were likely the resulting holes in the bridge surface. Below all of that sat a police boat, likely with a dive team scouring the waters around it.

I drew my head back down into the cover of the river grass and pondered my situation. It was, I decided, both good and bad. Bad, because the fact that a search was still in full swing would make it more difficult for me to avoid getting caught.

Good, because I was pretty sure that the divers would have been brought in at daybreak, which—I hoped— meant I'd only been missing for one night, during which they had almost certainly already searched the shoreline. How they'd missed me, I had no idea, but divers meant they were looking for bodies, not someone still alive and ambulatory.

Also good was the faint hope that Talia, Phoenix, and Sister Margaret wouldn't have had a chance to panic (too much) yet about my absence from our meeting place in Quebec City—assuming, of course, they'd been able to get there themselves.

Which was doubtful, since they were witnesses in a full-blown federal investigation. Not to mention connected to the crazy woman who'd cried *bomb*, stayed behind in the decoupled train car with the suspect, and then—from all appearances—been blown sky high with both. I winced at the last thought.

So, maybe they would be panicking a little. In between answering questions, that was, because there would be many of those. And that wasn't even counting the part where Talia was a Toronto cop who'd taken a leave of absence to accompany us here. So, *so* many questions.

But that was their problem right now. Mine right now

was not getting caught. And not getting lost. And finding shelter. And food. And getting to Quebec City. And—

I sighed. And this was getting me nowhere, and the sun was lower than ever, and I needed to move.

With a final glance at the bridge to be sure no eyes were trained in my direction, I crawled through the grass to the cover of the treeline, where I stood, squared my shoulders, and glumly settled in for an uncomfortable hike of unknown duration.

CHAPTER 11

The hike went faster than I thought it would.

As soon as I'd left the sound of the river behind me, a new, muffled roar from ahead had taken over. Before I knew it, I was staring at a divided and busy four-lane highway and wondering how I was supposed to get to the other side.

The highway stretched as far as I could see in both directions without any sign of an on or off ramp—or an overpass, apart from the one for the train. Traffic whizzed along steadily, much of it made up of transport trucks, and there were barriers along both sides of each two-lane section—a total of four of them, plus the grass median—that I would have to climb over in addition to risking life and limb darting between those trucks.

I knew from experience that it *could* be done. I'd proved that in Kingston when I'd crossed Highway 401 in pursuit of the goliath and Phoenix—in the dark, no less. The fact that I still had some daylight now didn't make repeating the stunt any more advisable. Plus, I had no idea what I would do when I got to the other side. Or where I would go. Or even if I wanted to be there, because where the hell was Quebec City from here, anyway? Perhaps if I'd paid more attention to the train's route map outside the business lounge in Montreal, I might have an idea, but I hadn't and I didn't, and—

And damn it, I was hungry.

I was hungry, because my coat with the sandwich in the pocket had blown up in the train, and I was thirsty, because nearly drowning had done nothing to slake that, and I was cold, because again, no coat, and damn it—I swiped a strand of cocoon remnant from my face—I was cobwebby, too.

And my feet were blistered from the wet boots that were two sizes too big for me.

And I had no money to throw at any of my problems, and no idea how in hell I was going to get to Quebec City from here, and—

I exhaled the ragged breath I'd sucked into my lungs and uncurled my fingernails from my cold palms. My issues list was long, yes, but panicking wouldn't solve anything. I needed to stay in control—if not of my situation, then at least my thoughts.

Once upon a time, a lifetime ago, when I'd been running the Mary Magdalene House for Women, I'd excelled at problem-solving. I just needed to remember how. I needed to remember who I still was beneath the tangle of cobwebs. To remember that I *was*, period.

I watched a series of semis roll by on the opposite side of the highway as I tried to prioritize my needs. Food, drink, and shelter were obviously at the top of the list, but there was no way to access them without money. The cash Talia had given me was zipped inside the inner pocket of the coat that had exploded with the train—along with my sandwich—and I doubted that the remains of the cocoon I wore would keep me alive if I remained outside. That left me with no choice but to find a way to where Talia and Phoenix and Sister Margaret were.

I blinked as another series of trucks rumbled past on the other side. Wait. Hadn't most of the ones I'd seen been heading that way? North, if I'd gotten my orientation right. Quebec City was to the north.

I stared up and to my right, at the railway overpass that crossed the highway and then descended toward …

I squinted at the flat, obviously industrial area on the other side of the tracks. It was no place for a train station, but our train had moved to side rails twice during the journey because the freight system it shared the track with took priority. And freight trains meant—

All systems in my brain fired at once. A rail yard. That was a rail yard, and a rail yard meant containers arriving and being offloaded onto trucks and those trucks taking them to their next destination and—and—and Quebec City had to be one of the destinations for at least some of them, right? And surely I could convince one of those truck drivers to take me along, right?

My knees wobbled in sheer, utter relief. I had a plan. Sweet Mary Magdalene, I had a plan at last. And it wasn't even one that I was cobbling together on the fly.

Well, maybe there was a little cobbling …

Fine. There was a lot.

But it was still a plan.

I MADE IT ACROSS THE HIGHWAY WITHOUT CAUSING AN accident, although I did incur the wrath of several truckers —expressed through long, drawn-out blasts on air horns that made my ears ring for long minutes after I'd dived over the last barrier and sprawled on my belly in the ditch. It turned out, however, that crossing the busy highway was the easy part.

Convincing a trucker leaving the rail yard to take on a dirty, cobwebby, suspiciously maybe-not-all-there old woman as a passenger? That was nowhere near as easy as I'd thought it would be. The language barrier didn't help.

I'd known that French was the primary language throughout the province of Quebec, of course, but in this region, it was apparently the only one spoken at all. And having grown up in Ontario in a bygone era, before French classes became compulsory in most Canadian schools outside Quebec, I'd never learned it. Any of it. Beyond the pretty much universally known *bonjour/hello, oui/yes,* and *merci/thank you,* I was lost.

In more ways than one, because after a very, very long time (according to my stiffening knees and numb fingers), I was still wandering along the service road where the trucks exited the rail yard. I'd been turned down by seventeen drivers already, and I was in increasing jeopardy of being reported to the rail police.

I limped over to a stack of wooden pallets at the side of the road and lowered myself down to sit on it. Whatever magick the stone had wrought on my insides to heal me and keep me alive, it hadn't extended to undoing the ravages of simple age, and I felt every single one of my years right now. The sun had long since disappeared below the horizon, dark prowled beyond the reach of the bright overhead streetlights, and I was facing a miserable, cold, and very hungry night as what had seemed like an obvious plan crumbled into dust.

"Hail, Mary Magdalene," I whispered through a throat made tight by exhaustion and the threat of tears. "If you're not too busy, I could really use a friend right now."

The rumble of another truck approached. Arms wrapped around my cramping, empty belly, I lifted my head to watch it, but I didn't get up. I didn't have another ask in me. Not tonight. I was too tired. And too cold. The wind had picked up, gusting across the flat terrain hard enough to toss loose pieces of lumber around, and the cocoon was no match for it. I'd live without food for the night, but I needed to find shelter somewhere—if not indoors, then at least away from the wind.

The truck slowed as it drove by, then stopped a little way past me. Its backup lights came on, and a persistent, high-pitched warning beep echoed along the service road as eighteen wheels rolled backward again and came to a stop beside me. The beep cut off, and the driver's window descended. A concerned, weathered old visage peered out at me.

A jumble of words followed in French.

"*Anglais?*" I asked hopefully. *English?* Oh yay, that made four words I knew.

The man in the truck shook his head and another spate of words issued forth. My shoulders slumped. I had no idea what he was saying, and I didn't have the energy to try anymore. Not tonight. I started to shake my head, then paused. *One last shot*, I told myself. *Just one.*

"Quebec City?" I asked, and then, seeing the now-familiar doubt creeping across the lined face, I added in desperation, "The Ursuline Sisters."

Doubt evaporated into delight, and the man's head bobbed. "*Les Ursulines*," he agreed, and I perked up.

Could this be it? Could this be my ride?

I placed a cold hand on my chest and nodded, too. "*Oui*," I said. "*Oui! Les Ursulines!*" Okay, I'd mangled that pretty badly, but I think we were communicating. I patted my hand against myself. "Me and les Ursulines."

That triggered another incomprehensible monologue, but it was at least an enthusiastic one, and I could have cried when it ended with him thrusting open his door and jumping out of the truck. Had I really done it? Had I found a way to Quebec City?

The truck driver gestured to me to follow, and on legs bowed by age or infirmity or both, led me with a rolling gait around the front of the idling semi. On the other side, he reached up and tugged open the passenger door.

"*Québec*," he told me, giving the city its French pronunciation of *Kay-beck* and nodding some more as he patted the seat that was level with the top of his head. "*Les Ursulines.*"

Perhaps he thought I needed the reassurance before getting into a massive vehicle with a total stranger in the dark. I did not. In fact, it was all I could do not to hug him as I smiled and nodded back my thanks. I threw in a *merci* for good measure, but it sounded more like mercy when I said it.

Which was also apt, I thought, as I reached for the handhold beside the door to pull myself up.

So apt.

We were underway in seconds, just as the digital clock on the dashboard turned over to 8:05. I shivered. It was no wonder I was cold. I'd been wandering around out there for at least five hours, if my judgment of the pale, half-hidden sun had been at all accurate when I'd woken up on the riverbank.

The driver wheeled the big rig off the service road and onto a main street, and then, driving several tens of thousands of pounds with one hand and half his attention, he twisted around to rummage in the compartment behind the seats.

I'd begun to wonder if I had evaded death in a flaming train wreck in favor of death in a flaming traffic wreck when he made a triumphant noise and turned back to drop a heavy jacket in my lap. Grinning, he gestured to me to put it on, then signaled for a turn.

The jacket was three sizes too big, in need of a wash, and smelled of pipe tobacco and stale sweat—and it was the most wonderful thing I'd ever worn in my life. I zipped it up and offered another tentative *merci*. Then, at my savior's urging—via more incomprehensible words and a few gesticulations that were only slightly less so—I put on my seatbelt.

Two expertly navigated turns later, we were on the highway I'd crossed to get to the rail yard, heading north. According to the sign that flashed by on our right, we'd reach Sainte-Foy in minutes, and Quebec City shortly after. I'd gotten that close.

The Mage had gotten that close.

But I'd stopped him, and as long as none of the other passengers who'd escaped had been another Mage, I'd slowed down their search for Methuselah.

I let my head fall back against the seat as the truck climbed a steep incline onto the bridge spanning the St. Lawrence River. The lights of my destination twinkled on the other side, and far below us, the dark waters of the St. Lawrence River flowed through the night. A container ship moved slowly against its current, its lights slipping beneath the bridge as we crossed above it. I was almost there. I was almost with Phoenix and Talia and Sister Margaret again. Almost on the trail of the elusive Methuselah and the answers to all of my many questions.

But that latter one was a tomorrow problem.

For tonight, I was almost there, and that was enough. The semi's tires bumped rhythmically over the expansion joints in the bridge decking as I closed my eyes and sent up a prayer of gratitude to Mary Magdalene and the Mother of All for getting me—us—this far. Not a request for more help—although another of those would almost certainly come later—but just a thank you for all that they had done.

And then ... then, I think my eyes just forgot to open again.

CHAPTER 12

When I jolted awake, the lights were gone. So was the river. I sat up from where I'd fallen asleep against the truck door and stared out at the dark trees scrolling past my window as the truck barreled down the highway and my muddled brain tried to deduce where we were and what had happened.

From behind the oversized steering wheel, the trucker —*who may or may not be a serial killer who's just abducted you*, my unhelpful imagination suggested—looked over and smiled, his teeth flashing in the light from the dashboard as he launched into a barrage of words. I wasn't sure quite why he insisted on using so many of them when I clearly didn't understand a single one, but perhaps he enjoyed talking?

As if he'd read my mind, he broke off in mid-sentence (I think) and chuckled. Then he placed a hand on his chest and announced, "Louis," before pointing at me and raising an eyebrow.

"Sis—" I began, but I stopped. Knowing the Mages would be trying to track us again, it might be best to drop the distinctive *sister* title. "Monica," I told Louis.

His eyebrow rose a little higher, this time with skepticism. "Sismonica?" he repeated dubiously.

"No. Monica. Just Monica."

His expression cleared as he nodded. More words followed, this time in question form. I recognized them as such because of the question mark I detected at the end— but I got no more than that from them, and I shook my head and shrugged my incomprehension.

He thought about it for a second, then inquired, "Pee-pee?"

That, I understood. I started to shake my head again but realized it might again be interpreted as a lack of understanding. "No," I replied. "No pee-pee."

The one side benefit to being dehydrated, I supposed.

"*Bon*," he said. He reached into a cooler bag on the seat between us and extracted a paper-wrapped bundle. Without asking, he dropped it into my lap, then handed me a travel mug from a holder on the console.

If he expected a polite refusal from me, he was sorely disappointed. I hadn't eaten since Talia had all but forced the train dinner on me, and that would have been the last time I'd had a drink, too. Although I imagined I must have ingested my share of river water while I was trying not to drown.

Displaying a great deal more control than I felt, I unwrapped what turned out to be a thick ham and cheese sandwich. I sank my teeth into it and very nearly moaned in bliss. It was home baked bread, too. Beside me, my truck-driver savior nodded approvingly, his grin widening.

I had several more bites interspersed with sips from the travel mug of what turned out to be hot, sweet tea. Then, when the pleasure haze triggered by the food had dissipated somewhat and I remembered where we were—or more importantly, where we *weren't*—I gestured at the windshield.

"Quebec?" I asked.

"*Saguenay en premier*," he responded.

He tapped the digital clock glowing on the dashboard —it currently displayed a time of 9:18—and then jabbed a thumb over his shoulder. My stomach gave a lurch of dismay. I surmised that he was on a schedule for the load he carried, but how far was Saguenay? Was he going back to Quebec City afterward?

"Saguenay," I said, "and then Quebec City?"

Loo-wee braced his elbows against the steering wheel and raised his hands, counting off destinations on the fingers of one. "*Saguenay, Trois-Rivières, puis Québec*," he agreed.

Heartily hoping that *pwee Kay-beck* meant *then Quebec*, I swallowed the information along with another bite of sandwich. I had no idea how far those destinations were from one another, but judging from the scenery floating by, I guessed that they weren't next-door neighbors. This was going to be a long drive, and a long night. Wistfully, I thought about how very close I'd been, then consoled myself that I would get there again—eventually.

Probably.

Maybe.

Talia, Phoenix, and Sister Margaret would be beside themselves with worry. But I had no way of contacting them, no way of letting them know that I was still alive, and so I did the only thing I could do. I finished eating, and with my belly full of ham and cheese sandwich and hot, sweet tea, I fell asleep again, wrapped in the scent of pipe tobacco and lulled by the steady hum of tires over pavement—and the sound of my new friend's off-key accompaniment to the lively Quebec folk music he'd begun blasting from the radio.

I was further than ever from where I needed to be, but for the moment, I felt only gratitude.

I WOKE ONCE, WHEN THE TRUCK SLOWED DOWN. I THOUGHT it was because we'd arrived in Trois-Rivières, but when I cracked open an eye, we were still in the middle of nowhere—civilization-speaking—and the truck was still rolling down the highway. Just a little more slowly than before. I thought about whether I had the energy to attempt another round of communication bingo, but even as I waffled about the idea, I saw the empty plastic bottle clutched in the left hand that Louis-pronounced-loo-wee rested on the steering wheel and heard the undoing of a zipper.

Sheer startlement made both my eyes fly open. I snapped them shut again before Louis saw that I was awake. He didn't need to know that I knew, and dear Mary Magdalene, I would much rather pretend I didn't.

That said, it took all the self-control I possessed not to snigger into the jacket collar like a ten-year-old when I couldn't block out the sound of urine tinkling into the bottle—or Louis's sigh of relief. At least he'd slowed the truck down in order to take care of business, right?

I listened to him screw the cap back on and then twist around in his seat to deposit his … deposit … in the back compartment. Three thoughts crossed my mind as the truck picked up speed again. First, how thankful I was to have been dehydrated and able to say no to his pee-pee query earlier, because I did *not* want to know how he'd intended for me to … well.

Second, how I'd just eaten a sandwich handed to me by the hand that had … also well.

And third, how ironic would it be to survive an exploding train, a fall into a river, and all the other disasters that had come before, only to be taken down by unhygienic food practices?

I probably would have laughed if I hadn't drifted back into sleep.

MY TRUCK DRIVER FRIEND DROPPED ME OFF AT EIGHT THE next morning alongside a parking lot on the shore of the St. Lawrence. A ferry was docked at a quay on the other side of the lot, and in the not-very-distant distance to my left, a long, high bridge spanned the river. I suspected it was the bridge that we had crossed many hours before, but decided I didn't need to know for sure, because even if it was only the half-hour walk away that it looked, I wouldn't have made it last night. All that mattered was that I'd made it.

A kind stranger named Louis had taken pity on me and shared his food and hot tea with me and let me sleep in his truck—he'd even given me his coat—and brought me to where I might find Phoenix and Talia and Sister Margaret, and that was enough.

It was more than enough.

That reminded me—I was still wearing Louis's coat. I reached for the zipper to return the garment to him, but Louis flapped both hands at me.

"*Non, non, non,*" he said, shaking his head along with his hands. More words followed. I still didn't understand those, but I'd spent enough time in this man's company to know what he was saying. I smiled and leaned across the truck cab to give him a hug.

"Mercy," I whispered, and I didn't even pretend that I was saying *merci*. I turned and opened the passenger door, then slithered awkwardly out and onto the pavement. I'd considered jumping down the way Louis did, but my knees and ankles had threatened retribution at the mere thought. It would be a while before they forgave me for the abuse they'd endured lately.

And I didn't even want to know how many blisters I had on my poor feet.

My hand was on the door, ready to slam it shut, when I remembered to ask, "Wait—the Ursulines?"

"*Ah oui, les Ursulines.*" He jabbed his finger out the window beside him, pointing upward. "*En haut,*" he announced. Then, impatient to be back on the road and on time for his next stop—I hoped it would be home for him, but I didn't know how to ask—he flapped his hand at me to close the door and slammed the gearshift into drive. I did as I was told and stepped back as the truck left the curb in a series of jerks. Louis gave a few quick blasts on his horn in farewell, and I waved until the vehicle had lumbered out of sight. Then, alone again, I turned to look across the street.

A row of stone buildings sat on the other side of a low stone fortification with cannons peeping out from it. Beyond the buildings were more buildings, all of them old and solid and speaking to centuries of stories, centuries of endurance. Beyond the buildings rose a hill that was dominated by an enormous, stately building, complete with towers and turrets.

It looked like a castle, but I recognized it as the Château Frontenac, a hotel and one of Quebec City's most iconic landmarks—and it was in the upward direction that Louis had pointed his finger. Which, I supposed, meant that I could add two more French words to my vocabulary: *en haut.* Up there.

By the time I'd limped through the warren of cobblestone streets that wound through the buildings to the foot of the hill, I'd surmised that Louis had dropped me off in the famed Old Quebec. It was probably as near to the Ursuline sisters as he could get his semi, because the streets in what had started as a French colony had not been constructed with transport trucks in mind.

Or cranky, tired old women, for that matter.

I stared up at the weird contraption stuck to the side of hill—kind of a cross between an elevator and a cable car— then eyed the building that appeared to be its entrance. It was called a *funiculaire*, according to the sign above the door, and a smaller, handwritten sign announced that the cost of a ride was five dollars each way. I sighed. I only needed to go one way, but the price might as well have been a thousand dollars for a woman who'd had to let a stranger buy her a donut.

I turned my head to look up and down the narrow, shop-lined street. I doubted that the *funiculaire* had been around in the early French colony days, and there were definitely more buildings on top of the hill, so there had to be another way up. Such as those stairs to the right. The rather long flight of stairs that my knees and blisters were not going to appreciate.

I sighed, straightened my spine in a semblance of an *I've got this* attitude, and began climbing.

The good news was that I was right about the stairs leading to the top of the hill. The bad news was that there were more of them than the first ones had led me to believe. A lot more.

At the top of the first set was a street with a pitch so steep that the sidewalk had a handrail along it. That led to a second set of stairs, longer than the first, which culminated in a short landing, and then *more* stairs. By the time I reached the top, I was hobbling, my knees and I were no longer on speaking terms of any kind, and I was sourly wondering yet again why the stone's magick couldn't compensate for at least some of my years.

But I'd arrived, and as I paused to catch my breath and flex an ankle that was almost as pissed at me as the knees were, I couldn't help but be captivated by the utter charm laid out before me.

We were a full month before Christmas, but the city was already decked out in lights and garlands that, even in daylight, lent it a magical air. The château towered to my left—up yet another set of stairs, so that wasn't happening —and a little park was before me, a tall monument in its center and a Santa display, complete with chair and photo backdrop, sprawled to one side. Beyond that, another warren of cobblestone streets and old stone buildings, and an utter swarm of people.

Suddenly, watching the Mage drown didn't seem as awful as it first had, because having him here, pursuing us and not giving a damn about who got in his way ...

That would have been worse by far.

So much worse.

With my knees and ankles as restored as they were going to get, I limped my way through a group of tourists who had stopped to point their phone cameras up at the château and headed for a nearby building with large letters on its side spelling out *Information*. Where better to ask where to find the institution of nuns who had helped found the city?

CHAPTER 13

If only it were that simple.

If only *anything* were simple.

If only this damned stone would stop making me so blasted cranky.

I pressed my lips together as I eyed the perfectly lovely, unbelievably obtuse young man on the other side of the counter and attempted to rein in my impatience.

"No," I said for the fourth time—in English, thankfully, because he was blessedly bilingual. Which meant that the issue was not a language barrier, it was him. I slid the pamphlet he'd given me back toward him, also for the fourth time. For an information bureau, they were remarkably unhelpful.

"You don't understand," I said. "I don't want to see the Ursuline museum. I don't want to see their chapel. I don't want to see the monastery that was converted to a hotel. I want to see *them*. The sisters themselves. Where can I find *them*?"

Because if the convent had been converted into that many things, where on earth had its former occupants gone?

"Madame," a new voice—a heavily accented female one with a haughty edge to it this time—said, "there is no misunderstanding. The Ursuline sisters are private women. They do not welcome ... tourists." That last word—and the deliberate hesitation that preceded it—was delivered with unmistakable disdain as a set of brown eyes raked over my unwashed hair and borrowed coat.

Unhelpful escalated to borderline rude, and I bridled

on Louis's behalf, but the woman was already speaking again. "Now, if there is nothing more we can help you with, you are holding up the line."

I looked over my shoulder at the single other person in the visitor center, who was currently perusing a collection of brochures. My irritation became a seethe that crawled beneath my skin, sending an unpleasant shiver down my spine. The stone was at it again.

For fucksake, I told it, *what do you expect me to do? Smack her on your behalf? Stop it.*

Smack her, a quieter part of me wondered, *or worse?* I withdrew my hand from the counter and tucked it into the jacket pocket, just in case. It might, I thought, behoove me to leave before *that* internal debate went further.

"Madame?" the woman behind the counter prodded. I turned back to her and she nodded pointedly in the direction of the exit. "Enjoy your stay in *Québec,* madame."

I gritted my teeth, gave her a tight, perfunctory smile, and stomped out of the building to take my search for the Ursulines elsewhere. Outside, I stopped at the foot of the stairs and looked down the narrow little pedestrian street.

A series of little wooden huts, laden with merchandise ranging from specialty wines to pet collars, lined one side, with little crowds milling in front of each and other people winding their way through. From the American-accented English I was hearing from all directions, a good number of them were tourists, which astounded me, because I wouldn't have thought Canada in November would be much of a vacation spot

Squaring my shoulders and straightening my spine— and ignoring the irritated little buzz tingling along the latter—I waded into the fray and began what was, essentially, a random meandering. Finding the Ursulines—or someone willing to tell me *where* I could find them—could take me hours, days, or weeks. Or it might prove altogether impossible. Who knew? But I had to start somewhere. And I had to hope that Talia, Phoenix, and Sister Margaret would have found them, too.

The reason for the crowds became apparent when I emerged from the crowded little pedestrian street onto the sidewalk of an actual paved one and saw an even more crowded square across from me. It, too, was filled with the little wooden huts, along with Christmas trees, strings of lights, fancy lighted deer, and what looked like—from where I stood—every artisanal product imaginable.

Above the entrance nearest me, a sign read *Marché de Noël Allemand*, which didn't require a whole lot of thought to translate. I knew *Noël* to be Christmas and could intuit from the booths that *marché* meant market, and I had been to the German Christmas market in Toronto enough times with the Mary Magdalene House residents to make an educated guess at *Allemand* meaning just that— German.

Look at you, acquiring a French vocabulary in your spare time, piped up my little inner voice.

I couldn't decide if it was being sarcastic or not, chose to ignore it, and crossed the street with a family pushing a baby in a stroller and pulling a wagon loaded with two other children and a pile of winter gear. They were speaking French, so on the other side of the intersection, I asked them if they knew where the Ursulines might live. But they were also tourists—here from Ottawa, they said— and had no idea.

The next two dozen people I asked said much the same, with only their location of origin changing. Well, that, and the amount of distance they tried to keep between themselves and what I'm pretty sure they believed to be an old homeless woman. My finding of well-known nuns in a city had become a search for the proverbial needle in a haystack.

After three hours of accosting strangers and walking up and down the sidewalks and cobblestone streets—I knew how long it had been by the ringing of the cathedral bells at noon—I was no closer to the Ursulines than I'd been when Louis had jabbed his finger skyward out the window of his truck. Ah, Louis. I tucked my nose into the jacket collar and breathed deeply of pipe tobacco. What I wouldn't give for another of those ham and cheese sandwiches on home-baked bread right about now. Or some of that hot, sweet—

A tug on the hem of the jacket drew my gaze, and I looked down at a fluffy hat that sported ears and a bear face and was tied beneath the chin of a small girl. She held out a paper mug with a lid.

"*C'est un chocolat chaud*," she said, her smile making her cheeks dimple. "*Pour vous.*"

I didn't need to understand the words (although *chocolat* was pretty obvious), but the offer was as unmistakable as it was heartwarming. And maybe a little overwhelming, I thought, blinking back a prickle of tears. I smiled back at her as I took the cup.

"Thank you," I said. "*Merci.*"

She giggled—whether at her own confidence or my pronunciation, it didn't matter—and ran down the sidewalk to join two men waiting arm-in-arm for her at the corner. I wanted to follow and tell them what a wonderful young woman they were raising, but they were French and I didn't have the words, and—

And then, striding purposefully past them and up a street marked as *des Ursulines*—how in all of creation had I missed that?—was a woman who caught my entire attention. A woman wearing a simple, mid-calf-length black skirt with tan stockings, a plain black coat with a matching scarf and gloves, and sturdy, no-nonsense brown boots. She was remarkable because of her sheer unremarkableness, and she moved so quickly, and I so slowly, that I almost missed her.

By the time I'd thrust my gift of hot chocolate into the startled hands of one of the dads at the corner, flung an apology to him, and turned down the street, the woman had already disappeared. I could see a bend ahead and, holding my breath that she hadn't already gone into one of the many doors lining both sides, I broke into an awkward jog, hampered by Talia's too-big boots and the blisters they'd caused. The thud of my footsteps echoed hollowly in my wake.

A little more than two-thirds of the way to the corner I aimed for, a wide, tunnel-like passage opened to my left, leading onto an interior courtyard of sorts. My footsteps slowed, and I hesitated for a split second in front of it, then ducked through the half-open iron gate. I arrived in the courtyard in time to catch a glimpse of the sensible skirt and dark coat that I'd been chasing as they disappeared behind a wooden door—a large, wooden door with no knob on the outside.

Like the doors used by cloistered nuns to keep out unwanted visitors.

I'd found them. I'd found the Ursulines.

I slumped to the pavement.

CHAPTER 14

I STARED UP AT THE STARK WHITE CEILING FOR LONG minutes. It was unremarkable, really. No light fixture, no distinctive features, no anything. It was like a blank slate, unlike my brain, which was cycling through so many thoughts that I'd given up trying to capture any of them in favor of just letting them roll past.

I found them ... I found the Ursulines ... they must have brought me inside ... but how? Sister Margaret said there were only four of them still living here, and they're all older than I am ... unless ... is Talia here, too? And Phoenix? Sweet Mary Magdalene, I hope they are ... you know, I'm getting really tired of passing out and waking up in places I didn't go to sleep in ... how long have I been out, anyway? Did someone wash me? I think someone washed me ... I don't smell like Louis anymore ... is that a spider? Maybe it's a fly ... no, it's too cold for flies ... it's definitely a spider ... damn, I'm itchy ... did they put a wool blanket over me? I'm allergic to wool ... wait, if they washed me, they had to take my clothes off first ... HOLY MOTHER OF ALL, WHERE IS THE STONE?

I sat bolt upright in bed at the same instant as a gray-haired woman opened the door with one hand, balancing a tray in the other. She shrieked, the tray went flying, thick orange liquid splattered against the wall, and I almost fell out of the narrow bed. The woman put one hand on the door jamb for support, the other over the wooden crucifix resting on her chest, and stared wide-eyed at me through dark-framed glasses. Out in the hall, a chorus of concerned voices approached, and what seemed like an entire posse crowded through the doorway and into the small bedroom I'd been given. Relief swamped me as I recognized three of them, and tears filled my eyes.

"You made it," I whispered, but my words were lost in the hurricane that was Phoenix.

"You're awake!" She threw herself onto the narrow bed with me and wrapped her arms around me. "And you're here. I thought—I was afraid—we couldn't—they said—"

I hugged her back, so fiercely that the air hissed from her ... but she didn't pull away, and I didn't loosen my hold.

"I'm glad to see you, too," I whispered when I could speak. I held her a little away, examining her face and searching her eyes for signs of trauma. "You're okay?" I asked. "You're not hurt?"

She snorted through her tears. "I'm the one who should be asking you that, don't you think? We hardly recognized you when you passed out. We thought you were some drunk who'd wandered in off the street—the sisters say it happens all the time. And that coat. Where did you get that? It smelled like you'd fallen in a pile of—" She stopped, glanced over her shoulder at the others gathered at the foot of the bed, and then finished, "Sister Bernadette burned it."

A razor-edged pang went through me at the thought of Louis's coat being so treated.

"Kindness," I corrected softly. "It smelled like kindness."

"What?"

I shook my head. "Nothing," I said, releasing my hold on her as one of the Ursulines stepped forward. "I'll tell you some other time."

Phoenix slid off the bed, and a nun beside me— different from the one who'd thrown the tray—peered over the top of a pair of wire-framed glasses, her gray eyes sharp and watchful.

"So you're the famous Sister Monica," she said.

I felt my eyebrows twitch and hastily smoothed out my expression. As greetings went, that hadn't sounded promising, but I thought I should return it anyway. I opened my mouth to at least thank her for looking after me, but what came out instead was a rather harsh and altogether too abrupt, "Where is the stone?"

Thin, gray brows twitched together above the wire frames, and there was a collective inhale in the room. I winced and thought about telling them that my response was out of concern for them, because of the danger the stone posed, but I didn't think they'd believe me. Hell, I didn't believe myself.

And I really, really wanted that stone back.

I *itched* with wanting it.

The nun looked across my bed at the others. They, in turn—including Talia, Sister Margaret, and even Phoenix —looked back at her. I frowned. What was I missing here?

Besides the stone, I mean.

Talia cleared her throat, and a stab of guilt went through me. I hadn't even said hello to her yet. Or to Sister Margaret. Was I that out of it after my ordeal, or—

"It's over there," Talia said. "It's still in the pocket of your jeans. We didn't touch it."

There were, I realized, all kinds of unspoken words underlying those few: *We know better than to touch the stone. You're welcome for picking you up off the pavement.* And something else. Something darker, born of a careful watchfulness.

I groaned inwardly and levered myself up to a sitting position to confirm what I was afraid of. Phoenix leapt to adjust my pillows so that I could lean back, and I thanked her absently. Then I did a head count. Talia, Sister Margaret, Phoenix, and one … two … three other nuns—although I only saw the back of the third one as she disappeared out the door.

Three Ursulines, when there should have been four.

Sister Margaret had given us a brief history of the Quebec Ursuline Monastery during the train ride between Kingston and Montreal, telling us that it had been the oldest school for girls in all of North America. Then, in the 1960s, the province of Quebec had taken over the running of both the girls' and boys' schools from the nuns and the Augustine monks respectively, as well as the hospital that they oversaw together. Having been made more or less redundant, the order had stopped taking new novitiates at that time, and attrition had done the rest.

When the massive property became too much for its dwindling, aging population, Sister Margaret had told us, they'd sold off the majority of it and most of the nuns had moved to a long-term care home. Most, but not all. Four nuns had remained.

Four. Not three.

"Fuck," I said wearily, because one of them was missing, and I was pretty sure I knew why. My gaze went to Talia, whom I trusted to give me the unvarnished truth. "How bad is it?" I didn't think any of them—remaining Ursulines included—looked upset enough for whatever I'd done to have had lasting consequences, but you never knew. "Please tell me she's okay."

The group exchanged another collective look. I didn't have to explain what I was talking about. They knew.

Talia sighed. "You were unconscious when we brought you inside, but when we started undressing you—when we got to your jeans ..."

"You were like a wild animal," Sister Margaret finished for her. "It took all of us to hold you down, and Sister Colette's face was unfortunately too near your elbow."

My expression must have revealed my utter horror at the idea of hitting an elderly nun—even by accident—because the Ursuline with the wire-framed glasses patted my arm.

"The doctor says she'll be fine in another day or two," she assured me. "I'm Sister Bernadette, by the way, and this is Sister Simonne. Sister Lise went to get you more soup."

I barely even heard the names, because Holy Mother of All, "You had to call a *doctor*?" I wheezed.

"Only as a precaution because of her age. She'll tell you herself that she has a hard head, though, and the nurse showed us how to change the bandages ourselves so that we don't need to take her back to the clinic. We might have freezing rain tonight, and it's difficult for her to get around on ice with her walker," Sister Bernadette said, and I wheezed again.

"Bandages?" I croaked. *Walker?* I thought.

"It was nothing, really," another of the Ursulines spoke up—a heavyset woman with steel gray hair cut in a straight, uncompromising chin-length bob and a pair of glasses hung from a chain around her neck. Sister Simonne? I couldn't remember. "Her glasses broke in the struggle, and there was a little cut on her forehead. Maybe two. They didn't even need to stitch it. They just used that fancy glue they have now."

Her tone was as reassuring as Sister Bernadette's—as if I deserved reassurance for having attacked one of their companions—but her words were less so. I'd broken the glasses and cut the face of a nun who needed a walker to get around. What kind of a monster was I becoming?

"You should have seen the blood," Phoenix said, her eyes wide with remembered awe. "It looked like someone died."

Not helpful, Phoenix. Not helpful at all.

I sagged against the pillows behind me, and Talia cleared her throat.

"You've heard enough for one day," she said. "You need rest. And you need to eat."

The remaining nun had returned with a fresh bowl of soup that she'd set on the bedside table before quietly and efficiently cleaning up the mess of the dropped tray. She straightened up from the floor at Talia's words and planted her hands on her hips, nodding at the bowl beside me.

"It's roasted butternut squash," she announced. "With white beans for protein. Hearty but not heavy."

I did a quick mental run-through the list of names Sister Bernadette had given. Lise, I thought this one might be, but my brain was getting tired, and I wasn't sure. I thanked her without risking it, and she didn't seem to notice.

"Can you manage on your own?" Talia asked.

I nodded. "But I'd like Sister Bernadette to stay," I said.

"Perhaps I should stay, too," suggested Sister Margaret. "I may be able to fill in some details for you as well."

It seemed to me that she should have already told me everything she knew, but I kept my sour response to myself, suspecting that it stemmed from my continued irritation over her relationship with Phoenix.

"A good idea," Sister Bernadette said. She picked up the soup and handed it to me. "But eat first."

I didn't even pretend to object. It had been a long time since Louis's sandwich, and I was starving. The soup was thick and creamy, perfectly seasoned, and had sat long enough to be drinking temperature. I waved away the spoon that Sister Bernadette offered—Sister Lise had put it in a mug for ease, bless her heart—and downed it in seconds. Then the work began.

"How much have you told her?" I asked Sister Margaret.

"Everything up to the train," Sister Margaret replied. "I don't know what happened there. None of us do." She looked around for a seat, but there was only one chair in the room, and it was on Sister Bernadette's side.

I motioned for her to sit on the end of the bed. She perched carefully and arranged her skirt around her. It looked like the ones the Ursulines wore. I wondered if they had one that would fit me—and if it had pockets—because my jeans must be thoroughly trashed by now. I had no doubt that Sister Bernadette would have burned them with the coat if it hadn't been for the stone.

My gaze slid past the Ursuline nun. Sister Bernadette's brow creased a little, but without comment, she reached for the jeans on the plain wooden dresser and handed them to me. I slid my hand into the familiar front pocket and closed my fingers around the smooth, cool square. Webs that I hadn't realized had drawn taut in me relaxed. If they'd been able to sigh, they probably would have.

I did it for them.

Having the stone with me again just felt … right.

But it was so, so wrong.

CHAPTER 15

I TOLD SISTERS BERNADETTE AND MARGARET THE TRAIN story in as little graphic detail as possible. My voice hitched only once, when I got to the part about the Mage drowning and my inability to save him, and a vivid image of the pale face, made murky by the water between us, filled my vision.

The face, and those eyes. Those wide, empty eyes that had stared at something awful. I realized that the room had gone silent—that *I* had gone silent—and sisters Margaret and Bernadette were waiting for me to continue. Each of their expressions was a study in conflicted emotions: distaste, presumably for the dying-Mage-in-the-water thing; cold anger, probably also for the Mage; and compassion, likely meant for me. I ended with Louis dropping me off down near the ferry and my subsequent search for the nuns.

When I finished, Sister Bernadette said, "I'm not surprised you collapsed when you got here. I'm just surprised you didn't sleep for the entire week."

That made it sound … I frowned. "How long have I been here?"

"Only a day," Sister Margaret replied. "But you were missing for two days before that."

I gaped at her, grappling with the numbers. And their implication.

"It's a wonder you even survived," Sister Margaret continued, shaking her head. "Talk about a miracle."

Not a miracle. Magick. The stone's magick. But I

hadn't mentioned the cocoon before, and I didn't see the point in backtracking now. We had bigger things to worry about. Like Mages.

"That means they've had three days to realize one of their own is missing," I muttered, "and to figure out where he was heading, if they didn't already know."

"And for Methuselah's trail to grow even colder," Sister Margaret added.

I'm aware of that, I almost snapped, but I caught the words back in time—and the out-of-context surge of irritation. There had been nothing in what Sister Margaret said that could remotely be construed as annoying, which meant that the stone was at it again. I'd wanted to believe that I'd been wrong about the influence I suspected it wielded over me—that it had just been the stress of the exploding monastery, or the goliath, or inadvertently killing Eldon Rusk, or the train trip, or all of the above. But the seething sense of aggravation that I'd experienced more and more often before the train trip—the one that had turned dark and terrifyingly ugly on the bridge when it had wanted me to kill the Mage—

All of that had returned, even though I was in as safe a place as I could possibly be right now. Which meant that it wasn't because of stress.

Sister Bernadette cleared her throat to get my attention. "The stone has had three days, too," she said quietly.

I'd sat up and pushed back the covers to swing my feet out of the bed, deciding we had no more time to coddle me, but the nun's words made me go still again. That had almost sounded like she *knew* ...

A chill danced across my skin as I met the sadness in her gaze. No, not sadness. Grief. Grief for ... me? I flicked a glance at Sister Margaret, who stared down at her clasped hands, avoiding my gaze.

A frisson of unease danced down my spine. I lowered my weight back down to the bed. "Three days to do what?" I asked.

A tight-lipped Sister Bernadette got up to close the door, then returned to her chair. Sister Margaret came around the bed to sit beside me. The frisson became a chill that seeped toward my core.

"If there's something I need to know, can we please just spit it out?" I asked. I tried to summon a smile but suspected it was more of a grimace.

The Ursuline nun placed her hands on top of the sensible skirt covering her lap. "I'm not going to lie, Sister Monica. There have been a handful of times in the history of our Obsidian Sisterhood that someone has touched one of the stones. It has never gone well for them."

Oh hell, I thought wearily. Now what?

"Define *not well.*"

"Sister Margaret told you that the stone feeds off the darkness inside anyone that it binds to?"

"The darkness inside its *victims*," I said. "As in the ones that it cocoons." I turned my head to look at Sister Margaret. "You said nothing about the ones like me that it just binds to."

"Just" binds. That was rich. I scowled. Especially since, technically, it had also cocooned me on the river shore.

"I wasn't sure it would happen to you," Sister Margaret said, her voice not nearly as apologetic as I thought it should have been, "and I thought you had enough to deal with."

Fury, entirely out of keeping with the situation, began to boil in my belly. My hands twitched with the desire to strike out, to strike *her.*

Or to strangle her, and not just metaphorically speaking.

My sheer shock at the violence of my thoughts acted as a counter to them. I curled my right hand into the blanket, a woolen one as sensible as the Ursulines' skirts, and tightened my left around the stone that it already held. Slow, inexorable understanding dawned, and for a moment, the room wobbled around me as the blood drained from my head.

"There is darkness in me," I whispered, "and the stone has bound itself to that?" Spiderwebs knitting me together had been one thing, but this was a whole other level of—

Sister Bernadette leaned forward in her chair to place a wrinkled hand on my knee, and a very faraway part of me belatedly noted that I was wearing a flannel nightgown like the ones I'd worn when I was still part of St. Paul's. Then it thought about the ruined building and dead nuns I'd left behind there, after I'd returned to it. Then it thought about the trail of destruction that I'd left in my wake since then, and the trail of destruction that had started all of this, and my growing irritation with Phoenix and Talia and the world in general—and Sister Margaret in particular.

"There is darkness in all of us, Sister Monica," the Ursuline nun said gently, interrupting my downward spiral into horror. "You know that. You may not hold with the majority of the teachings of the church—holy Mother knows most of us don't—but that teaching, that one you can believe. The stone did not bind to you because of that, but…"

Still horrified and not at all appeased, I lifted my gaze from her hand to her face. "But what?"

"But it can and will amplify that darkness, if you let it."

I stared at her, processing the revelation. Something visceral in me wanted to deny what she'd told me. I wished I'd never laid eyes on the infernal stone, never mind hands. I wanted to take it and heave it out the window, but heaven knew who might pick it up next, or what might happen to them, and oh hell, who was I kidding? It belonged to me, and I belonged to it, and dear sweet Mary, I felt like goddamn Gollum with the ring right now.

Closing my eyes, I drew a deep, shuddering breath. Then another. And a third. Slowly, I coaxed the fingers of my right hand to relax their hold on the blanket. I tried to do the same with the fingers of the hand holding the stone, but they—or perhaps it—refused. I inhaled a fourth breath.

Sisters Bernadette and Margaret waited, neither of them pushing me to speak, both allowing me the space I needed to come to grips—no pun intended—with the stone's hold on me. Slowly, the tightness in my chest eased, and I remembered what else Sister Bernadette had told me.

"Tell me about the others," I said. "You said others in the Sisterhood had touched the stones and been bound to them. What happened to them?"

Sister Bernadette sat back again. "Most were eventually encapsulated by the stone's own webs, as all the victims are. Some lasted longer than others, but ..." She trailed off, but I didn't need her to finish. I'd more than caught the gist of her words.

Perhaps the cocoon at the river hadn't been quite as helpful—or innocent—as it had seemed. If I hadn't woken when I had, if I hadn't moved ...

Another shudder rippled through me. Then, after a long, numb moment, I gathered what few scattered wits I could still find in my head. There weren't many. Or if there were, they were hiding from the voice that was screaming somewhere deep inside my psyche.

"You haven't said anything about getting rid of it, so I assume that's not an option? Wait." I frowned as one of my remaining wits flagged me down. "You said *most* were eventually cocooned. Not all?"

"If the stories are right, two were saved before it got that far," she said. "By Methuselah. A very long time ago."

"Before he …?" It was my turn to let my words trail off, because I didn't yet know that much about the alien. I supposed that should be next on the agenda.

"Before he forgot who he is," she said. "Yes."

Definitely next on the agenda. But first, I needed to be sure … needed to understand the full ramifications … needed to know just how screwed I was. I plowed ahead with my questions.

"And he's the only way?"

"If you mean the only one who could unbind one of the stones, then yes. He was the only way."

The change of verb tense didn't escape me. I closed my eyes and let the inevitability that had been building in my heart wash over me. Sister Bernadette's hand returned to my knee, and Sister Margaret slipped a not-unwelcome arm around my shoulders.

When I was ready to continue—as if one could ever be ready for this—I inhaled a deep breath into my belly, then released it in a sigh and opened my eyes again.

"How long do I have?"

"Until the stone takes over completely?" Sister Bernadette shrugged, withdrawing her hand a second time and settling back in the chair. "I don't know. The stories are old—very old—and have been told and retold so many times that we can't be sure what is true and what was embellished."

For an instant, a heartbeat, hope flickered in my chest. If the stories were that old and that unverifiable—

I squashed the little flutter. Down that path, I was certain, lay folly. Not to mention the kind of distraction I couldn't afford. That *we* couldn't afford. For all we knew, the Mages were already in the city, and if they weren't, they would be soon enough. Our Methuselah-clock was ticking. Which led me to the next item on my agenda.

"Tell me about him," I said. "Tell me everything."

CHAPTER 16

THEY'D LOST HIM IN INCREMENTS, SISTER BERNADETTE told me. He'd disappeared in slivers here and there, mostly, but sometimes whole chunks had dropped away, like the one Sister Agatha had witnessed on the day that John F. Kennedy was assassinated. They had no idea why, and by the time they'd seen the pattern and connected the dots, he had lost too much of himself to be able to tell them. Over the millennia, he had gone from being a brilliant, insightful being delighted with his place on our planet to little more than the equivalent of a human child, Sister Bernadette said, but … less than. He still thrilled at the small things in life, but only when he noticed them—and he was noticing them less and less.

In the last months that he had been with them, he had taken to sitting more often and for longer periods in his room. They'd given him the largest of the bedrooms—it would have belonged to the Mother Superior, when one had served here—because he'd seemed to enjoy his solitude. He'd sat in a chair by the window overlooking the courtyard for hours at a time, simply staring out. Sometimes he'd needed to be reminded to eat and drink, and to use the bathroom. The nuns had changed him into his pajamas and tucked him into bed every night, but when they rose at their customary six a.m., he was back in the chair, his slipperless feet like ice, and Sister Bernadette wasn't sure that he slept anymore.

As to where he might have gone, they had searched everywhere they could think of. They continued to hold out hope, because that was who they were, and it was all they had.

It was precious little.

"Which one of you spent the most time with him?" I asked Sister Bernadette, remembering the coaching Talia had given me on the train about what questions to ask. "If I can talk to her, she might remember something small, something that seemed insignificant, but—"

But Sister Bernadette was crossing herself—mostly out of habit, I suspected, given her reference to the holy Mother earlier—and shaking her head.

"Sister Agatha was his favorite," she said, "and you're probably right. She would have known him better than the rest of us. But she passed away in her sleep a week after he disappeared."

I dug through annoyance at discovering another dead end in search of the compassion I *should* be feeling instead. There was precious little of that, too.

"I'm sorry," I replied, hoping I sounded more so than I felt.

"She was with him that day," Sister Bernadette said quietly. Her fingers toyed with the plain wooden crucifix she wore on a cord around her neck, identical to the one I'd noticed on Sister Lise. Sister Simonne's had probably been hidden beneath the glasses hanging from her chain. The Ursulines had no veils like that of Sister Margaret, but their church roots still ran deep.

I brought my attention back to the nun's words. "They walked together every day," she was saying. "Sister Agatha used a cane and couldn't go very fast, but he was so patient with her. That day, however, he kept going further and further ahead, and she couldn't keep up. He turned a corner, and by the time she got there, the street was empty and he was gone. She blamed herself, but none of us could have seen that coming. He'd been content, and there was no reason—"

She broke off, pursed her lips, and met my gaze with a resigned one.

"But that doesn't excuse us for losing him," she said. "We got complacent. I knew that Sister Agatha was having difficulty keeping up with him, but I didn't have the heart to tell her so. One of us, someone more capable, should have been there. Perhaps then we could have stopped him."

Sister Margaret's arm was still around my shoulders, and she gave me a tiny squeeze of what I suspected was a warning. I didn't need it. I didn't disagree with Sister Bernadette's assessment, but despite the irritation burrowing beneath my skin, there was no purpose in lashing out. Or in assigning blame. Instead, I rose from the bed and crossed to the window, giving myself time to wrestle my little would-be demons into submission.

The room I'd been given was on the second floor—it must have been a task and a half, wrestling me unconscious up a set of stairs—and its window overlooked a quiet street. Brick and stone buildings lined the other side, separated by alleys that might have once accommodated horses but were too narrow for cars. Meticulously maintained white trim surrounded the windows. Cheerful Christmas wreaths and swags adorned the ornate, red-painted doors.

A black-and-white tuxedo cat strolled across the pavement, then sat down in the middle of the street and proceeded to bathe itself. I watched it for long seconds, letting its tranquility, its calm, its focus become my own. The borrowed equanimity seeped into me, softening the webs that tried to pull my every fiber taut. *I can do this*, I thought.

"You're sure?" I asked at last. "He's that far gone? There's no chance you're wrong or that he'll—I don't know—find his way back, somehow?"

"I wish he could, *ma belle*," Sister Bernadette said sadly. "I truly wish he could, but it's been almost eight months, now. I fear he has truly lost his way."

I heard her push up from her chair and turned as she set it back in its place against the wall. She patted my arm and tried to give me a smile, but the heaviness in her eyes weighed down the corners of her lips, and she just shook her head instead.

"We will talk more later," she said, going to the door and waiting as Sister Margaret rose to join her. "Rest now."

She opened the door and stepped out, but Sister Margaret paused to look back at me. "Would you like me to send in Talia? Or maybe Phoenix? They've both been so worried about you."

I'd been worried about them, too. But right now, I needed time. Time and space. To think about Methuselah, yes, but mostly to think about the stone that had attached to all the parts of me that I had tried so hard to suppress over my lifetime. To figure out how—and if—there was a way I could slow down its feeding. To control it, myself, both.

I wasn't particularly hopeful, given the sadness with which Sister Bernadette had delivered the news, but neither was I willing to give up. Stubborn, my father had called me as a girl. Pig-headed. He'd leveled the words as accusations, failings, but Mother Joan had taught me to instead think of these qualities as determination, one of my greatest assets.

And I had it in spades.

So I summoned the weakest, most pathetic smile that I

could manage, told Sister Margaret that I thought I should lie down for a while first, and waited for the door to close behind her. Then I uncurled my fingers from around the stone, held it out in the flat of my palm, and glowered at it.

"Right," I told it. "Time to get a few things straight."

CHAPTER 17

Morning brought nothing in the way of miraculous epiphanies conjured by sleep or dreams. It did, however, bring watery sunlight struggling through the curtainless window—a perfect companion to my general crankiness— a soft tap at my bedroom door, and Phoenix, bearing coffee, no less.

I pulled myself up against the pillows and back-pocketed my bad mood as she set the mug on the bedside table and perched beside me on the narrow bed, leaning in to give me a hug.

"You look better today," she said with more hope in her voice than the ring of truth.

I hugged her back and pasted on my best smile, because just seeing her had already improved my morning. And the aroma of coffee didn't hurt, either.

"Bless your heart for this," I said when she released me and I could reach for the mug. "It has been literal *days* since I had coffee."

"Don't thank me yet," she said. "The nuns only have instant here." She shuddered and pulled a face. "I don't know how they survive. Are nuns that poor?"

I sipped the coffee. It was as awful as Phoenix had warned, but it was still like an elixir to my caffeine-deprived body.

"We—*they*—" I corrected myself, because yikes, where had *that* come from after all these years? "—take three vows: chastity, poverty, and obedience. Some orders take their vows to extremes, others just buy instant coffee."

She scowled. "That sounds like oppression."

"It is oppression."

"Why do you—they—agree? This is the twenty-first century, for fucksake."

"Tradition. Habit."

"Indoctrination?" she suggested sourly.

"Especially that. The patriarchy runs strong in the church, my friend." More accurately, the patriarchy *ran* the church, I thought, but that could be a discussion for another day.

"But the ones in the Obsidian Sisterhood are so different—how do they put up with it? How do they stay nuns when they don't agree with the rules they have to follow?"

The phrase *self-preservation* sat on the tip of my tongue, but that was too easy—and it didn't do the sisterhood or the women who formed it the justice they deserved. There was so, so much more to it than that. I took another drink of my coffee, which was cooling rapidly because frugality in monasteries too often meant a dearth of heat, too, and thought back over my own years in St. Paul's. My reasons for joining, my reasons for leaving, my reasons for stubbornly retaining the title of—

"Sister?" Phoenix prompted.

I started at the way she'd inadvertently finished my thought.

"Service," I said. "The overarching point of our vows is service. Some believe that means service to the institution, others of us choose to think that it means service to humanity. The Obsidian Sisterhood has been in service to humanity since before the church existed—or any other faith that we have in the world right now. They're not so much staying in the monasteries and other religious institutions as they are hiding in them."

"Kind of like in plain sight?"

"Exactly like that."

"Huh," she said. "I still think they should buy decent coffee, though."

I drained the last of the brew she'd brought me, shuddered faintly, and muttered, "Hear, hear."

Phoenix took the mug from me. "Want me to bring you more? Sister Margaret said she'd bring breakfast up to you after we're done ours."

Snorting, I swung my legs out of bed on the opposite side from where she sat. "I'm tired, not dead," I retorted. "I think I can manage going downstairs to eat."

She returned my snort as I stood up to a chorus of audible snaps and cracks from my knees and back. "You sure about that?"

"I'm sure, smart-ass. Now hand me that robe." Shivering in the distinctly cool air, I pointed at the thin gray robe hanging on the back of the door, choosing to remain in place while my ankles sorted themselves out and my hips got on board with the whole *upright* idea.

Phoenix stood and fetched the garment, returning to hold it out to me. But when I reached to take it from her, she didn't let go. I looked askance at her but waited for her to speak first.

"You know that you almost were, right?" she said at last, her voice small.

"Almost what?"

"Dead," she said. "You were almost dead. We thought you *were* dead."

Her eyes had gone shiny with the threat of tears, and she blinked rapidly. Then she sniffled, and I hesitated. This wasn't something I could brush off with an *I'm fine, just look at me* kind of assurance. This was more, and it deserved better than that. Phoenix deserved better. I took the robe from her and set it on the bed, then grasped her shoulders gently.

"Yes," I said simply. "I was almost dead. And I can't tell you that I'll survive whatever happens next, Phoenix. Not because we all die someday—although we do—but because what we're doing—what *I'm* doing—is dangerous. Very dangerous."

Phoenix's shoulders tensed beneath my hands as her breath hitched, and I gave her a second to rebalance herself. She lifted a hand to wipe away a tear that had escaped, then nodded her readiness to hear the rest.

"But whatever happens to me, sweet girl," I continued, "remember that you have good people in your corner. Talia and Sister Margaret aren't the kind to walk away and leave you, Phoenix. You won't be alone."

Another tear, another swipe of a hand. A sniffle.

"And if something happens to them, too?" she whispered. "What then?"

I stared unflinchingly into the anxiety shadowing her eyes. I knew it came not from the twenty-three-year-old who expressed it, but from the child who had grown up feeling unloved and alone because of who she couldn't be, and from the teen who had ended up on the streets because her family refused to accept who she was. When Phoenix had come to the Mary Magdalene House for Women, the family she found there had helped to fill that void—to give her the security she had so desperately needed—and now they were gone, too.

"Then," I said with quiet conviction, "you still have the most important person—you."

Disappointment and hurt flashed across her expression, and I tightened my grip against her attempt to be rid of me. I knew my words weren't the ones she wanted to hear. They were, however, the ones she needed to hear.

"You're not her anymore, Phoenix," I said. "You're not the woman who came to the shelter. She's still a part of you, yes, and she always will be, but you are so, so much more now than you were then. And with or without me and Talia and Sister Margaret, or whoever else comes into or leaves your life, you will always have you. *This* you." I gave her a tiny, gentle shake. "The you who has learned to love herself and stand up for herself and *be* there for herself. Yes, you might feel alone sometimes—in fact, I guarantee you will, because that's just a part of the human condition. But you're not, because you will always have *you*. And that, my beautiful, sweet girl, is everything."

The disappointment in Phoenix's face became disillusionment, and her eyes turned hard. "Sister Margaret said you'd say that, but you're wrong. It's *not* everything. And it sure as fuck isn't enough."

Before I could recover from my shock, she pulled free, whirled, and ran from the room, leaving the door hanging open in her wake. I stared after her, my mouth hanging open, until Sister Bernadette cleared her throat in the hallway outside my door.

"Is everything all right?" she asked, as she came into the room. "You look …"

Pissed off? I thought. Probably because I was. I just couldn't say with whom, because right now Phoenix, Sister Margaret, and I shared that honor in roughly equal parts. But I stiffened my spine, put on my metaphorical big-girl panties, and made myself pick up the robe from the bed.

"Everything is fine," I said. "Thank you."

She regarded me for a moment, then set the stack of clothing she carried on the chair.

"Sister Simonne washed your things yesterday," she said briskly. "The jeans can be salvaged but will require mending. Your shirt and underthings are beyond repair."

She pointed at the pile. "We did our best to guess at your size until we can get new things, but Sister Lise can make adjustments if you need them. There's underwear and hosiery under the blouse. Breakfast is at eight o'clock, if you'd like to join us."

She left again, and I went to poke at the clothes, which were, unsurprisingly, identical to the ones the Ursulines all wore. Not quite a habit, but not quite not. A neatly pressed white blouse, a dark, sensible skirt—I couldn't decide in the reluctant daylight if it was black or navy—a thick, gray cardigan, a bra that I was pretty sure my less-than-generous bosoms would swim in, and—oh, look at that.

I held up a pair of plain cotton briefs and surveyed them sourly. I now had an actual pair of big-girl panties to go with my metaphorical ones—just like the ones we'd been given to wear at St. Paul's. As if they'd scorched my fingertips, I dropped the underwear onto the other things and wiped my hand against the robe I still held. My skin crawled at the thought of putting on the uniform of a nun again.

My sense of pissed-off-edness wasn't soothed by it, either.

Short of wearing my nightgown out to search for Methuselah, however …

"Fuck," I told the room. Then, donning the robe and scooping up the very sensible clothes, I headed for the bathroom.

"You okay?" Talia asked under her breath as I eased

into the dining room chair beside her. "You look like you should be back in bed. Or in hospital."

I managed a tight smile, the result of a shower, shampoo, and hearty lecture to myself on patience, gratitude, and not letting myself cave to the stone's bindings. "I'm fine. Just a bit bruised, is all."

"Physically, or emotionally?" Her voice was dry, and when I flashed a surprised look at her, she nodded across the rectangular table at Phoenix, who was seated beside Sister Margaret and studiously ignoring me. "I heard there were … words."

I lined up the knife and teaspoon beside my plate, an exact half-inch from the edge of the table. *"Details,"* Mother Annunciata said in my memory. *"A life well lived is in the details. None is too small."*

I pushed the utensils awry again. "Is that what we're calling it?" I asked Talia, looking sideways at her. "Words?"

"Sister Bernadette's description," she said. "What happened?"

"Nothing major. She"—I nodded at Phoenix, trying not to scowl—"wants assurances I can't give."

"Ah." Talia leaned back in her chair. "She's scared, is all. She'll come around."

I watched Sister Margaret lean in to say something to the young woman, and Phoenix gave the giggle-snort that always made me smile. That used to always make me smile. Right now, it made me want to cry. Or throw something. Preferably at Sister Margaret.

I realized I was twisting my napkin in my hands. Sighing, I moved to put it back beside my plate, then hesitated. Maybe it was better to hold something soft, in case the stone's annoyance got away on me.

Because sweet Mary Magdalene, it was a struggle to

keep this thing under wraps. Or, more precisely, to keep myself under wraps. It was as if the explanation Sister Bernadette had given me last night had been some kind of secret permission that the stone had been waiting for to *really* let its presence be known. Or maybe I was beginning to admit to myself just how entrenched it had become.

And to come to terms with my new reality, in which I would slowly be corrupted by a stone that would then cocoon and kill me.

I clenched my fist around the napkin in my lap. Yes, keeping something soft in hand was a good idea right now.

A door to the left swung open, and Sister Bernadette came into the dining room bearing a platter of scrambled eggs. The other two nuns—the ones who weren't confined to their beds on doctors' orders because of me—followed. Sister Lise carried a plate of ham slices in one hand and a bowl of beans in the other, and Sister Simonne brought a plate of toast and a carafe.

I suppressed a shudder at the thought of the coffee contained in the latter. I really was going to have to do something about the *instant* problem.

"Do you want me to talk to her?" Talia's question drew my attention back to her.

I shook my head. "No," I said. "It's been a long few days for her. Let's just give it time."

"It's been a long few days for all of us," Talia reminded me, "and a long few weeks before that."

I grunted. "True, but we're older and wiser, remember?"

That made her laugh. "Right," she said. "Wiser. I forgot about that part." She started to turn her attention toward the nuns and the food they'd brought, then paused to sweep a narrowed gaze over me. "You think if I give them the money and you tell them your size, one of the Ursulines might hit up a clothing store for you? If you want, that is."

"Oh sweet Mary, yes," I muttered. "*Please.*"

CHAPTER 18

When breakfast ended, Phoenix offered to help with the dishes and was promptly swept off to the kitchen by sisters Lise and Simonne, and Sister Bernadette took a tray up to the missing Sister Colette.

Talia, Sister Margaret, and I headed toward the living room. I hesitated in the hallway as we crossed it, looking toward the front door and the neat entryway with its row of coats hung on hooks along the wall, and the line of boots beneath them.

Talia looked back at me from the living room doorway. "Don't even think about it," she said. "He's been gone for almost eight months. He can wait one more day while you get your feet back under you."

"I'm—" I bit off the word *fine* as she scowled. For a moment, I was tempted to scowl back—and to argue with her—but she had a point. While the stone's magick seemed to heal my more catastrophic injuries faster than ever, it had not yet found a way to address the finer points of recovery. The lingering stiffness, the fatigue, the I'm-getting-too-old-for-this-shit issue. While waiting another day wouldn't matter—hopefully—where Methuselah and the Mages were concerned, it would matter a great deal to me. In the good sense.

"One day," I agreed. "But only one."

And so I retired with her and Sister Margaret to sit beside a crackling fire in the living room, each of us in one of the rocking chairs around the wood stove while, outside the window, a flurry of tiny snowflakes swirled past.

For a little while, we rocked in silence, just three old

women—well, two plus an up-and-coming one, because Talia was still in her fifties—in their chairs by a fire on a cold November morning. It brought back memories of Sister Ernestine and the others, then of the Mary Magdalene House. Nostalgia, sharp and bittersweet, caught at my throat. My first instinct was to push it away, but I stopped myself.

My friends—all of them—deserved better than to be forgotten, and I deserved better than to forget them. I closed my eyes and let my mind wander back to happier times. To the Magdalene women who had lugged home that ridiculously large dining table and spent days restoring it. To the first meal I had shared with them around it. They'd been so proud of themselves, and I'd been amazed at how something as simple as eating together could cement the ties of found family the way that it had.

And then there were the meals at the Sisters of St. Mary's, where Sister Ernestine had taken me in as a boarder and I'd been welcomed as one of their own, *sister* title and all. I remembered the Yule dinners in particular, when we wore silly hats and celebrated the season and one another before launching into preparations for the holiday dinner that the sisters assisted with at the local men's shelter.

So many memories filled with so much good. So very much.

"You're smiling," Talia said. "You haven't done much of that lately."

I roused myself to find her and Sister Margaret both watching me, their expressions quizzical. I let my smile remain, not ready yet to let it go.

"Memories," I said. "Good ones."

"The shelter and St. Mary's?" Talia asked, nodding her

own head when I nodded mine. "Good. I'm glad you're able to remember them that way."

"Me, too," I said. But my nostalgia, like the ephemeral thing it was, had dissipated, and the present waited for me. I stopped rocking. "They'll know by now where we are."

"The Mages?"

Talia stopped rocking, too, and then Sister Margaret. Something about discussing an imminent threat just didn't pair well with the comfortable back-and-forth motion. The brief moment of respite that we'd found, however, had been … nice. It would make for another memory filled with goodness, and I filed it away as such. I had a feeling I would need all the goodness I could hold onto in the coming days.

"You think they'll come after us here?" Sister Margaret frowned, glancing around at the cozy room filled with decades of memorabilia. "Maybe we should find somewhere else for the Ursulines to stay. They're too old to tangle with them."

I swallowed a snort, refraining from pointing out that she and I were no spring chickens ourselves. Talia had a better—and more informative—response.

"Doubtful," she told Sister Margaret. "If the Mages have the ties to police that we suspect—and, given their ability to track Monica's bank card the way they did in Toronto, I'm pretty sure that's a given—they'll have known where we've been since the train incident. Our names are all over the system as witnesses and victims. Hell, the *Sûreté* themselves drove us here, so if they wanted one—or all— of us, we wouldn't be sitting here by the fire right now."

The *Sûreté* was the Quebec provincial police force, I knew. They wouldn't have had jurisdiction over the train attack, but they would still have been involved in the investigation.

"I think they're waiting for us to find Methuselah," I said, referring to the Mages. "They'll be watching every move we make, and when we find him, that's when they'll make *their* move."

"Good luck to them," Talia muttered. "I mean, after eight months, our chances of finding Methuselah at this point are roughly what, nil?"

"Perhaps slightly better than that," Sister Bernadette said, coming into the room with another tray, this one holding several mugs.

A whiff of chocolate reached me, bringing up more memories. Steadfastly, I diverted a fresh pang of nostalgia. I'd had my moment, and now, having safely landed with the Ursulines and my friends, I needed to get on with finding the proverbial needle in a haystack. A sentient one. With powers. Who was intent on avoiding us.

"Oh?" I responded to Sister Bernadette as she handed me one of the mugs. Its warmth told me that it was perfect sipping temperature, just the way Sister Ruth used to serve it at St. Mary's. I set the mug to one side. "You know where he went?"

"No, but I think he's at least still here in Quebec City," she said. She passed two more mugs to Talia and Sister Margaret. "And more specifically, in Old Quebec."

Sister Margaret sat forward in her chair, and Talia shot me a *what the hell, I thought you said you'd talked to her* look. Then she set her mug down on the floor beside her chair and turned a stern gaze on the Ursuline.

"Explain," she said in her best cop voice.

Sister Bernadette flashed her a startled look over her wire frames, seemed to remember who she was, and nodded. "Of course. Sister Colette and I were talking just now, when I went to pick up her breakfast tray—she's feeling much better, by the way, Sister Monica—and she reminded me that Methuselah had no money with him when he left. So he can't have gone far, right?"

We were silent for a few ticks of the clock hanging on the wall above the doorway, careful not to look at one another. At least, I was careful. It was the only way I could hide another of my skirmishes with irritation. Once again, Talia stepped into the breach.

"That won't really limit him very much," she said. "He could have asked someone for a ride, panhandled enough for a bus ticket—"

"Oh," Sister Bernadette interrupted with a flap of her hands. "Methuselah would never do either of those things. He's terrified of vehicles. We walked everywhere with him."

"Well," said Talia.

"Well," said Sister Margaret.

And you couldn't have thought of this earlier? my irritation demanded. Fortunately, it used its inside voice, because in truth, Sister Bernadette wasn't to blame for holding back these details. It was on me for not having asked the questions in the first place. The ones that I'd thought about asking yesterday, when I'd told Talia that I'd talked to Sister Bernadette and Sister Margaret. But then I'd dropped them, unvoiced, because the nun who had spent the most time with Methuselah—Sister Agatha—had died, and it hadn't occurred to me to ask them of Sister Bernadette.

What the hell, indeed.

Sister Bernadette looked at me expectantly, waiting for my reaction, but it took three deep breaths before I could trust myself to speak past the irritation at myself.

"Right," I said, "when the others are done, we'll go over whatever else any of you can remember about him. Does that work?"

"Of course," said Sister Bernadette.

"And maybe Talia can ask the questions?" Sister Margaret ventured. "Just so we don't miss anything?"

Not even my irritation could argue with that—but hey, at least we had that place to start that I'd been missing.

BETWEEN THE NEED FOR NAPS AND ALL THE ERRANDS THAT had to be done—Sister Lise needed to go for groceries, Sister Bernadette was delivering a care package, and Sister Simonne had gleefully accepted the task of clothes shopping for me—Talia quickly gave up on the idea of a single conversation with all three nuns at once.

"It's honestly better this way," she told me as she paused in the hallway leading to the main-floor bedroom assigned to Sister Colette, who was the eldest of the remaining Ursulines. Because, of course, I'd had to hit *that* one.

"A one-on-one conversation always yields more information than a group discussion," Talia continued. "In groups, everyone is contradicting everyone else, and you end up more confused than when you started. This way, we can compare notes and see what the similarities are."

The explanation sounded reasonable—and also like she was over-explaining.

"Why do I get the feeling you're telling me that because you just don't want me sitting in?" I asked dryly. I hadn't really expected an answer, and I regretted the question as Talia folded her arms and leaned against the wall.

"Because I am," she admitted. "You haven't been the easiest person to talk to lately, Monica."

I tried—and failed—not to feel defensive. "Um, thank you?"

She ignored me. "What is going on with you? And I don't just mean since you got back, because it's been longer than that. You've been—"

"Sister Monica?" Sister Simonne practically danced down the hallway toward us from the kitchen, waving a pad of paper and pen in one hand as the glasses hanging on their chain bounced against her ample chest. "I'm ready to take down your order. Ooh, I'm so excited! I haven't been shopping for clothes in *decades*. Sister Lise makes all of ours, and—" She broke off as she took my arm with her free hand. "Detective Dawson, you don't mind if I steal her away, do you? I want to be back in time to help with lunch, and—"

"Of course," Talia said, her voice warm but her smile tight—and not reaching the eyes that met mine—as she added, "We can finish later."

I followed Sister Simonne into the living room, wondering if that had been meant as a reassurance or a threat.

CHAPTER 19

I kept to my room as much as I could for the rest of the day, carefully avoiding being alone with Talia. With my search for Methuselah beginning the next day—Sister Bernadette had said she'd accompany me—I didn't immediately need to know what answers Talia had gleaned from her conversations with the others, and I had no intention of opening myself up again to the questions that I knew she had for me.

First, because I didn't know how to answer those questions other than to tell her what Sister Bernadette had shared with me, and second, because I didn't *want* to answer them for the same reason. Talia and I had become friends, yes, but despite our proximity over the last weeks, not close ones. I wasn't entirely sure why. The woman had, after all, walked away from her job to join my crusade, I genuinely liked and respected her, and in many ways, we were a lot alike.

Huh. Maybe too alike, I thought, reflecting on how we both liked to be the one running the show.

Fortunately, whether it was because she was preoccupied with her information-gathering, or she sensed my reluctance to talk—although *that* had never stopped her before—she did not come looking for me, and I was able to get some of the rest that it turned out I really did need. Hours of it.

I ended up napping most of the day, waking when Sister Simonne returned with my clothes and when lunch was served, but that was it. When Sister Lise knocked at my door to tell me that it was almost dinnertime, she woke me out of a deep slumber, and it took several groggy minutes to talk myself out from under the warm covers. I felt like I could have slept through the entire night, and I was grateful that I'd agreed not to go after Methuselah until the next day.

I was late getting downstairs for the meal, because I'd had to remove the tags from the new clothes that Sister Simonne had delivered to my room. The good news was that I felt like myself again in blue jeans and a warm, serviceable gray sweatshirt (Sister Simonne had made careful note of my dislike of ironing, and there had been no blouses bought). Perhaps most importantly, I had a bra that fit.

The bad news was that the platters of food were already on the table, and almost everyone was already seated and waiting, which limited my seating options. Sisters Lise and Simonne flanked Talia on either side in what I realized were their usual chairs—because of course I hadn't thought to ask the day before, and they'd been too polite to say anything. There was an empty chair on the other side of Sister Simonne's, but it was too close to Talia for me to be able to avoid her, and so I murmured an apology for my tardiness and headed around the table toward the remaining two unoccupied chairs to the left of Phoenix.

Not ideal, if that black look she leveled in my direction was anything to go by, but it was still preferable to Talia worming things out of me that I wasn't ready to tell her yet. Maybe.

I'd only made it a few steps, sidling between Sister Simonne's chair and the wall, acutely aware of Talia's narrow-eyed disapproval, when Sister Bernadette arrived in the company of the until-now-absent Sister Colette.

The stooped, round-shouldered nun sported an unruly

mass of gray curls above a bright white bandage over her left eyebrow. She had two black eyes, which were actually varying shades of purple, dark blue, green, and yellow, and a swollen nose that shared the same color palette because, apparently, I had a thing for hitting people in the nose.

And yes, she really did use a walker.

The air left me in an audible hiss, and the guilt that I'd managed to set aside rushed in to take its place. Sweet Mary Magdalene. Seriously? Decking the emergency nurse in Toronto hadn't been bad enough?

It was a damned good thing I didn't believe in hell.

Sister Colette looked my way, tipping her head back to stare at me through glasses that were taped together at the nose bridge and so thick that they distorted her blue eyes, making her look like a fierce owl. "*You,*" she said.

Part of me shriveled up inside, and my mouth went dry. I swallowed. "Sister Colette," I began, "I am so, so—"

"You pack quite a wallop, young lady," she informed me. Then, eyes dancing behind the glasses, she smacked the handgrip on her walker and let out a whoop of laughter. All the Ursulines joined in except Sister Bernadette, who guided the elderly nun to the empty chair behind which I stood.

Still cackling, Sister Colette patted my hand with her much wrinklier one and then plopped herself into the chair. I automatically pushed it in for her—dear sweet Mary, the woman weighed next to nothing, and I'd *hit* her? I took a steadying breath and leaned down.

"I am so, *so* sorry," I told her earnestly. "I didn't—I wasn't—"

"Pfft!" she responded. "That was more excitement than I've seen in a lifetime around here. Plus, I had my first ride in an ambulance."

I thought I was going to throw up. They'd had to call an ambulance?

Beside Sister Colette, Sister Simonne hastened to reassure me. "It was just a precaution," she said. "She wasn't unconscious or anything, there was just so much *blood*, and—"

Sister Colette flapped a hand in her colleague's face to silence her. "Hush!" she exclaimed. "You're making the poor girl feel bad."

Sister Bernadette, who had followed to take Sister Colette's walker off to the side and out of the way, heaved a sigh and patted my shoulder as I gritted my teeth and internally counted to ten.

"You'll get used to Sister Colette," she said, rolling her eyes at their eldest member. "And Sister Simonne is right, the ambulance was purely a precaution. We'd actually called it for you before you woke up and—well. Detective Dawson told us it was best that you remain in the monastery, and since the paramedics were already here, we had them look after Sister Colette."

"The very good-looking paramedics," Sister Colette corrected, cackling some more.

Sister Bernadette rolled her eyes again, then pointed me toward the empty chair on the other side of the table, next to Phoenix. "Sit," she said, "and let's eat before *all* the food goes cold."

I nodded, and with Sister Colette's laughter and Sister Bernadette's mutters of *incorrigible* following me, went to sit beside Phoenix ... who promptly half-turned her back on me and struck up a conversation with Sister Margaret on her other side. Fortunately, there wasn't even time for the lump in my throat to fully form before Sister Bernadette, who had taken her seat on my other side, waved an invitation at the food.

"Please," she said. "Guests first."

Phoenix needed no other invitation and reached for a large bowl of spaghetti topped with meat sauce. She served herself and then, when prompted by Sister Margaret, passed the bowl grudgingly in my direction. Between the quiet hostility rolling off her and sitting across from the elderly Ursuline I'd tried to kill, my appetite was hovering somewhere between non-existent and I-think-I'll-puke-if-I-eat-a-single-bite, but I took a small scoop of the spaghetti and passed the bowl along.

Surprisingly, I managed to eat the pasta, along with some of the salad that came my way and a slice of garlic bread. I even had seconds when the bowl made the rounds again, making Sister Lise, who had been the cook for tonight, beam across the table at me. Then, between sips of coffee and slight shudders—because we still needed to address the *instant* issue—I looked over at Sister Bernadette.

"Can I ask why you all speak English so well? I'm grateful, of course"—that was an understatement, because trying to get the answers we needed would have been a nightmare otherwise—"but I'm surprised."

"Three of our sisters came over from England in 1963," she replied. "They were the last to join our order. We all spoke the language fairly well already, as English and French were both taught in our school, but we refined it extensively when they joined us. Sister Catherine is the only one remaining of the three, now. She's in the home with the others."

"Moving them out of here must have been hard for you," said Phoenix, surprising me by leaning forward to join the conversation, "and for them."

"It is always difficult to say goodbye, whether to a place

or a person," said Sister Bernadette. "But ultimately, that is how we all end, yes?"

"Yes," said Phoenix, her voice softening. I knew she was thinking of the Mary Magdalene House and the women there who had been her family—and that she was watching me—but something else had reached for my attention, pulling me away from the voices around the table.

A heaviness.

A heat.

A warning.

I thrust back my chair and stood, my hand going to my jeans pocket. "Someone's coming," I said, and seven forks clattered onto seven plates.

THE SOMEONE TURNED OUT TO BE A NEIGHBOR, WHO HAD come to ask the sisters if they were aware that Methuselah was currently sitting on the front steps of the *funiculaire* entrance in the Petit-Champlain district, the lower part of Old Quebec City where Louis had dropped me off.

Sister Bernadette had answered the door, with the rest of us crowded into the little hallway behind her. Sister Lise pushed her glasses up on her nose as she translated for me in a hushed whisper.

"Guillaume says they were coming back from dinner with friends when they saw him," she murmured. "They asked if he was all right, if he was lost, but he just walked away—further into the district."

French words continued to flow back and forth through the open door, along with a gust of wind that danced through the hall, briefly distracting me with renewed gratitude for the jeans I was wearing. I had no idea how the Ursulines managed winter here.

Sister Lise's translation continued. "They stopped for a glass of spiced wine at the Christmas market on their way back, so Guillaume thinks it was about an hour ago that they saw him." She sighed. "He could be anywhere by now."

"He's certain it was him?"

"Yes. He is certain." Sister Lise nodded as Sister Bernadette began another string of words interspersed with an occasional *merci* as she waved Guillaume off into the cold.

At last, the door closed, shutting out the wind, and Sister Bernadette turned to lean against it as she looked at us. My eyes met hers.

"I'll need a coat," I said. "And something warmer than the boots I arrived with, please. The closest to size eight that you have."

At the fringe of the group, Sister Simonne slipped away.

"I'm coming, too," said Talia. "We can split up and cover more territory."

"And me," Phoenix and Sister Margaret said in unison.

"No."

It came out as a snarl, and Phoenix drew back in surprise, trying to hide her hurt. I gritted my teeth and wrestled control of myself away from the stone. Her offer of help had been akin to an olive branch, and I'd just snapped the damned thing in half. Go, me.

Softening my voice, I said, "It's better if the rest of you stay here. Too many of us might scare him, and if you do happen to find him, there might be a Mage on your tail. None of you are equipped for that."

"Neither are you, with the stone not working," Talia pointed out.

"No, but at least it will make sure that I survive an attack. I can't be worrying about you *and* Methuselah."

She scowled, and I braced for an argument, but Sister Margaret put a hand on her shoulder. "She's right, Talia. It's better that we stay behind."

"I will come with you," said Sister Bernadette. "I can show you the way, and he knows me."

I nodded to her, and she turned to get her coat as Sister Simonne came back with laden arms. She handed me the boots first—the same sturdy kind as those lined up in the front entrance. They were a bit big on me, but smaller than Talia's were, so at least I would avoid getting new blisters—or, hopefully, reopening the old ones.

The coat was next. It smelled strongly of mothballs. Phoenix drew back with a wrinkled nose, but after living for a day and a night in Louis's pipe-tobacco-and-sweat-scented coat, I hardly noticed. Olfactory adventures in coats were just how I rolled these days.

Sister Simonne handed me a toque and scarf, then a pair of mittens, all made of scratchy wool. I hesitated for only a second before donning them, because beggars couldn't be choosers, and I didn't have time—or money—to find myself a department store right now.

"Are you ready?" I asked Sister Bernadette, who was similarly outfitted. She nodded and pulled open the door, and I stepped outside. Not until the heavy wooden door closed behind us and we were halfway across the courtyard did I realize I'd left without so much as a "fare thee well" or backward glance.

Damned stone.

CHAPTER 20

The snow flurries of the morning had amounted to almost nothing. What little had fallen had been swept away by the wind that gusted through the courtyard and wrapped Sister Bernadette's skirt around her legs, but she didn't seem to notice.

"This way." She pointed down the street to the left as we exited the passageway from the courtyard. I followed in her wake, one hand rubbing at the itch of wool against my forehead. Tomorrow, I promised myself, I would ask about a different hat.

Sister Bernadette moved at a brisk pace along the sidewalk, making a right-hand turn when we reached an intersection. "This is the shortest route," she said over her shoulder, "and there will be fewer people."

"Are there a lot of people out at this hour?" I scurried to catch up with her. I'd made a note of the living room clock before we left and knew that it was a little after seven. "Isn't it a weeknight?"

"Thursday," she confirmed. "But the Christmas market is open until nine from Thursday through Sunday all this month and next."

"Even down where your neighbor saw Methuselah?" I asked, thinking, *please, no.*

She shook her head. "No, the market has four locations, all in this part of the city, but there are still a lot of tourists in the Lower Town, too. The shops stay open to take advantage of the traffic."

Of course they did. Awesome.

A group of men came toward us, huddled into their

coats and scarves and spread across the width of the sidewalk. They showed no sign of having seen us or planning to step aside, and out of habit, I stepped off the curb and into the street. Sister Bernadette, however, was having none of it. She aimed herself squarely between the two leaders, bent her arms so that her elbows stuck out slightly from her body, and barreled through—much like a snowplow.

I stepped back onto the sidewalk and ducked behind her at the last second, thoroughly enjoying the voices raised in surprise as the leaders realized we weren't moving aside and the men behind them hastily parted. The best part, however, were the apologies that followed us down the sidewalk. I fell back into step beside the nun.

"That was rather impressive," I said.

"There was a time, when we wore our habits, that people saw us," she said. "They don't anymore. I used to move for them the way you just did, but one day, I saw a woman—not a nun, but she was about my age—do what I just did. I haven't stepped aside since."

Huh. I knew that many other women of our generation did the stepping-aside thing, and I rather liked her solution. I sent her an amused look. "I may have to start doing the same."

An instant's hesitation on her part made me remember that I might not be around to worry about it for much longer, but she recovered as we turned another corner— left this time—and leaned into the veritable gale blowing down the street.

"Do," she shouted over the wind, clamping a hand onto her hat to keep it from lifting off her head. "We can start a revolution."

The remainder of our walk was made mostly in silence, except when Sister Bernadette suggested we change direction or go somewhere in particular. I recognized some of the landmarks from my arrival and search for the monastery: the Château Frontenac, of course; the information office that was now closed for the day; the Santa display at the foot of the tall monument with a lineup of children and their parents waiting patiently.

Sister Bernadette had been right about the Lower Town still being crowded. It, too, was all decked out for the holidays, although I hadn't noticed that after Louis dropped me off because I'd been too focused on putting one foot in front of the other and making it up the hill. It would be hard not to see the decorations now, however, as they bounced and danced wildly in the gusts of wind blasting in from the river. I adjusted my toque and scarf to cover as much of my head as possible without obscuring my vision.

"Is it always this windy?" I asked. We'd stopped at the bottom of the final stairs descending into the Petit-Champlain district, and Sister Bernadette was scanning the street stretching before us.

"At this time of year, yes," she said. "In the summer, when we need it to break the heat? Never." She pointed to our right, and I recognized the front of the *funiculaire* building with its wide stone stairs. "That's where Guillaume saw him."

Quickly, I assessed the possible routes Methuselah might have chosen. I could see two streets from here, and I remembered from my arrival that a veritable rabbit warren of others spread out from those. Plus, there was the possibility that he'd gone up the stairs after neighbor Guillaume had left.

"Awesome," I said. I pressed my lips together, inhaled deeply through my nose, and then blew out the air in a gust that the wind snatched away from me. "Well. We may as well get started."

Looking about as optimistic as I felt, Sister Bernadette started down the street that lay ahead.

We searched for hours. The streets emptied first of families, then of the remaining tourists, then of the locals as everyone headed inside to warmth and bed. I was chilled to the bone, and I decided that if I never had to walk another cobblestoned street in my life, it would be too soon.

Two things kept me going as long as we did. One was, obviously, the threat of the Mages. The second was Sister Bernadette's description of our quarry.

As we'd started down the first street, she'd told me to look for a tall man wearing a trench coat and fedora. I'd shot her a horrified look, almost tripping over the rough stones.

"A fedora and trench?" I'd echoed. "In this weather? He'll freeze to death!"

She'd returned my incredulity with calm equanimity. "Except he cannot die, *ma belle*," she reminded me.

Right. I knew that. But I was beginning to think that I couldn't die either—at least, not easily—and I'd still been half frozen outside with no coat or hat, before Louis had taken pity on me. And I'd had all my faculties about me— well, most of them, anyway. Enough to be able to seek shelter, at the very least. But the way the Ursulines had described Methuselah?

Without further comment, I'd hunched my shoulders

against the bitter wind, picked up the pace, and sharpened my vigilance. Sister Bernadette had lengthened her stride and followed.

By the time we gave up, we were the only ones awake in all of Old Quebec. Or, at least, the only ones awake and foolhardy enough to still be outside. The wind hadn't died down in the least—in fact, I was pretty sure that the gusts had increased in both intensity and frequency—and my fingers and toes had long given up any feeling.

Sister Bernadette had accompanied me uncomplainingly, but as I paused in front of the Santa display again and waited for her to catch up with me, I saw that her face was pinched with cold. She looked exhausted, and my conscience gave a twinge at keeping an eighty-plus-year-old woman (a) up this late, and (b) outside in this weather for so long.

We'd completed four circuits of the Petit-Champlain district, climbed the stairs back up to the Upper Town, walked every street there at least three times, and then repeated the entire route. It was time to admit defeat.

"We should call it a night," I told Sister Bernadette when she caught up with me. How had I not noticed that she'd slowed down so much? "We can try again tomorrow, in the daylight."

She nodded wearily, tucked her mittened hands into her coat pockets, and began a homeward shuffle. Joining her, I tucked my arm through hers and slowed my pace to keep step.

"I'm sorry I kept you out so long," I said. "I forgot that you're—"

Sister Bernadette snorted. "This is no later than I've been out searching before." She looked sideways at my surprise. "You thought we'd just sat back when he disappeared?"

I had, but I hadn't let the stone's influence let me say so. "You didn't say anything."

"I didn't think I needed to."

Ouch. And touché.

"You're right," I said. "I apologize."

"Also?" She slanted me another glance. "I'm eighty-three, *ma belle*. Not dead."

I smiled and tucked her arm closer. "Noted," I said.

Sister Simonne and Sister Lise were waiting up for us when we got back to the residence. They stripped off our coats and scarves when our own numb fingers fumbled, hung the garments on the hooks, and knelt to help us off with our boots. They'd sent the others to bed at midnight, Sister Lise told us as she lined our boots up with the others, with a promise to wake them and let them know when we returned safely.

They pattered off in their slippers and flannel nightgowns to fulfill that promise while Sister Bernadette and I went into the kitchen for the tea they'd kept warm for us— chamomile, Sister Simonne said, to help calm our nerves. Whatever the outcome.

I was too exhausted to feel nerves of any kind, calm or otherwise, but the tea was hot and sweet with honey, and it was delicious. We drank it in silence, and I listened to the soft footsteps moving overhead as sisters Simonne and Lise delivered their missives and then headed for their own rooms. Sister Bernadette finished her tea first and went to set her cup in the sink for washing up tomorrow—or make that today, I corrected myself, as the mantel clock in the living room gave two soft chimes. She paused in the doorway to look back at me.

"We *will* find him," she said. "It's just a matter of time."

Her optimism should have been heartwarming, but it wasn't. Because time was the one thing we didn't have.

Well. We didn't have much of a plan, either. Or a way of fighting off the Mages if they found us. Or a home. Or money. Or a car. Or—

I folded my arms on the table and rested my forehead on them, because *shit*.

CHAPTER 21

I felt the chill as soon as I stepped through the gates and into the massive square covered in paving stones, and my steps slowed and then stopped. Sister Simonne carried on ahead of me, still chattering away to herself, but her voice was muffled here, swallowed by the vastness of the space and the buildings rising on its every side. It was the third day of my search for Methuselah, and she had accompanied me in place of Sister Bernadette, whose arthritic hip had flared up after our long, cold trek on the first night, followed by a second long day of searching yesterday.

Wracked by guilt, I'd apologized profusely to the head of the Ursulines, but Sister Bernadette had waved away my words, telling me that some things were more important than the aches and pains of an old woman. Still, it had been a reminder that I was at least fifteen years younger than most of the monastery residents. Today, I'd insisted that Sister Simonne and I take frequent breaks to rest and warm ourselves in one of the many restaurant entries or beside the propane fires burning at each of the Christmas market locations, especially given the nun's greater bulk.

Too frequent, perhaps, because during our last stop, Sister Simonne had regarded me with hands on wide hips and a frown of concern as she told me that if I needed to return to the monastery for a nap, she could continue on her own. Hiding a smile, I'd demurred, cut our break short, and plunged again into the crowds of people that filled the sidewalks and park spaces, filling the air with happy voices and infectious, uplifting energy.

But here in this square, there were no people. It was empty, silent, and oppressive as hell. And yes, the weather was cold in general, because it was the end of November, but this cold, this soul-deep chill, felt different.

I hunched my shoulders as I turned slowly in place, looking up at the rows of mullioned windows—dozens of them—that ran across the face of each of the buildings, then at the set of double doors that led into each of them.

What was this place? There had been a sign at the gate as we'd come in, but I'd been too focused on watching for a fedora and trench coat to pay attention to it. We'd been directed here by one of *les perdus*—the lost ones—as Sister Simonne called the three men sheltering in one of the doorways along St. Jean Street.

Not because *they* were lost, she'd hastened to assure me, but because society had lost *them*. Once, the Ursulines had brought sandwiches and tea for them every few days and had kept their feet warm with new, knitted socks every winter, but without new blood coming into the monastery, the aging nuns hadn't been able to continue meeting the need.

"And so," Sister Simonne had said as she finished her explanation, her voice husky and her brown eyes watery, "*Perdu encore.*"

Lost again.

But that hadn't dampened the men's delight at seeing her, and even though I hadn't understood a word of the French they'd spoken, their worry had been obvious—and genuine—when Sister Simonne had asked if anyone had seen Methuselah. It had taken some doing, but I'd convinced the Ursulines to take their search into their community and ask for help, pointing out that at this point, we had little to lose. The nuns had agreed, albeit reluctantly, and word had spread rapidly. There had been a steady stream of concerned neighbors stopping by with promises to keep an eye out, and to ask if the nuns needed any assistance in the monastery with Methuselah gone—as if he had been looking after them, instead of the other way around.

From the discussion and many gesticulations that had taken place between *les perdus* and Sister Simonne, it had been clear that Methuselah was well known beyond the nuns' immediate neighborhood, that he was thought of with great fondness down here on the streets, and that, yes, *les perdus* were sure they'd seen him.

When Sister Simonne had finally received as definitive an answer as she'd said we were likely to get, given the differing opinions that had seemed to be held, she had pressed a few coins into each of the men's weathered, street-stained hands and repeated *merci* more times than I could count. Then, we had continued on our way.

And now we were here.

I felt a presence at my shoulder and turned to see that the nun had retraced her steps to join me.

"What is this place?" I asked.

The nun pressed her lips together, and her gaze, too, traced the lines of windows. "Now?" she asked. "It's a branch of the university."

"But it wasn't always."

"No." She shook her head, and a shadow crossed her eyes. "No, it was not. At least, not as we think of learning now. It was originally built as a seminary, and then it became a boys' school for a time—including for Indigenous children. The man who founded it was known for his austerity and adherence to the church's most dogmatic rules. I don't think this was a happy place."

I didn't think so, either—and judging by the weight inside my mitten right now, neither did the stone.

I gave a little start, because *mitten*? Since when had I taken the stone from my jeans pocket and put it inside my mitten?

"You look unsettled," said Sister Simonne. "Can you feel them, too? The ones who cried out for their mothers and fathers?" She wrapped her arms around herself over her coat, even though it wasn't that cold today. "Sister Bernadette says that I'm imagining things, but I don't like this place. Not at all. I don't think Methuselah would be here."

I was still trying to figure out how I'd managed to take my mitten off, reach under my own coat and into my jeans pocket, and remove the stone without being aware of any of it. I shivered. I didn't like the way I was losing moments to this thing. But Sister Simonne was right. The very walls of this place felt as if they were steeped in misery and pain, and if Methuselah had come here …

I swept my gaze over the massive square one last time, but there was nowhere for a man to hide in here. Not so much as a shadowed crevice marred the facade. If Methuselah *had* come here, he was gone now. There was a drop-off to the left of us, down to what looked like another level, with stairs at the side and who knew how many streets intersecting beyond them.

Sister Simonne suggested we continue our search elsewhere, and I nodded acquiescence and followed her back to the black iron gates. We would make the most of the daylight we had left, and then we would head back to the monastery to have dinner with the others. After that …

I slipped my mitten off, lifted the hem of my coat, and replaced the stone in my front pocket. After that, we would see.

WE WALKED FOR ALMOST TWO MORE HOURS INSTEAD OF the one I'd expected. Sister Simonne took me to the far end of the enormous Dufferin Terrace in front of the Château Frontenac, to where a long staircase rose up into the trees. It was the start of the Governors' Boardwalk, she said, and it—all three hundred and eight stairs of it, plus almost a kilometer of walkway, according to the sign at its base—would take us up to the Citadelle overlooking the St. Lawrence River.

Methuselah had loved going there, she told me as, belying both her age and her size, she made the climb seemingly without effort, stopping only to ask the few people we met along the way if they'd seen anyone matching Methuselah's description. I huffed along in her wake, resolving to add stair climbs to my exercise regimen. When I had an actual regimen again, that was, and I wasn't just trying to prepare myself for a battle I had no hope of winning.

The boardwalk and the Citadelle were both new territory for me. Sister Bernadette hadn't brought us this way because of her hip, and because it seemed logical that we'd have more success looking for our missing alien where he would be more likely to find at least some shelter and food.

I was more than willing to expand the search, however, and perhaps beginning to feel just a bit desperate. Or more accurately, more desperate. Privately, I was beginning to think that, alleged sightings aside, Methuselah wasn't even in the city anymore—at least not this part of it. Which meant expanding our search beyond the gates of Old Quebec into the city of more than half a million people, and who knew how far beyond that.

I dreaded the idea, but we were running out of options. And time. And, right now, daylight, too.

It was almost dark by the time we reached the Citadelle itself. The boardwalk ended with a final short set of stairs and then a fork in the path. Forward led to a gazebo overlooking the river, and right took us toward a walking path that doubled back on the boardwalk and led toward the fortification. Sister Simonne turned right, and I followed.

She stopped at the edge of a deep, wide trench, on the other side of which sat a row of stone buildings topped with roofs of grass, their second-story windows at eye level with us. A handful of lights had come on along the buildings' outer walls, and lampposts dotted a distant walking path that sloped down to what seemed an endless sweep of lawn—the Plains of Abraham, Sister Simonne told me. None of the lights did much to combat the semi-gloom that accompanied the transition from day to night. They weren't quite needed for overall illumination yet, and they weren't powerful enough to reach into the encroaching shadows.

She tugged off her mittens, lifted her chained glasses to her nose with one hand, and pulled an ancient pocket watch from her coat pocket with the other. She angled the watch to peer at its face by one of the lights on the stone building across from us. A mutter of annoyance escaped her.

She pocketed the watch again and sighed. "I should have checked the time before we came," she said. "The museum and tours have shut down for the day. We won't be able to go inside the fortification."

I frowned. "You think he'd be hiding in a museum?"

"Not the museum, no, but the Citadelle is huge, and he

could be hiding in one of the other buildings. It's also an active military base, home to the Van Doos—the Royal 22nd Regiment—and the only way inside is either through the museum or with a tour guide. There are cameras everywhere. Only a handful of the regiment stays here, but…"

Sister Simonne trailed off with a shrug that I concurred with, because we really didn't need to be explaining ourselves to one of Canada's most famous infantry regiments. *Merde*, indeed.

I looked down into the trench beside us again, my gaze traveling its length from one end to the other, both of which were sharp turns toward the center of the fortification's famous, lopsided star shape. Phoenix had actually shown me an aerial view of it just this morning, when I'd gone to Sister Bernadette's office to say goodbye to her before Sister Simonne and I left for the day.

The young woman had been ensconced in there with Sister Bernadette's elderly computer every waking hour since she'd discovered its presence, Talia had told me last night, playing endless games online. She'd asked if we should worry about it, but I'd shaken my head and told her that it was Phoenix's way of dealing with stress and uncertainty—and heaven knew she had enough of that in her life right now.

"Leave her be," I'd said to Talia, and then, as an afterthought, added, "but maybe suggest that she be extra careful about covering her tracks. She might not be as invisible as she thinks."

I hadn't wanted to mention security to Phoenix myself, because we seemed to have established an uneasy truce that I didn't want to disturb. And knowing how anxious she was about our safety—mine, Talia's, and Sister Margaret's included—any mention of potential danger could have brought down that truce like a house of cards.

Which was why she'd surprised me so much with the whole Citadelle thing.

"Look," she'd said, when she showed me the monitor. She'd pointed to the way the Citadelle's front gate wasn't actually the entrance but was instead the beginning of the fortification's first line of defense—not counting the cannons you'd already had to bypass, she'd amended. She traced a finger over the picture on the computer monitor, showing how the gate opened onto a wall that was actually a triangle.

"See? You had to go around it to get to the real front gate—assuming you survived the rifles all along here"—she pointed at slits in the square-cut stone walls lining the trench—"and here. They called it a kill zone. It's ingenious, don't you think?"

Well. That had certainly been one word for it, but before I could point out the horror behind the whole concept, Phoenix had added, "So? Would it work?"

"Would what work?" I'd asked.

"Going there." She jabbed the screen with her finger hard enough to make it rock on its stand. "To fight the Mages. We could defend ourselves. Hide. Take them out before they even knew we were there."

I still remembered the feel of my jaw dropping open as I'd stared at her. I hadn't known how to respond. There had been so very many layers in her suggestion: her desire to help; her acceptance that I could not protect her—or any of them; her lack of understanding—even after all we'd been through—of just what it was we faced; her change from sweet, gentle, wouldn't-hurt-a-fly young woman to someone who thought of murder as a viable option.

I mean, she wasn't wrong about any of that, but dear sweet Mary Magdalene, that it had come to this …

Sister Simonne had come looking for me, then, and I'd used her as an excuse to avoid answering Phoenix. At least for the time being. I'd given the young woman a quick hug, promised her we'd talk later, and left so fast it was a wonder I didn't run someone over on my way out the door. And after having a whole day to think about it, I still didn't know what to say.

Computer games would have been so much easier to deal with.

"Sister Monica?"

I jolted out of my reverie to find Sister Simonne a dozen feet along the path, looking back at me in askance as she waited. "Sorry," I said. "Did you say something? I didn't hear you."

"I said we'll walk the perimeter," she replied, "and then call it a day. *Les perdus* will watch for Methuselah and come to the monastery if they see him. It is the best we can do for now."

I let my gaze travel the deep, paved trench again, and then the wide sweep of lawn. Both were empty. I nodded at the nun. "Yes," I agreed. "You're right."

Tomorrow, we would start again.

CHAPTER 22

Talia woke me at nine with coffee and a look of determination that told me we were about to have a discussion. I was tempted to roll over and feign more sleep, but I'd already bolted upright at her sudden barging in, and I didn't think she'd buy it. So I heaved an aggrieved sigh instead.

She plonked the coffee mug onto the bedside stand. "Do *not* give me that," she said. "You've been dodging me since your first day here, and we need to talk."

"I've joined you for every meal that I haven't been out looking for Methuselah," I pointed out. "And I've gone to the living room with everyone after dinner when I've been here, too."

She wasn't buying that, either.

"Where I haven't been able to ask you anything beyond how you're feeling because Phoenix has been there, too, and you know it." She hooked a foot around the leg of the chair and dragged it forward, then sat down and put both feet up on the bed beside me, her own cup cradled in hands resting against her midriff. "Now talk."

I could have prevaricated, but that would have been a waste of both time and words, because I knew what she was asking, and I really was going to have to tell her sooner or later. And Sister Simonne and I had agreed on a later start today, so sooner appeared to be the choice.

I shifted my backside up in the bed and leaned against the pillows.

"The stone is bound to me," I said. Then I hesitated, because regardless of timing, this wasn't going to be easy.

Talia frowned. "Didn't we already know that?"

I took a deep breath, glanced at the door to be sure that it was fully closed, and dropped my voice. "Permanently," I said. "It's bound to me permanently."

Silence met my bombshell. Seconds dragged into a minute, and then into an eternity. Someone passed by in the hall outside. A toilet flushed. Sister Bernadette's voice called up the stairs in search of Sister Lise. A truck rumbled by on the street below my window.

Talia still didn't speak.

For lack of something better to do, I reached for the coffee cup she'd set on the bedside table and took a sip. A faint shudder went through me as it rolled over my tongue. I wondered if we would be here long enough for me to get used to instant. Perhaps I should consider adding cream and sugar to take the edge off of it—or maybe something stronger. I'd never been a drinker, but I suspected that even the holy Mother herself would forgive me for starting now. Except I had no idea what kind of alcohol I would like, and I could hardly request an assortment be brought in for me to sample. Unless maybe one of the nuns kept a bottle for medicinal purposes the way Mother Joan had in my early days at St. Paul's. Brandy, I thought it might have been.

Talia cleared her throat, jolting me out of my disjointed ramblings and back to reality. "How long have you known?" she asked.

"The day I got here—well, when I woke up."

"Sister Bernadette and Sister Margaret stayed to talk to you. I remember." She nodded, staring down at her own cup, and I realized that she hadn't looked at me since I'd told her. "So Sister Margaret knew before then?"

"Yes and no," I prevaricated. "She knew, but she said that she hoped that once we found Methuselah …"

The brown gaze flicked up to meet mine. "Once we found Methuselah, what?"

Before I could answer, she dropped her feet to the floor with a *thunk* and sat forward in her chair. Coffee sloshed over her hand, but she ignored it. "Wait. He can undo it? He can unbind the stone?"

I clenched my teeth, my lips pulling tight, and shook my head. "Sister Bernadette doesn't think so. He would have been able to once, but he's …" I trailed off.

"Too far gone," Talia finished.

"Yes."

She blew out a long, slow breath. "Shit."

"Yes."

"She's sure?"

I nodded, and she muttered, "Shit," under her breath a second time. Then she scowled. "Hold on, how do they know this? Has it happened before? The stone binding to someone and him undoing it, I mean?"

In as few words as possible—because really, rehashing the details of my predicament was *not* my idea of fun—I summarized what Sister Bernadette had told me. When I finished, Talia rose from her chair and went to stand at the window, a dark silhouette against the bright day unfolding outside.

I would need to get moving soon, if Sister Simonne and I were to leave at noon as planned. We had no way of covering all the streets at all times of the day, so we'd decided to alternate our hours. Yesterday, we had gone out as soon as breakfast was done. Today, we would go out after lunch and stay out through dinner.

Talia's voice broke again into my thoughts.

"Should we tell Phoenix? She'd want to know."

"I will," I said, "but not yet. She's too fragile. I want

her to feel …" I trailed off, not sure how to put my thoughts into words. My heart into words.

"Like she'll be okay without you?" Talia asked, her voice gentle.

Tears prickled behind my eyes, and I blinked them back. "Yes."

"She's stronger than you think, you know."

"I know," I said. "But I don't want her to have to be strong about that. Not yet."

Talia sat for a moment, staring at the hands she'd folded together in the lap of her outstretched legs. I wondered how her wrist was doing—which reminded me about Phoenix's eye, too. Sweet Mary, some friend I was, not checking in with either of them. I opened my mouth to ask now, but her next question knocked all thought of injuries and healing right back out of my head again.

"Why is Phoenix so important to you?" she asked. "I mean, I know that she was a part of the shelter, but your relationship to her—it's more than just a friendship. Why?"

So we'd reached that level of sharing, had we? I set my coffee mug on the bedside table again, choosing my words with care. Not to protect myself, but rather to make the story as short, succinct, and matter-of-fact as possible.

Which, I thought wryly, would absolutely protect the long-buried feelings part of me.

"My mother died in childbirth when I was twelve," I said. "The baby was born intersex, and my father was … well, conservative would be an understatement. He told us that the child was an abomination, and that my mother had died as punishment for giving birth to it. The nuns from St. Paul's—that's where I went to school—stepped in and tried to mitigate things as best they could. They thought Father would be more accepting of a son, so they had the baby christened as Joseph. As the eldest sibling, I stood in for my mother, and we raised him as a boy. *I* raised him as a boy, because Father still refused to have anything to do with him.

"Father tried to pull me from school so that I could stay home as a surrogate mother, but the law was against him, and the nuns enlisted the priest's aid in convincing him that I needed to graduate. By the time I did, Joseph was starting school at St. Paul's as well, and I knew that we'd made a mistake in the gender we'd assigned to him. But Mother Joan had offered me a place as a novitiate at St. Paul's and to pay my way through teachers' college. She said it was best that Joseph remain as he was, so that he could keep his place in the family. She assured me that she would look out for him and, for a while, I thought everything would be okay."

My mouth twisted. "More accurately," I said, "I desperately wished that it would be. She was kind to him, and the others followed her example." I fell silent, gathering my courage to speak the rest of my story. Of Josephine's story. Talia waited without prodding or prompting. After a moment, I continued.

"Then Mother Joan died, and Annunciata was assigned to St. Paul's in her place, and everything changed. By that time, I was teaching at the school, and I tried to run interference where I could, but Annunciata allowed no contact with family outside of school hours—or conversation with the other nuns outside of the allotted social time that she personally supervised. Joseph lasted there until he was sixteen, and then he ran away from home and went to Toronto. He—she—changed her name to Josephine and wrote to tell me she'd found friends and a job, and that she was happy."

I took another break. It was no wonder I never told anyone about this. Even keeping it short and matter-of-fact, it was hard. This time, Talia prodded, as if sensing I needed a nudge to continue.

"But she wasn't," she said. "Happy, I mean."

"No," I said quietly. "No, she wasn't. It turned out that her *job* was working the streets, and she was an addict. She died of a drug overdose when she was eighteen."

"Hell." Talia's voice was even quieter than mine had been. "I'm so sorry, Monica."

"So am I." My gaze went past her to the window. I couldn't see much of the sky from here, but I could tell that it was sunny. I wondered if the wind of the last two days had died down at all. Then I wondered what time it was, because I really should get moving and back out there looking for Methuselah. Oh wait, Sister Simonne and I were going out later today. I forgot.

Talia sat forward in her chair and put a hand over the one I'd twisted into the covers. "It wasn't your fault, Monica. You were just a child yourself and, Jesus, you were in a bad place. There was nothing you could have done."

"There was much I could have done," I corrected, "and now I'm taking care to do it. There's a difference between guilt and remorse. One will eat us alive from the inside, the other will help us make better choices. I failed Josephine. I will do everything in my power not to fail Phoenix."

"That's why you don't want to tell her about the stone, yet?"

"That's why I don't want to tell her at all," I responded. "But I will at some point, because I know I have to."

"And in the meantime?"

"I'm going to do the only thing I can," I said. "I'm going to find Methuselah before the Mages do."

Not until she had left me to get dressed, taking my empty coffee cup with her, did I remember that I still hadn't asked about her wrist.

CHAPTER 23

ON DAY FIVE OF THE ENDLESS, FRUSTRATING, FRUITLESS game of cat-and-mouse, I changed tactics. If I couldn't go to Methuselah, I decided, perhaps Methuselah would come to me. Or at least to a cup of hot chocolate.

Even though there were only four of them remaining and no one—least of all me—would have blamed them for sleeping in a little, the Ursulines still gathered for morning lauds at five. When Phoenix had expressed horror at the idea of rising so early, Sister Colette had patted her cheek and told her that their rising was such a habit at this point, they wouldn't be able to sleep anyway, so they might as well pray. Especially as they had much to pray about right now.

Somewhat fascinated by the idea, Phoenix had joined them yesterday morning, but she had immediately decided that she wasn't cut out for the ecclesiastical life long-term.

"I don't know how you survived," she'd muttered between yawns as she and I did the dishes after dinner that night. "But I will say that it was … intense."

"Intense?" I'd raised an eyebrow as I'd handed her a pot to dry.

"There was an energy," she'd said, her voice thoughtful. "When they were praying together. You could feel it. Was it like that for you?"

"It was," I'd said. "Once."

"But not anymore?"

I'd paused to consider the question, because I did still pray—*Hail Mary Magdalene*—and surely I wouldn't have continued to do so if I didn't think there was something to it. Something … more.

"All of us are witches at heart, Sister Monica," whispered Sister Margaret's voice in my memory, *"whether we want to know it or not."*

"I do feel something," I'd told Phoenix. I wouldn't lie to her. Not about that, anyway. "But it's complicated."

"Is that your way of saying you don't want to talk about it?"

It had been my way of saying that I didn't think I was quite comfortable with equating prayer with magick, and I didn't want to talk about that. But I didn't suppose I needed to be quite so precise with her.

"It's my way of saying that I'm going to bed early," I'd countered, handing her the dishcloth. "Make sure you wipe the counters when you're done."

"Sister Monica?" Her voice had followed me to the kitchen door, and I'd paused to look back at her. She'd been drying a fork, and her entire focus had appeared to be on the task—except for the darting glances she'd kept shooting at me.

"Yes, Phoenix?"

She'd nibbled on her bottom lip. "Are we … are you and I … are we okay? I mean, I know I was mad at you about what you said, about me always having myself for company, but—are we okay now?"

Oh sweet Mary Magdalene. She'd thought *I* was angry with *her?*

The stone's familiar irritation had rippled through me, and I'd told it in no uncertain terms to piss off as I'd recrossed the kitchen and taken the young woman in my arms for what I'd realized was a long-overdue hug.

"I'm not angry with you about that, Phoenix. I'm not

angry with you about anything. It's just ..." I'd trailed off, uncertain how to continue—because *no lies*—but I'd meant what I'd told Talia. I couldn't tell Phoenix the truth, either.

"You just have a lot on your plate," Phoenix had mumbled into my shoulder, "and it makes you impatient. I know. That's what Sister Margaret said, too. I just ... I just wanted to be sure."

I'd held her away, cupped her face in my hands, and stared into the blue eyes that were so familiar—and so very dear. "You can be absolutely sure," I'd told her. "And I'm sorry I gave you reason to think otherwise. I tell you what —you have my word that if I'm ever annoyed or irritated with you, I will tell you. Fair?"

Liar, I'd imagined the stone whispering. Except it hadn't been a lie, because the irritation and annoyance were *not* mine, and I refused to own them. Except maybe the part that stemmed from watching Sister Margaret's seemingly effortless relationship with the person I most treasured in all the world. That part was entirely on me.

Phoenix had nodded. "Fair," she'd said. "And thank you."

"Thank *you*, sweet lady, for making me accountable for my actions of late. I'll try to do better."

The accountability for my actions idea had followed me down the stairs and tiptoed with me into the entry hall at ten past five this morning, but I ignored it. If there were consequences later, so be it. I would face them then. But for now, I was going to try to find Methuselah my own way.

I pulled on my coat and boots in the dark as I listened to the murmur of prayer from behind the closed living room door a few feet away. Then, when the four nuns' voices warbled into a singsong chant, I took my scarf and hat from the hook, opened the front door, and slipped outside. The handle-less door closed behind me.

There was no turning back now. Not without waking the neighborhood, anyway.

THE NEARBY COFFEE SHOP OPENED AT SIX THIRTY DURING the week and at seven on weekends. Today was Monday, by my admittedly flawed time calculations. Flawed because my days and nights since arriving here had flowed together into an unending stream of walking, sleeping, eating, and walking the streets in search of an elusive old man who wasn't a man at all.

Rinse. Repeat.

I felt reasonably certain that the Christmas market had been open for the past four days, although I wobbled on the details when it came to counting them. But if I was right, those had been Thursday through Sunday, which theoretically made today Monday. I would find out when the coffee shop either did or didn't open at six-thirty. Regardless of what day it was, it was too early to go there just yet—but that was part of my plan. Because I actually had one, for a change.

It was still dark at this hour, and only a handful of people were up and out already, most if not all of them bound for work. Except the die-hard runners, but I wasn't convinced that they ever slept at all. I shrugged deep into my coat against the chill and meandered the streets, nodding to the few other hardy souls I encountered, peering into shop windows, looking at the decorations.

The mostly empty streets worked in my favor, making

me easy to see and easy to follow. Not by the Mages, but—if I was right—by Methuselah.

And I felt sure that I had been, because half a dozen times over the last two days, I had caught a glimpse of him. Or at least his fedora. It was never more than a block or two away, and I hadn't even mentioned it to anyone, because blinking is automatic in humans, and every time I blinked, what I thought I saw would disappear again. Initially, I'd felt nothing but frustration—and the concurrent irritation that came with stone management—but then … then I'd become curious. Analytical.

Until, by the end of yesterday, I was convinced I was right. All this time that we'd thought we were looking for Methuselah, he'd been watching us. Watching, but not approaching, even though he knew the sisters well. So was it me or them that he shied away from?

There was only one way to find out. Today, I planned to send him as clear and nonthreatening an invitation as I could, in the form of what Sister Lise had told me was his favorite drink, hot chocolate.

So I walked and browsed store windows and made myself *not* look around for the now-familiar fedora. When the coffee shop opened at six thirty—because, *yes*, I'd guessed the day right—I was waiting at its door with a handful of other patrons.

At the counter, I ordered a coffee for myself and a large hot chocolate for Methuselah, getting both drinks in to-go cups. Then, as an afterthought, I bought a half-dozen croissants. If my plan worked, the alien might be hungry; if it didn't, the croissants would be appreciated back at the monastery. I paid cash, using the money Talia had given me to replace what I'd left behind in the train explosion. She'd cautioned me that we were running low on funds, and I'd promised to use it only for an emergency.

Croissants totally counted as an emergency, right?

With a cup in each mittened hand and the bag of croissants tucked under one arm, I ventured back out onto the sidewalk, murmuring *merci* to the woman who held the door for me. Outside, I took stock of my seating options. I was inclined toward the enormous wooden terrace that ran along the front of the Château Frontenac. It would be mostly unpopulated at this hour (except for those runners) and had several gazebo-like structures with benches beneath them, plus other benches along the railing that overlooked the St. Lawrence, so there were ample seating choices.

But I hesitated. I'd felt exposed standing out on it, and Methuselah might, too. He would have nowhere to watch from while he decided whether or not the hot chocolate was worth the risk. I needed someplace smaller, where he would have hiding places, and—

My gaze fell on the park across the street, where dozens of Christmas market kiosks were closed until Thursday. I hadn't been paying particular attention when we'd gone through it over the weekend—I'd been too busy looking for a fedora—but I thought that there had been benches tucked away into corners there. There must be, because people needed to sit and eat and—

A flash of movement by the corner of the kids' hut caught my eye. He was there already.

I adjusted the bag a little more securely into the crook of my arm and headed toward the market, taking a detour down the opposite sidewalk and coming in through a different entrance. I had to play this carefully so that I didn't spook him.

Between the multi-globed streetlamps surrounding the park and the many Christmas lights, the market space was bright enough to navigate with ease—and shadowy enough to make my eyes twitch from side to side as I walked. I found an unlit propane fireplace surrounded by logs that had been turned on end for seating and chose one of those. The fireplace was ringed by an aluminum shelf. I set the drinks and croissants on that and moved the hot chocolate a little apart from me.

Then I waited.

CHAPTER 24

By the time the sun came up, my coffee was gone, Methuselah's hot chocolate had turned stone cold (so had my toes), and I was ready to concede defeat.

A couple of dozen people had made their way through the market, passing through on their way to work. They were easily distinguishable from tourists by the computer bags slung over their shoulders, and by the way most were walking with their head down as they looked at the phone they carried in one gloved hand and sipped from the travel mug they held in the other.

My own hands were shoved into my armpits inside my coat. They were faring better than any other part of me, but there hadn't been a fedora—or even a glimpse of one —in the entire hour and a half that I'd been sitting here. If Methuselah *had* been watching us the last couple of days, it wasn't me that he wanted to see, and he wasn't going to take my offered bait. I'd take the croissants back to the monastery, have breakfast with the others while I thawed my toes, and then—

The scuff of a boot against pavement behind me made me stop breathing.

Long seconds ticked by while I wrestled with the urge —no, the drive of self-preservation—to turn around and see who was there. Because if that wasn't Methuselah, if it was a Mage …

A fedora settled onto the propane fireplace shelf beside the bag of croissants, and a second later, a tall, lanky man sat down on one of the log stools opposite me. His face was blurred by the circular window of the fireplace between us, and it took all the restraint I possessed not to lean to the side for a better look. If this was going to work, it had to be on his terms, not mine.

"I like hot chocolate," said a child's voice.

I did a double take. Well, that was unexpected. When Sister Bernadette had said Methuselah was the equivalent of a human child at this stage, I hadn't dreamed that she meant an *actual* child would be housed in an old man's body. I held myself back a second time from leaning around the fireplace, and managed what I thought was an admirable job of keeping my voice steady—or at least neutral—as I replied, "I'm afraid it's gone cold now, but we can get another one, if you'd like."

In response, the figure opposite me pulled a hand from a coat pocket and reached to take the paper cup from the shelf. Long, thin fingers wrapped around it, pink light glowed briefly, and a wisp of steam curled up from beneath the fold-back tab.

"It's fine," the child said. "Thank you."

I muttered a distracted, "You're welcome," as I tried to get my bearings. Talia and I had meant to ask about powers, but the question had gotten lost amidst too many others. I'd forgotten about it, and no one had mentioned an ability to heat things up by touch, or that the most ancient being on the planet sounded like he was eight years old at most or—

I remembered the croissants and thrust the bag at him. "I thought you might be hungry, too," I said.

After a moment, the long, thin fingers accepted it, and I heard the bag rustle as it was opened. A croissant appeared around the firepit, like an offering being held out to me. My stomach was too tied in knots to be hungry, but I accepted it anyway—because *Methuselah*—and we both ate in silence.

"So you're the one," a new voice said as I picked flaky crumbs off my coat front. An adult voice—and, more specifically, that of an old man.

I half shot to my feet before I realized that the voice came from the same being as the child's had. From Methuselah. I settled back onto the log, my heart doing a breakdance kind of thing halfway between my chest and my throat.

"The one?" I echoed, trying to wrap my head around this new development. Was it a split personality thing? Could aliens have split personalities? Or was he just two beings in one form? Were all his kind like—

"Show me," he said.

"Show—?" I bit off the second echo. I really needed to pull myself together here. I was supposed to be earning Methuselah's trust, not making like a parrot.

A loosely clustered group of people strolled into the marketplace alley where we were sitting. These were very much tourists, and I suppressed a flare of annoyance at the intrusion as they wandered along the closed kiosks on one side, then the other. I understood nothing they said in whatever language they spoke, but their disappointment at finding everything closed was obvious, and after a short debate amongst themselves, they departed back the way they'd come.

My shoulders descended back down to where they belonged. Except for a brief glance at the intruders, I hadn't taken my gaze off Methuselah, and now I leaned very slightly to my left, bringing his shoulder into view around the fireplace's glass surround.

"My name is—" I began.

"Show me," he interrupted. "I know you have it."

Well.

Well.

I hesitated, not particularly wanting to bring the stone out in a public place like this, and not at all sure what he wanted with it. Was he planning to take it from me? Could I let him? Could I *stop* him?

Even as I vacillated, however, Methuselah also leaned around the fireplace, letting me see him for the first time. He was strikingly ordinary in appearance … for the most part. His face was creased with the passage of years, but not the number of years I knew he'd lived. He looked to be about seventy or seventy-five, with a bushy mass of pure white hair that stuck out in every direction and hung half across his forehead. A long, narrow nose sat above a mouth that tilted up at the corners a little, as if he found me amusing.

I wouldn't blame him if he did, given that I was pretty sure that I was gaping at him in shock. And then I met his gaze, and ordinary gave way to astonishing, because his eyes—oh sweet Mother of All, his eyes.

They were pale blue, and at the same time, crystal clear. It was as if I gazed into a bottomless pool of water, but this pool contained …

Stars.

He had stars in his eyes. No. Not just stars. Galaxies. He had entire galaxies in there, and they went on forever, and I wanted to follow them, and sit among them, and be astounded by them, and—

"Show me," he said once more, and this time, it didn't even occur to me to hesitate.

I stood and unzipped my coat so that I could reach my jeans pocket beneath, and then, with surprisingly steady fingers, I withdrew the stone and held it out to him on the flat of my palm. He unfolded his lanky frame from the log stool and stood.

Even hatless, Methuselah towered over me. I still hadn't taken my eyes from his, and when he dropped his gaze to the stone in my hand, the loss of the galaxies within them was like a knife to my belly. And yes, I knew what that felt like, because I'd once almost lost a knife fight with a pimp, back in the days of running the Mary Magdalene House for Women. Almost.

But that was an eon ago, and this was now, and Methuselah was reaching for the stone, and I was no longer looking into those amazing eyes, and—

My fingers snapped shut as his hand hovered above mine. What the hell was I doing? He couldn't have the stone—he couldn't have any of them. The Ursulines had been adamant about that, and unanimous. They'd all agreed that his mental capacity made him—

"Dangerous," Methuselah said on a sigh, visibly deflating as if he'd tapped into my thoughts. His hand trembled, then closed into a fist and drifted back to his side. The amazing eyes met mine again, but now they were … ordinary. They were still a clear, crystal blue, but that was all. No stars resided in them. No galaxies. Not even a sparkle.

Only sadness.

"I've become dangerous, haven't I?" he asked.

I hesitated, not knowing quite how to proceed. Perhaps I should have brought one of the Ursulines with me for this after all, but it was too late now. I slipped the stone back into my jeans and zipped up my coat again. Then I stuffed my hands into my pockets. Methuselah was waiting for an answer.

"Yes," I answered honestly. "I think you might have."

He stared into the propane fireplace's glass surround, pressing his lips together. His chin quivered, and another pang went through my belly. Whoever—whatever—Methuselah originally was, his was a gentle soul, and it hurt me to hurt him.

"I'm sorry," I continued. "None of this is your fault."

He laughed at that. A short, sharp, bitter bark of laughter that made me take an involuntary step back. His gaze flicked up to me, then back to the fireplace.

"It is more my fault than you can possibly imagine," he murmured. "More than any of you can imagine."

Cold fingers crept down the back of my neck. Wind, I told myself, huddling into my coat collar. It was just the wind. And Methuselah was just waxing melancholy because I'd told him he was dangerous, and—

"It likes you, you know." The child's voice was abruptly back, and the tall, lanky alien—man—whatever—was spinning on the spot, arms spread wide to keep his balance.

I blinked, trying to keep up with the rapid change. "What likes me?" I asked.

"The stone. That's why it hasn't killed you yet."

Right, so no knife stab, that. It landed more like a fist in my gut, making me wheeze. I took a mental step back and readjusted what I knew. Again. I hadn't expected the child Methuselah to have the same knowledge as the adult one. I wasn't sure exactly what that would mean, but the equivalent of an eight-year-old (give or take) who knew that I carried a stone of incredible power and could decide to take it back at any moment?

There was no way that could be good.

"Methuselah," I said, injecting a lightness into my

voice that I most certainly was not feeling at the moment, "how about we go home? Would you like that?"

The tall old man spun faster, and a woman passing by hesitated, concern etched in the brow peeking out from under the edge of a fuzzy pink toque. I gave her a smile paired with a shrug and a *what can you do* expression, and she gave me an uncertain smile and a pitying look in return as she continued on her way. I turned my attention back to the spinning old man-child.

"Well?" I asked. "Would you like to go home?"

"Can't," he replied. "No one's there anymore." Abruptly, he stopped spinning and giggled. "My head feels funny."

He staggered, and I leapt forward to catch him and steer him back to his log. "You've made yourself dizzy," I said, crouching beside him. "Put your head down and rest for a moment, and you'll feel better."

He did as he was told, lowering his head to his knees and wrapping his arms around his shins.

"What did you mean, no one is home anymore?" I stroked Methuselah's back in slow circles as I would have done if he really had been a small child. It was what I had done for my siblings when I had been the only mother they'd had left. I tightened my lips and made myself face the present rather than the past.

Methuselah hadn't answered, so I asked, "Is it because Sister Agatha is gone? I know you miss her, but the others are still there. Sister Bernadette, and Sister Colette, and Sister Lise, and—"

"That's not home," said the adult Methuselah from within the folded arms. "Home is lost. Everything is lost. I couldn't find them, and I couldn't find Grandmother, and I'm here and it's too late."

I was going to need way more information than that,

but my knees were beginning to protest my prolonged squat, and I was going to need some assistance with navigating through a conversation with him. The speed with which he switched back and forth between child and adult was making *me* dizzy. I eased myself to my feet.

"Okay," I said, "not home, then. Let's go back to the sisters. We can get warm and—"

"Will there be more hot chocolate?" child-Methuselah asked, lifting his old man head.

"I'll make sure of it," I promised. Before my words had faded, he'd already leapt up off the log and skipped down the alleyway between kiosks. Swearing under my breath, I snatched up the empty cups and the bag of remaining croissants and jogged after him.

"Race you!" he called over his shoulder.

Dizzy, I thought again, picking up my pace. And exhausted.

When we reached the foot of the stairs leading up from the courtyard to the nuns' plain, handleless wood door, Methuselah tugged me to a stop. His gaze was earnest when I met it—and unmistakably childlike again.

"I like you, too," he said. "So I won't kill you, either."

CHAPTER 25

THE SPEED WITH WHICH SISTER BERNADETTE YANKED OPEN the door when I thumped on it made me wonder whether someone had seen us coming down the street from the living room window—but her utter shock at seeing Methuselah by my side said otherwise.

For an instant, she simply gaped at him, but then she stepped aside and waved us both into the little hallway, which promptly shrank three sizes because Talia, Phoenix, and all the other nuns—Ursulines and Sister Margaret included—crowded into it as well. The Ursulines all exclaimed over Methuselah's reappearance, with sisters Colette, Bernadette, and Simonne stripping him of his coat and hat and ushering him into the living room while Sister Lise practically jogged into the kitchen to make him his treasured hot chocolate.

Those remaining had words to say about my *dis*appearance. Talia, in particular.

"What in the *hell* were you thinking?" she growled at me, snatching the toque from me that I'd just taken off and thrusting it at Sister Margaret along with my coat. "No note, no nothing? We didn't know if you'd been taken by Mages or that goliath thing or what the hell had happened. I couldn't even call the local cops, for chrissake, because I don't know who the hell I can trust, and—"

Her words dropped off mid-sentence as Sister Margaret put a hand on her shoulder. She pressed her lips together and took a deep breath.

"We were worried," she finished, her voice quieter. Her

scowl suggested that she was far from done with me yet but would restrain herself for the sake of the others.

"I didn't want anyone to come looking for me," I said. "I had an idea for drawing out Methuselah, but I needed to do it alone."

Talia rolled her eyes. "Dear everyone," she said with a sarcastic air of drama, "I have an idea for finding Methuselah. I'll be back soon. Please do not follow me. Signed, Monica."

Well, when she put it that way …

"I'm sorry." I sighed. "And yes, you're right. I could have—*should* have—left a note. But"—I pointed past her to the doorway through which the Ursulines and Methuselah had disappeared before she could get going again—"it worked. I found him before the Mages did."

"You *still* should have left a note."

We already established that, my irritation grumbled, because apparently she couldn't be stopped, but I dug deep for patience and understanding. "I'm sorry," I said again. This time, my gaze encompassed them all. "Truly."

Phoenix edged past Talia to give me a hug. "It's okay," she said. "We're just glad you're okay."

I squeezed back gratefully, then released her and stooped to remove my boots and place them with the others. When I straightened, Talia still looked sour, but at least her arms were no longer crossed. Phoenix had stood back again, her gaze darting between me and the living room door.

"Do you think …" Her teeth played with the ring piercing her bottom lip. "Can I go meet him?"

"Of course," I said. "Just …"

"What?"

"He's a bit … unusual," I said, and the young woman rolled her eyes ceilingward.

"Duh," she replied with a snort. "He's an alien. Of course he's unusual."

With that little gem of wisdom, she slipped through the half-open living room door. Talia grunted in the wake of her departure.

"Damned if she doesn't have a point," she muttered, smoothing a hand over the tightly pulled-back hair she favored.

I didn't think I'd ever seen her with it *not* pulled back, come to think of it. Not even at the cottage. It made me wonder whether the detective who was so good at digging up other people's issues might have some of her own. But that thought was for another time. Right now, I desperately needed another coffee—even if it was instant.

I moved toward the kitchen, but Sister Margaret stood in my way. She was frowning. "Is he … what we expected?" she asked.

"Yes … no … maybe?" I said, spreading my hands and shrugging. "I have no idea what I expected, to be honest. But if it helps at all, he says he and the stone both like me, so they won't kill me."

She and Talia inhaled a collective breath, and both held it as they stared at me with widened eyes. *Oh good,* I thought, *at least I'm not alone in that reaction.*

Talia released hers first, with a grim, "Fucking hell."

Sister Margaret stood aside, clearing the way to the kitchen. "I'll get Sister Bernadette," she said, "and meet you in the kitchen."

Sister Lise was adding miniature marshmallows to a mug of hot chocolate when Talia and I entered the kitchen, but she abandoned her task in favor of wrapping her arms around me in a fierce, unexpected hug.

"You found him," she whispered. "I can't believe you found him! We searched everywhere, and I know that Sister Bernadette said we never gave up hope, but—" Another hug. "You found him, and he's okay."

I hugged back, realizing that to his Ursuline caretakers, Methuselah had been much more than just a responsibility. "It was your tip about hot chocolate that did it," I told her. "I bought one for him and then just sat and waited for him to come to me."

"Like bait," she said, stepping back to take a pressed white handkerchief from the sleeve of her sweater. She lifted her dark-framed glasses up and swiped the handkerchief under her eyes.

"Exactly like bait," I agreed.

"I'm *so* glad it worked." She sniffed and blew her nose, then stuffed the handkerchief back up her sleeve.

"But I had to promise him another one for when we got here." I tilted my head toward the mug on the counter, and she followed my gaze with hers.

"Oh," she said, and then, "Oh! Of course. I'll take it to him now. And Sister Monica ... thank you."

Not giving me a chance to respond, she picked up the hot chocolate with the melting marshmallows in it, leaving the open bag of the latter on the counter, and charged through the kitchen door, narrowly missing sisters Bernadette and Margaret.

Talia rounded on me, not waiting for the newcomers to close the door.

"What the hell," she growled, snatching the jar of instant

coffee from me that I'd taken down from the cupboard, "have you not told me? *Kill you?* He couldn't really do that, could he? Not without the stones, right? I mean, he's powerless without them, *right?* Answer me, damn it."

"I would answer you, if you'd let me get a word in edgewise." I took the tin back, then lost it again to a tightlipped Sister Margaret, who set it on the counter and reached for the kettle. I reluctantly turned my attention back to a spitting-mad Talia. "And ..."

"And what?" she demanded.

At the sink, the faucet came on as Sister Margaret filled the kettle. The sound of running water threatened to drown out anything I said, so I waited for her to be done. By the time she turned off the tap and put the kettle on the stove, Talia had sunk into one of the two chairs at the rarely used little table. Rarely used except by me, that was, because I'd taken to having my morning coffee in here while the nuns gathered in the living room for lauds. I felt no desire to join them, but there was a sense of familiarity in listening to the chants that was comforting. Perhaps Phoenix had been right about the power raised in prayer. And if Sister Margaret had been correct about the Obsidian Sisterhood being witches who didn't practice magic ...

Well. Perhaps spellcraft, like prayer, relied on intent more than it did on words.

"What happened?" Talia asked. Her voice was calm, but her tightly folded hands on the table before her belied her underlying tension.

Sister Margaret took four mugs down from another cupboard. Sister Bernadette shifted her weight, and remembering her arthritic hip, I motioned her toward the other chair. I'd sat long enough in the Christmas market that it would do me good to stand for a while—and maybe pace the room a little. Or a lot.

Sister Margaret selected a spoon from the cutlery drawer.

"Monica," said Talia.

My gaze traveled over each of them, and then briefly, my tone flat, I told them about the warming-of-the-hot-chocolate incident in the Christmas market. And about how wildly Methuselah had swung from child to old man and back again in the space of a heartbeat. And about how he'd recognized himself as dangerous.

When I finished, Talia rested an elbow on the table and pressed her fingers to her lips.

"Christ," she muttered from behind them, staring at me.

"Tell me about it," I said. I moved out of Sister Margaret's way so that she could open the fridge for the milk. I didn't like standing where I'd been, anyway, because I couldn't see out the window from there. It turned out that I couldn't see it from my new position by the microwave, either, and I moved restlessly back to the counter beside the fridge.

The chair Talia occupied was my preferred place, because I could keep an eye on more of the street outside from it. But I supposed having her there was the next best thing, because Talia-the-cop never really shut off, and I knew she'd see anything out there as quickly as I would.

"Did you know?" Talia asked, then waved away a response and answered her own question. "You must have. But why didn't you tell us? Or warn us? I mean—hell, I don't know what I mean."

"Yes," Sister Bernadette said. "We knew."

"About the dementia or the power?" Sister Margaret

asked at my elbow, making me jump. Sometimes the nun was so unobtrusive, I forgot she was even in the room.

"Both," admitted Sister Bernadette.

"And you didn't think it was important to say something about it?" Talia snarled, coming half out of her chair, her fists on the table between them. "Anything could have happened to Monica out there."

Sister Bernadette leveled a look at her that would have given Mother Annunciata a run for her money in the disapproval department. The very annoyed cop set her jaw in a stubborn line and tried to look unfazed, but a subtle shrinking-down in her chair said otherwise. I remembered when Sister Ernestine had stared her down at the hospital in much the same way when we'd first met.

Sister Bernadette and Sister Ernestine, I thought, would have liked one another.

"If *Sister* Monica hadn't taken it upon herself to venture out alone," Sister Bernadette replied, her voice tart, "one of us would have been with her. Even if she'd just left a note, we could have gone after her."

I ignored Talia's *I told you so* expression and accepted the coffee that Sister Margaret handed to me, my grip on the mug tighter than it needed to be. The stone's influence had me straddling a line somewhere between defensiveness and belligerence. With an effort, I resisted the desire to pick a fight and returned the conversation back to the point.

"How bad is it?" I asked Sister Bernadette.

Talia looked annoyed for a second, as if she'd wanted a fight, too. The Ursulines had breached her trust with their lack of communication about Methuselah, and she would not readily forget it. She did, however, press her lips together and let me take the lead.

"Methuselah, I mean," I clarified when Sister

Bernadette didn't immediately answer. "What is he capable of?"

The nun waited while Sister Margaret set coffee cups in front of her and Talia, then she stood and went to a small closet at the end of the kitchen. After removing two brooms, a mop, and a bucket from it, she rummaged a little further in the back and emerged with two folding chairs. She set the chairs to one side, put the cleaning things back in the closet, and then passed one chair to me and the other to Sister Margaret.

"Sit," she said. "We need to talk."

CHAPTER 26

"WHAT THE FUCK DO YOU MEAN, NO ONE KNOWS HOW powerful he is?" Talia snarled at Sister Bernadette, biting off the words as she stared across the table at the nun. Her hands clutched the coffee mug before her, but I was pretty sure she'd rather that they were wrapped around the sister's throat.

I couldn't blame her, because mine itched to do much the same. I held my temper for two reasons: first, Talia had beaten me to it, and second, despite the stone's urging, I knew anger would get us nowhere. It would have helped greatly if Sister Bernadette could have led with something a little less blunt—and a lot less inflammatory—than *"The truth is, we have no idea how powerful he is, or what he's capable of. No one does."*

The Ursuline nun, for her part, ignored the police detective altogether and focused on me. "Whatever stories might have been passed down, whatever might have happened in past—"

"The archive fire," Sister Margaret interjected. "They were lost in that."

Sister Bernadette nodded. "Along with almost every written record we had, from what I understand. Yes."

Would we ever not feel the repercussions of the explosion that had taken the Obsidian Sisters' archive and the life of its curator, Sister Helen Louise? I frowned at a new thought.

"So how do you know any of what you told me?" I asked. "About the ones who bonded with the stones?"

"Some stories were passed down verbally among the keepers. They needed to be, to keep us safe."

"Such as?" Sister Margaret leaned forward on her flimsy folding chair, her arms resting on her thighs and coffee mug cradled in her hands.

"Such as, we know that Methuselah held incredible power when he arrived on Earth, and that not all of it belonged to the stones. When he realized that we had none of the abilities that he had, he refused to use his. It was his idea to separate the stones from himself, and to live as one of us. He asked for shelter."

Talia snorted. "Right. The big, bad alien asked a bunch of women to protect him. From what?"

"From himself. He was afraid that he would inadvertently show his hand, and that the power mongers would come searching for him."

I frowned. "But if they had, couldn't he have just … I don't know, taken care of them?"

"He could," Sister Bernadette agreed, "but where would it end? He had no aspirations for ruling our planet, Sister Monica. He was … broken … when he arrived, and he needed help. We gave it."

"For thousands of years?" Talia asked, skepticism continuing to lace her voice.

"Yes," Sister Bernadette said, turning calm eyes on her. "For thousands of years, because that is what we promised."

"To keep him safe from the wannabe despots."

The nun chuckled without humor. "You don't get it, do you?" she asked. "It was never about keeping Methuselah safe from us, it was about keeping us safe from Methuselah. As long as he wasn't threatened, he didn't need to use his powers. We buried his secret as deeply as we knew how, and we kept it buried."

"Until you didn't," I said softly.

Sister Bernadette stirred her coffee without answering for a moment, the spoon *tinking* gently against the ceramic sides. Then she looked up at me, her expression sad.

"Until we didn't," she agreed. "We thought they were just … memory glitches at first. They were so few and far between that the keepers before us were able to move him before the Mages could track the power and find—"

"Wait. The Mages can track his power?"

"Yes. There needs to be a significant use of it—a death or a bringing back to life, or something of that nature."

Bringing back to life? I heard Sister Margaret take a quick inhale beside me, and Talia and I exchanged glances.

"Anything less than that seems to be relatively safe," Sister Bernadette continued. She sighed, shaking her head sadly. "He really has tried to follow his own rules, but sometimes he forgets. And lately … before he left, he forgot a lot."

My head ached. It was no wonder, given how tightly my jaw was clenched. My shoulders ached, too. And my arms, I realized. In fact, every muscle in my body had tensed, all the way down to my—shit. All the way down to my fingertips, because my hands were locked together in my lap, and the stone had found its way into them, and—

Hell.

I tried to surreptitiously slide it back into my jeans pocket, but all three of the other women tracked the movement. I ignored their concern—Talia's written in a scowl across her forehead, Sister Margaret's in her pursed lips, and Sister Bernadette's showing as a faint shadow in the depths of her eyes—and finished tucking the stone back where it belonged.

"So," I said, my weariness unfeigned, "let me get this straight. Methuselah is capable of who-knows-what-power that isn't even connected to the stones. *And* he's the only one who can control the stones' powers, too. Which is why the Mages need him. But they've been unable to find him until now, because they haven't been able to track him, because he hasn't been using his powers. But if he's started again, and if they get out of hand and he does something big enough, I won't be the only way the Mages have of tracking him."

"No," Talia murmured, "but you're definitely the fastest way. Because now you've found him."

I stared at her, and then, my voice as quiet as hers, I said, "I have, haven't I?"

CHAPTER 27

I WAS MISSING SOMETHING HERE. I DIDN'T KNOW WHAT, BUT I could feel it. For the umpteenth time, I replayed the conversation in the kitchen over again in my mind as I stared out the window of my room at the darkened street below.

Powers. Sister Bernadette had said that Methuselah had powers the Mages could track, but he never used them—at least, not at a trackable level—and so the Mages had needed another way to find him. Me. Or rather, us, since Phoenix had been the one to read the journal Sister Anne Louise had given me.

The latter part hadn't come as any surprise, because we'd all known that the Mages wanted to track us, but …

But I still felt that I was missing something. I frowned at my faint reflection in the window, letting my mind play back over the chain of events that had brought us here after I'd killed Rusk. First, the length of time we'd stayed undiscovered at the cottage—which had been just long enough to let everyone heal well enough to travel— followed by a chain of events that … I frowned.

A chain of events that, in retrospect, seemed almost to have encouraged us to make our next move. As if we'd been funneled here by design. I mean, yes, we'd planned on coming to Quebec City all along, but … why was I getting the sense that the schedule we'd followed hadn't been our own?

The goliath watching us. The attack on the cottage. The train.

That damned train. The delays along the track, our

missed connection, our bump up into business class, where fewer seats and fewer people meant we'd be easier to keep an eye on. The man who'd been responsible for being that eye.

I hadn't been supposed to notice him. I knew that now. His offer had been hastily assembled, put forward to preempt the attack he feared I might make on him—and to distract me from the fact that he hadn't made his move long before the bridge outside Charny. Because if he'd been willing to pay in the first place, he would have just said so long before that, without jumping through the hoops that he had.

But he'd been just another cog in a machine that had very carefully funneled us here, to where Methuselah was, and I had cooperated all the way.

Except, maybe, for the way the train incident had ended. I'd bet *that* had thrown a wrench in their works.

In the window, my pale reflection's lips twisted at the thought, but my smile-grimace quickly faded. Because I might have put the Mages off my scent for a short while, but our reprieve wouldn't last forever. They would know by now that Talia and Phoenix and Sister Margaret had taken refuge with the Ursulines, and they would be watching. Perhaps they already *had* been watching, and—

I cut my own thoughts short, because no, if that were true, I wouldn't be standing here dithering. I'd already be fighting for my life and for every other life in what remained of this monastery. Including Methuselah, because I could not—would not—let him fall into their hands.

But if that was the case—if they weren't already here, if they weren't watching, then where were they, and what the hell *were* they doing?

And what in the name of Mary Magdalene herself was I still missing?

A soft tapping sounded at my door. Arms crossed, I jerked my head around and scowled at the interruption. I was tempted to ignore it, but a small voice followed.

"Sister Monica?" Phoenix called. "Are you all right?"

I closed my eyes. Because that? That was a whole other problem, and I so did not want to deal with it right now.

"Sister?"

I exhaled a slow, shaky breath and uncrossed my arms, then went to open the door. The young woman on the other side stood with her hands shoved into the pockets of her hoodie and her shoulders hunched, watching me guardedly with eyes that were too big in a pinched, worried face. Methuselah stood behind her.

All right, *that* was unexpected. I hesitated, then stood back to let them both into the room. Methuselah bounced past Phoenix, folded himself into a cross-legged position on the floor by the bed and took a dragon figurine from the pocket of the trench coat he still wore. Appropriate dragon noises ensued as he ignored us and moved the dragon along the hills and valleys made by his legs.

Phoenix met my gaze—I tried to keep it only semi-star-tled—with a grimace and a shrug. "He likes me," she said. "Sister Bernadette says I make him feel safe."

"That could be a good thing," I told her, "as long as you're okay with it."

Another shrug. "I suppose. It's just a little weird, him being so old and so childish at the same time." The corner of her mouth quirked into a smile. "The nuns have a bunch of picture books for him. He likes stories."

I nodded, watching the man-child on the floor. "I saw you reading to him in the living room when I came upstairs," I said.

I'd been hell-bent on getting some alone time to process my chaotic thoughts, so I hadn't stopped, but I'd seen enough to know that Methuselah was well looked after. All the Ursulines except Sister Bernadette—still in the kitchen I'd just left—had been clustered together on the sofa, talking quietly amongst themselves as Phoenix and Methuselah sat on the floor before the fire, and every nun's gaze had been locked on their charge as if afraid he might disappear again if they looked away.

Phoenix gave a soft snort. "Like I had any choice. He chose a book and dropped it into my lap, then sat down beside me. It reminded me of—" She stopped and swallowed, and her expression hardened. "Never mind. It doesn't matter."

It did matter. It mattered a lot, the way Phoenix had lost her family because of who she was. I knew she missed her younger siblings every moment of every day—not because she'd ever said so to me, but because that was how I missed Josephine, too. But there would be a time and a place for talking to her about it when she was ready, and she needed to choose both. Just as there would be a time and a place for me to tell her about my own family. For now, however … for now, she was eyeing me with a frown.

"I'm stronger than you think, you know. And smarter."

"Stronger, yes," I agreed. "But not smarter." I held up a hand as she opened her mouth, bristling with indignation. "You couldn't possibly be smarter than I already think you are."

"Oh." She snapped her mouth shut again, a flush of pink tingeing her cheeks. Then her frown deepened. "Then you should let me help. There must be something I can do—computer things, maybe, and—stop shaking your head at me! I'm an adult, damn it, and I can make my own choices. I choose to help."

"It's not that easy, Phoenix."

"Why? Because you're so fucking overprotective?"

It was on the tip of my tongue to deny the accusation, but she and I both knew I'd be lying. I sighed.

"I *am* overprotective," I admitted, "but there's more to it than that."

"Like what?" she demanded. "Why can't you let me do something?"

Irritation, all too familiar now, mingled with guilt and self-doubt and a dozen other emotions I didn't want to be feeling. Needed not to feel, if I had a hope of keeping a clear head. I raked my fingertips through my short hair, leaving it standing on end much the way my nerves were doing right now, and wheeled away to stalk the very short distance to the door and back before I faced her.

"You want the truth?" I asked, curling my hands into fists to keep from taking the stone from my pocket. "The truth is that I haven't got a clue what *I'm* doing, let alone what to ask you—*any* of you—to do."

Phoenix blinked at me, startled by my words, my vehemence—or perhaps both. On the floor, Methuselah stopped playing with the dragon figure and watched me in narrow-eyed concern as I wrestled with the seething at my center.

"So it's true, then," she whispered. "What Talia told me is true. You and the stone … you can't get rid of it. It's eating you from the inside."

I stared at her. Talia had told her—?

The seething grew, becoming a clawing at my insides, as if trying to tear its way out of me. From behind it, I met Methuselah's calm, clear eyes.

"It likes you," he said, just as he had in the market, with his child's voice and his ancient knowing. He nodded, as if in agreement with himself—or satisfaction

—and added, "It likes your darkness. You know how to feed it."

My jaw dropped. I knew how to—did he mean *on purpose*? But before I could sort through the shock enough to formulate a question, Phoenix rounded on him, horror etched in her expression and the rigid lines of her body.

"Jesus fuck," she snapped. "Do you know how creepy that sounds? Don't say that to her!"

"Phoenix," I intervened, but it was too late. Methuselah's face sagged. He jumped up from the floor and, dodging the hand I put out to stop him, fled the room, leaving the dragon figurine behind on the area rug by the bed.

"Hell," I muttered.

"What?" Phoenix spread her hands wide in a gesture of innocence, but her gaze wouldn't meet mine. "It was rude. *And* creepy. He shouldn't have said it."

I didn't have time to argue. I snatched up the dragon toy and headed after Methuselah, pausing in the doorway to look back at Phoenix. She hadn't moved. Guilt and anger fought for the upper hand in her expression. A sense of betrayal overwrote both in the hunch of her shoulders, the protective hug of her arms across herself. I hesitated. I would pay dearly for this—and so would she—but I could *not* lose Methuselah again. And I couldn't stop for explanations.

"I'm sorry," I said. "We'll talk later."

And then I ran out the door.

CHAPTER 28

I found him without having to alert the others—
well, most of them, anyway. I'd almost run over Sister Margaret in the hallway, but she flattened herself against the wall at the last second.

Hell.

"You heard?" I asked.

"Some," she said. "Enough." She pointed down the hall toward an unused door at the end that was now hanging open. "He went upstairs. Go. I'll look after Phoenix."

I wondered what it said about me that I didn't hesitate —not for so much as a heartbeat.

The Ursulines lived in a small wing of what had once been a huge complex of buildings. The rest of this building still stood, of course, but it had been walled off from the Ursulines when the rest of the property had been sold. And while the nuns only used two floors of their residence, all of the buildings, including this wing, had three floors— plus an attic.

Thankfully, Methuselah had only gone as far as the deserted third floor and not beyond. He was seated, unmoving, in a rocking chair in front of a cold, empty fireplace in the third room that I looked into. I tapped on the doorframe.

"It's me," I said. "May I come in?"

There was no response. I waited a moment, then quietly crossed the room to join him. There was no other chair, but I found a small, wooden footstool of questionable sturdiness and eased myself down onto it, hoping for the best. It held, and I released the breath I'd been holding. Then I reached out and set the dragon figurine on the armrest of the rocking chair beside Methuselah's elbow.

"You left this in my room," I said.

He didn't reply.

I tried again. "Phoenix didn't mean to be short with you, Methuselah. She was just trying to protect me, that's all. She was worried that my feelings would be hurt when you said—" I broke off, trying to remember his exact words.

"That you know how to feed it?" he whispered.

"Yes," I agreed, grateful that I seemed to have tapped into the grownup version rather than the child. I just hoped it would last long enough to get some answers. "When you said that. What did you mean? How do I feed it?"

He rolled his eyes at the question. "You let it in," he said, "but you don't let it have all of you. You're still there, too. The others gave up too fast because they were frightened, and then it ran out of darkness to eat. You're not frightened. You're strong, so you put up a fight. It likes that."

A chill crept down my spine. I pulled my hands inside my sweatshirt sleeves and hunched my shoulders. Was it just me, or did that sound even creepier than his words to Phoenix had done? Sweet Mary Magdalene, he made it sound as if it—the stone—and I were playing some kind of cat-and-mouse game. And I sure as hell wasn't the cat.

I wasn't sure about the *strong* idea, either. Or the *not frightened* part, because I knew that if I peeked into the future—into what was waiting for me, what was inevitable—I wouldn't just be frightened, I'd be terrified.

I wasn't strong, I thought. I was just willfully blind.

I choked back an inappropriate snort of laughter.

There was a time and a place for my dark brand of humor. This was neither. I went back to my gentle probing for information.

"Does the stone like you, too?" I asked Methuselah.

"Yes," he nodded. "It was my friend once, when it was all one piece, but then I broke it and everything turned bad."

The stool and I both wobbled. There was so much in there that I wanted—and needed—to unpack, that I didn't even know where to start. *All in one piece? One piece of what? What broke? What turned bad? Was this what he'd been talking about in the market when he said that him becoming dangerous was his fault? Why he'd left home?*

A dozen more questions piled up behind those ones, but first—first, I had to pursue the tack I'd begun. I had to know. I took a shaky breath.

"Can you stop it?" I asked. "Can you stop the stone from eating me?"

Methuselah took the dragon figurine from the rocking chair's armrest and, rocking gently, held it in one hand while he traced its lines with the fingertips of the other. He didn't answer for so long that I thought I'd lost him again. Fuck.

Fuck, fuck, fu—

Methuselah stopped rocking. He lifted his gaze from the fireplace and looked at me for the first time since I'd come into the room. His eyes were filled with stars again.

"I can't stop it," he said. "But you can. Remember, you know how to feed it."

Sweet Mary Magdalene, I had questions. So many questions. But before I could sort them out in my head, let alone make my tongue and voice cooperate, there was a tap at the door, and Sister Margaret and Phoenix came into the room.

Within the blink of an eye—less, because I saw it happen—Methuselah devolved into his child-self again. He slid off the rocking chair and onto the floor and began bouncing the dragon toy across the fireplace hearth to the accompaniment of quiet roars.

My first impulse was to order the interlopers out again and try to draw him back, because holy Mother of All, I'd been *this* close to an answer—to something that might actually help for a change. That might help *me*. But Phoenix looked as if she'd fall apart if I so much as sneezed in her direction, and Methuselah …

I sighed, watching him move his dragon over the mountains of his outstretched legs. Methuselah the grownup was already gone again, and I could do nothing more than wait for him to return.

And hope that he did.

"Are we intruding?" Sister Margaret had stopped just inside the doorway. "We can come back, if you'd like."

"No," I said, keeping back the *it's a little late for that, don't you think?* It wasn't their fault that Methuselah regressed in the blink of an eye. I watched him shift his weight a little, turning his back to Phoenix, and rephrased the thought. It wasn't entirely their fault, but there was certainly something there with regard to Phoenix.

Sister Margaret put a hand in the small of the young woman's back and nudged her forward. Careful to avoid looking at me, Phoenix walked over and dropped cross-legged onto the floor beside the old man.

"I'm really sorry," she said. "I didn't mean to hurt your feelings."

His dragon roared faintly.

"And I don't think you're creepy," she added. "You're just ... different. I'm different, too. But that doesn't mean either of us is bad, okay?"

There was no answer at all this time. I was about to suggest that she leave it and try again later, but she reached inside the zippered front of her hoodie and brought out a picture book with a puppy on the front.

"I brought a book," she said. "Do you want me to read you a story?"

The child Methuselah considered the offer for point two seconds, then stuffed the dragon into his coat pocket and slid closer to Phoenix. "I like dogs," he said.

"Me, too," she replied, flipping to the first page. "Know what else I like?"

"What?"

"Methuselahs."

It would never not be bizarre to hear a child's giggle come from an old man's body, I thought. Not ever. But here we were.

Sister Margaret caught my attention as Phoenix began reading. She raised her eyebrows in query and tilted her head toward the door. Did we want to leave them? I looked at the young woman and the old man sitting cross-legged on the floor. Later, Phoenix and I would have to talk—as would Methuselah and I, if and when his grownup came back—but for now ... for now, they were both okay. And they were safe.

Absorbed in his story, Methuselah didn't so much as glance my way as I eased myself to my feet. Phoenix's gaze flickered in my direction, but too briefly for me to make eye contact. I followed Sister Margaret out of the room and down the hallway toward the staircase to the second floor.

"Are you sure you're all right?" she asked. "You looked … upset when Phoenix and I came in. Did Methuselah say something?"

I hesitated. I'd been knocked sideways by the alien's claim that he could tell me how to use the stone, and I didn't think I was ready to share that with anyone just yet. Not until I knew if it was true. I wasn't worried about disappointing anyone, but if I had to hear one more *give it time* as someone patted me on the shoulder …

I shook my head. "Not really," I answered Sister Margaret. "I hadn't been there that long before you and she … came in."

"Well," she said. "At least he and Phoenix have patched things up. I'm glad of that. But Phoenix told me that you and she had another fight."

Oh, she did, did she?

"Hardly a fight," I disagreed. "She was rude to Methuselah, he ran off, and I came after him. End of story."

"Then you do blame her." Sister Margaret sighed, her thin face sad.

"I think blame is a strong word," I replied in surprise. "And I think it's between me and Phoenix."

"Oh," said the nun. And then, blinking too quickly, "Oh. I didn't realize I was stepping on toes where she's concerned. I just thought—she seemed—" She twisted her hands into the folds of the sensible skirt on loan from the Ursulines, and her expression turned despondent. "With you being so busy, I thought she could use a friend. I'm sorry if I overstepped, and I'll be more careful in future. You have my word."

Stiffly, she turned and started down the stairs, leaving

me to stare after her, feeling like an ogre. My conscience prodded me, wanting me to go after her and apologize, but the stone—the stone's influence, the part of me under the influence, whatever—had had its fill of drama. It was tired, I was tired, *we* were tired, and …

And fuck it, I thought sullenly as I plodded down the stairs behind her. Not just *fuck*, but *fuck it*. As in all of it. The stone's attachment to me—or mine to it—or however the hell it worked. Methuselah's oblique declaration. Phoenix's clinginess. Talia's pissiness. Sister Margaret in general.

Not for the first time, I resented the shit out of her easy relationship with the young woman whom I considered my charge. Also not for the first time, I knew I should be grateful, because Phoenix needed a champion more than ever with all of the upheaval in her life, and I could not be that. Not right now. Maybe not ever.

Fuck that, too, I snarled inwardly. *No, fuck that especially.*

But I still breathed a little sigh of relief when I got to the bottom of the stairs and Sister Margaret had already disappeared, so that I didn't have to face her again.

CHAPTER 29

I left a note in Phoenix's room asking her to come and see me when she came back downstairs from the third floor with Methuselah. She knocked on my door just before dinner. I opened it, and we stared at one another for a minute. Her gaze left mine first, her expression inscrutable.

Dropping my hand from the doorframe, I stood back to let her enter. I spoke first. I'd had a good hour to get over my Sister Margaret fixation and come to terms with certain facts where Phoenix was concerned, and the truth was that the Methuselah incident had been a symptom of a greater problem, one that originated with me. We needed to clear the air.

"I'm sorry," I said, and she shot me a surprised look.

"*You're* sorry? For what? I'm the one who was rude."

"You were," I agreed, "but I was the reason behind it. And I'm sorry for that. I'm sorry for not talking to you myself instead of making Talia do it. I'm sorry for being overprotective. And I'm sorry for not being able to protect you more."

"That doesn't even make sense," she said.

"I know," I said. "But it's how I feel, and the point is—"

"I know what the point is," she said. "And it's fine."

A part of me would have liked to believe her and let it go at that, but a smarter part of me disagreed. Probably the one channeling my inner Talia.

"It does matter," I said, "because you deserve better.

You deserve to hear the truth, and after all we've been through, you deserve to hear it from me."

She stared at me, the piercing in her bottom lip betraying the tremble there, and then her entire face crumpled. Abandoning her stoicism, she leaned against my chest and let my arms wrap around her. Her words were delivered into my shoulder between sobs and hiccups. "I know what you said earlier, but you really are all I have left, you know."

I rested my head against hers and rocked us both back and forth as my own tears wet her bright pink hair.

"I know," I whispered, my voice breaking. "And I'm so sorry, Phoenix."

"And you're not even trying!"

Wait, what?

I pulled back to stare at her. "Excuse me?"

"Methuselah told me that you know how to use the stone, but you're not even trying. We're just sitting here, waiting and waiting, and—"

Wait, *what*? And how dare he tell her something like that? Now *I* wanted to be rude to him.

"I can't stop it. But you can."

What in the name of Mary Magdalene herself was all of that even supposed to mean? That, and *you know how to feed it*? As if I had any control over what it took from me, or what I—

My entire brain stopped to hold its breath as something in my thoughts tried to crystallize … to coalesce. Something was there. Something I was missing. Something—

Phoenix sniffled, jerking my attention back to her. "What?" she asked. "You have that look."

"What look?" I replied distractedly.

"The one that says you thought of something."

"I—" I frowned. "Maybe?" I loosened my arms and let them drop away from her. "I don't know yet, but if your offer to help still holds, I *have* thought of something you can do."

"Anything."

"Help me look after Methuselah."

She rolled her eyes. "Babysitting? *That's* how you want me to help?"

"Hear me out," I said. "You're right that what Methuselah said was creepy, but he didn't mean it that way, and he didn't mean to be rude, either. And even if he did, it's a piece of information that I didn't have before, because he carries more inside him that I—than any of us —can ever possibly know. Especially about the stones."

"Ohhh." Lips rounded, Phoenix drew out the word as understanding dawned. "He might be able to save you!"

I hesitated. I wanted to let her believe that—hell, I wanted to believe it myself, but—

"But that's not going to happen, is it?" she asked, deflating again. She swiped at a new tear that had spilled over onto her cheek.

I drew a deep breath, following the cool air as it flowed in through my nose and into my belly, then again as it left, warmed by my body. By me. By my presence. Then, in the moment of stillness that it left behind, I shook my head.

"No, my sweet. It's not. The stone—the stone and I are too bound together now, and Methuselah isn't strong enough to separate us. But he can help me save you, and that—that, Phoenix, is everything to me."

I thought she would reject my words again, the way she had earlier, but she gave a defeated little sigh and shoved her hands into her hoodie pockets, curling her shoulders forward.

"Fine," she said. "I'll do it. But I'm not giving up, you

know. There might be another way that we don't know about."

Reaching deep, into the very fiber of my being, I dredged up a smile for her. "Of course," I said. "Who knows? Anything is possible."

WE WERE A SUBDUED BUNCH AT DINNER THAT NIGHT. Methuselah had chosen to remain in the solitude of his bedroom, Phoenix picked at her plate, neither the Ursulines nor Talia seemed much interested in conversation, and Sister Margaret …

Sister Margaret was just plain frenetic. She dropped her napkin and picked it up. She shifted her chair closer to the table and then further away. She adjusted and readjusted her utensils so many times that I wanted to reach over and take them away from her. She shifted her chair again. And she ate even less than Phoenix.

I blamed myself in part, because our last exchange had been … well. Unpleasant was one word for it. Acrimonious was probably a better one. I didn't, however, think that the fault for her mood—or any of the others'—lay entirely with me.

We could all feel it, I thought, watching the faces around the table. There was no laughter tonight. No sharing of stories from the day, or discussion of plans for tomorrow. Words were exchanged in murmurs—most of them involving a *please* and *thank you* for passing something across the table—and gazes were downcast, fixed on the plates before their owners. Now that Methuselah had been found, the question of *what next* hung over us like a pall.

No, more like one of those pendulum scythes, inching closer with each sweep that it made above us while we watched in fascinated horror, knowing it was a matter of time before it sliced into us, and then—

And then, we had no idea what would happen. Which was also part of the problem.

Sweet Mary Magdalene, there were a lot of problems.

Not least of which was Methuselah's cryptic statement that I already knew how to use the stone—and my certainty that he was right, but that I didn't know *how* to know how. It felt as if my understanding were comprised of two ends of rope that I needed to tie together, but the ropes were a fraction of an inch too short to meet, and the harder I pulled on them, the more they retracted. It was frustrating, and it was exhausting, and—

Sister Margaret shifted her chair for the fourth time, and I snapped.

"*Will* you stop fidgeting!" I burst out.

Instant silence dropped over the room. Sister Margaret froze, half out of her seat with her hands gripping the chair on either side of her and her mortified gaze locked onto mine—along with every other gaze in the room. Slow heat swept up from my toes and suffused my entire being.

I was losing it, I thought sadly. With every moment that I remained tied to this damned stone, I was losing a little more of myself. A little more of my patience, my compassion, my good. I was strong, Methuselah had said, and I wanted to believe him. I did believe him. But I was tired, too, and I didn't know how much longer I could hold out.

With quiet precision, I folded my napkin in half on my lap, then in half again. Then I set it beside my still-full plate and pushed my chair back from the table.

"I'm going to have an early night," I said, "but we should talk in the morning and see where we go from here.

I'm—" I broke off and shrugged, because *tired, out of ideas, lost, frazzled, wiped, stymied*. Take your pick, because I was all of those and more, and I didn't have it in me to list everything, nor did the women here need to hear it. But there was one that seemed to fit the bill.

"Done," I told the room. "I'm done."

CHAPTER 30

I woke with a start that gave way to near heart failure when I saw the shadowy figure looming against the light coming through my bedroom window. It took what felt like an eternity—but was probably only a second or two—to see that the figure's outline included the shape of a fedora and a long coat.

And to remember to breathe.

"Methuselah?" I groped for the lamp on the bedside table and turned it on, blinking in its glare. "What are you doing in he—"

"They're coming," he said, in his Methuselah voice. "Run."

My heart slammed against my ribcage. I pulled the stone out from under my pillow and scrambled out from under the covers, reaching for the clothes I'd slung over the chair the night before—if it had been the night before. I hadn't looked at the clock when I'd turned on the lamp, and I couldn't see it from this angle. I had no idea what time it was. It didn't matter.

"Who?" I demanded of Methuselah. "Who is coming?"

"The ones who want me," he said. "And something else."

My hands stilled with my jeans pulled onto one leg but not yet the other. *Something else?* My immediate thought was the goliath, but then I remembered the mini fire-starters on the train. The Mages had more than one monster at their fingertips. Stone still clutched in my fingers, I pulled the other jeans leg on, wriggled them over my hips and zipped them up.

"Can you tell what it is?" I asked. My hand hovered over my bra, then passed it up in favor of my sweatshirt. I didn't have time for societal expectations. Turning my back to Methuselah, I shucked my nightgown over my head and dropped it onto the bed, then pulled on the sweatshirt.

He hadn't responded by the time I was dressed, and I turned back to find him fogging the windowpanes with his breath and drawing stick figures on them. *Oh hell,* I thought. *Not now.*

"Methuselah?" I prodded gently. "Can you tell what's coming?"

He turned a child's round, wonder-filled eyes on me. "Christmas," he replied happily. "Christmas is coming. Phoenix said so!" Then, giggling, he skipped out of the room, and I heard him run down the hall.

I stared at the dark, empty doorway, my wobbly knees very much wanting me to sink onto the edge of the chair as the adrenaline surge dissipated. What the hell. And what now?

I made my wobbly knees carry me to the bedside table and the clock. I picked up the latter and blinked at the time. It was only eight thirty-five? That meant I'd been asleep for no more than half an hour. How was that even possible?

I set the clock back down and sat on the bed. My heart and thoughts were both racing and out of synch with one another, and I took a deep breath, trying to calm them. To center myself. To figure out what the actual *fuck*.

Talia looked up from her book—a mystery she'd found tucked away in the bottom back corner of the bookshelf—as I entered the living room. Surprise lifted her eyebrows.

"I thought you were going to bed early," she said.

Sister Bernadette glanced over at me from the sofa she shared with Sister Lise, Sister Margaret, and Sister Simonne, pointed the remote control at the television they'd been watching, and muted the volume. "Something happened," she said.

"Phoenix?" I asked, not wanting her to overhear.

"Upstairs in my office," said Sister Bernadette. "With Methuselah."

That's what you think. I bit back a chuckle-snort, because he was likely back there now. But I closed the door anyway, then leaned against it for good measure. I wanted no interruptions.

In a recliner near the window and perpendicular to the four nuns wedged together on the couch, Sister Colette set her knitting in her lap. Six pairs of eyes all locked on me.

"I was in bed," I told Talia, "until Methuselah came in to tell me that they were here."

"They? They who?" she asked.

"Beats the hell out of me," I said. Briefly, I told her and the sisters about Methuselah's little wake-up call.

When I finished, Sister Bernadette was the first to clear her throat and speak.

"I know it's concerning," she said. "But before we jump to conclusions, we need to remember that Methuselah is …"

She trailed off, and Sister Colette finished dryly, "Unreliable?"

Sister Bernadette nodded. "At best." She sighed and grimaced at me. "This might be some figment of his imagination. He's made many wild predictions in the past. None have come to fruition that we know of, and we've learned to take them with a large grain of salt."

The others nodded agreement, but when I checked in with the stone in my pocket, it felt … on edge. Heavy. Hotter than usual. Not … right.

"Well," said Talia, "at least we know that if they *are* here, they don't know where to find us."

"Yet," I countered. "They don't know where to find us *yet.*"

"Perhaps," said Sister Colette, who'd cocked her head toward the window beside her, "they hope to draw you out."

The eyes that had been fastened on me turned to her as she tucked her knitting into the standing bag by the chair and levered the footrest down.

"I hear sirens," she said, heaving herself out of the recliner. She reached for her walker. "Police. Fire. More than one."

The stone in my pocket turned to lead.

CHAPTER 31

Sister Bernadette and Sister Lise voted themselves fastest and most able to act as scouts to determine whether Sister Colette's theory was right, but they'd barely been gone five minutes when they were pounding at the door again. I wasn't sure whether the scant time or the frantic pounding was worse.

Talia wrenched open the door for them, and they fell into the hallway in a tangle of arms and legs and other nuns leaping forward to help them. All except Sister Colette, who leaned grim-faced on her walker in the living room doorway.

Sister Lise was first to catch her breath enough to speak. "The Mages are here," she panted out. "We met Guillaume coming back from the Christmas market—he had burns all over his clothes. He said there are fires everywhere. Things are dropping from the sky and bursting into flames whenever they touch something—or someone. The Christmas markets are in chaos. Oh, and he said something is in the tower of the cathedral."

"Something?"

"A person-snake."

Talia and I exchanged glances. The fire things we knew, but the other?

"A person-snake?" I repeated. Not doubtfully, because having met the fire things in person—not to mention the goliath—I knew better, but as a request for more details. Because *person-snake* sounded … bad.

"He wasn't making much sense. He said it was like a serpent, but huge and with multiple heads—of people."

Oh, yeah. That sounded bad, all right.

"As far as we can tell, it's just the old city so far," Sister Bernadette picked up the story. "Sister Margaret, you didn't see anything when you went out?"

"Nothing," said Sister Margaret. Then, catching my eye, she assured me, "I only walked to the corner and back—it's all I've ever done."

I stared at her in shock. She'd left the monastery? On a regular basis? By herself? Holy Mother of All, what had she been thinking? And what had Talia been thinking, allowing it?

Hot, angry words hovered on my tongue—*are you goddamn kidding me?* being the primary ones—but I held them back, because the horse had already disappeared from the stable, and it was a little late to be slamming doors shut now. But we would absolutely talk house rules later.

If we had a later.

"Then," said Sister Bernadette, either unaware of or not caring about the sudden undercurrent of tension, "we should assume that Sister Colette is right. They know you're in the area, but they don't have an exact location. They're trying to draw you out."

"I told you so," grumbled Sister Colette. She turned her walker around and headed back into the living room, adding, "I'll get the supplies ready."

Supplies? What supplies? And *shit*. What was I supposed to do? I could hear the sirens through the door now. There were so many of them. I could hardly remain here while the Mages waged war on the unsuspecting city, but how could I leave Methuselah and Phoenix? And no matter what I did, what could I *do*? I'd barely absorbed Methuselah's words of this morning, let alone had time to process them or attempt to use the stone again in their wake.

I would be no better than any of the nuns, marching out of here to fight a battle they couldn't hope to win against whatever the hell a *person-snake* was. And on the flip side, I couldn't hope to protect the monastery in their absence, either.

"Go with them," said Sister Margaret, pushing my coat into my arms as if to end my dilemma. "They'll need your help."

I looked down at the heavy woolen garment hanging from my half-hearted grasp. "But the stone," I mumbled, "and Phoenix and Methuselah." I meant that I still had no control of the stone, of course, and that I had to protect Phoenix and Methuselah, but finding words through my mounting dismay was almost impossible.

Sister Margaret tipped my chin up until I met her calm, steady gaze, then clasped my shoulders. "I'll stay here," she said. "The Mages don't know where we are, and I'll keep Phoenix and Methuselah safe. You have my word."

PERHAPS AFTER SEEING SISTER ERNESTINE UNVEIL AN armory hidden in the fireplace mantel of the home I'd shared with the St. Mary's nuns in my former life, it shouldn't have surprised me to learn that the Ursuline sisters had a defense plan of their own. Although I had to say, the explosive cargo they were tucking into their skirt waistbands and coat pockets seemed a little more on the side of attack than defense.

"Molotov cocktails?" Talia yelped as she joined me in the living room and saw the cache of liquid-filled bottles in a cavity behind a bookcase the nuns had pulled away from the wall.

What was it with nuns and secret hideaways in living rooms?

"Self-igniting ones," Sister Bernadette agreed. She held up one of the bottles and pointed to the test tube taped to its side. "As soon as they both break, boom. Relatively speaking."

She shoved the bottle into her pocket beside another, and Talia and I both flinched at the alarming *clink* of glass against glass.

"Are you out of your mind?" Talia stared at her in appalled horror, and then at the cache, and then at Sister Bernadette again. "You have—how—you can't—"

"Honey," Sister Colette said, reaching up to pat her cheek as she wheeled her walker toward the door to the hallway, "you are either with us or against us. Choose."

Talia's jaw flapped soundlessly, and then she turned on me. "Monica, you can't possibly let them—for chrissake, *do* something."

I did. I made a decision.

"Talia is staying here," I told Sister Bernadette, "with Phoenix and Methuselah and Sister Margaret."

"Wait, what?" Talia's head whipped around and she scowled at me. "Are you kidding me? I'm not letting you and a bunch of old ladies wander off alone into who knows what the hell that commotion is"—she gestured at the living room window—"with enough volatile explosives to blow up half the city."

Her gaze swiveled back to the nuns, and she added, "No offense," then back to me, and she growled, "No way."

"None taken," Sister Bernadette murmured, calmly buttoning up her coat over the bottles secured beneath it.

"Talia—"

"*No*," she snarled.

"Please."

Her mouth opened for another refusal, then snapped shut. She ran both her hands over her always-smooth, tightly constrained hair, then over her face. "You're killing me here, Monica," she said. "You're doing exactly what the Mages want, for fucksake. At least let me have your back."

"I'm sure we'll be okay on our own here," Sister Margaret said. "The Mages don't know where we are, and—"

"I can look after my own back," I said, ignoring Sister Margaret and speaking to Talia. "But I need to know that my heart is safe." I nodded toward the doorway, where Phoenix stood watching the proceedings with Methuselah. Well, she watched. He ran his toy dragon up one side of the frame and down the other, whispering quiet roars as he did. I reached for Talia's hand and gave her fingers a squeeze. "Please."

"And them?" Talia asked, the sweep of her free arm encompassing the motley crew of elderly Ursulines who'd moved into the hall and were tugging on toques and mittens. "Who will look after them? This is insanity. Goddamn dangerous insanity."

Sister Bernadette came to stand in front of her, turning her away from me and placing a mittened hand on each of her shoulders.

"We," she said with steel in her voice, "are the Obsidian Sisterhood. We are not here to look after ourselves or to be looked after. We are here to keep *him* safe"—she nodded past Talia at the dragon-wielding

Methuselah—"because that is what we do. It is what we have always done."

Talia puffed up like she would launch into further argument, and then she deflated. "Fine," she muttered. And then said again, "*Fine*. But you'd damned well better come back in one piece. *All* of you."

Sister Bernadette pulled her in for a quick, uncharacteristic hug, making the bottles in her pockets clink together again. Talia's eyes went wide, and she hastily disengaged herself and stepped back, then back again. I had no idea how much effort she was exerting to stay quiet, but it looked like a lot.

"We should go," Sister Bernadette said to me, heading for the others in the hall.

I shrugged into the coat I still clutched, tugged my toque from its pocket, and stepped around Talia to follow.

IT FELT AS IF IT HAD TAKEN THE NUNS FOREVER TO GET everyone loaded up with explosives, but as I glanced at the living room clock on our way out, I saw that it had only been minutes. We made it as far as the front door before another hurdle occurred to me.

"Wait—how are we getting there?" I asked. I pointed at Sister Colette's walker. "You can't possibly walk all the way."

"Of course not," Sister Colette snapped, rolling her eyes at me as if I was daft for even suggesting the idea. "We're taking the car."

They had a—

The blare of a horn cut across my surprise. I peered

over Sister Lise's shoulder into the brightly lit courtyard and did a double take at the sight of an ancient station wagon sitting there, its engine rumbling roughly, with Sister Simonne at the wheel. In the kerfuffle of coats and mittens and explosives, I hadn't even noticed she was missing.

Sister Simonne revved the engine as the vehicle sputtered and coughed, and a cloud of blue smoke spewed from the tailpipe, scattering the group of neighbors who had gathered, presumably, to confer about the attack on the cathedral.

"Talk about déjà vu," Talia muttered at my shoulder. "Are those things standard issue for nuns, or something?"

I didn't answer, plunged for a moment into the past and an almost identical car that the St. Mary's nuns had owned. St. Jude, they'd named it, after the patron saint of lost causes. Sweet Mary, I missed that car. And I missed—

Sister Simonne honked the horn again, and Sister Bernadette nudged me from behind, plucking me out of the past.

"The Mages will be waiting," she murmured. Her voice was gentle, as if she knew I struggled.

Which I did, just on more levels than she realized.

I blinked back a sheen of tears, swallowed the lump in my throat, and nodded. I turned to say goodbye to Phoenix as Sister Lise carried Sister Colette's walker down the stairs to the cobblestones, and with extreme caution— because *self-igniting Molotov cocktails?*—Sister Bernadette and Talia edged Sister Colette herself down to join it.

"You'll be back," Phoenix whispered fiercely in my ear, wrapping me in a hug so hard that I could barely breathe. "Promise you'll be back."

"I promise I will do everything in my power," I said, pulling back to look at her. "Everything."

Her grimace told me that my words weren't what she

wanted to hear, but she straightened her shoulders, set her jaw, and gave me a firm nod. "I know," she said.

In the entryway just behind her, Methuselah moved his dragon through the air like an airplane, complete with zooming noises. He stopped when he sensed my gaze on him, and his eyes met mine. There were no stars in them.

"They're coming," he murmured. "Run."

As soon as he'd delivered the words, he returned to his "airplane," and Phoenix shuddered.

"Tell me again how he's not creepy as fuck?" she muttered. But she waved away my response and heaved a sigh. "I know, I know. And I promise I'll look after him while you're gone," she said. "But after that, he's *your* responsibility."

I ruffled her pink hair. "Deal," I said. "And do me a favor? Look after you, too."

I turned away to join the nuns, but not before Talia caught my eye one last time and held aside her borrowed cardigan to expose the sidearm I hadn't seen since the cottage. She meant it to be reassuring, I knew, but the sight of it made me want to throw up.

We were officially ready for war.

CHAPTER 32

THE URSULINES AND I MADE IT TO WITHIN A BLOCK OF THE chaos before we had to abandon the vehicle. A barricade had been set up across the street, with another built of garbage for next day's collection blocking the sidewalk, leaving us no room to get by. The street was comparatively empty otherwise and would have counted as little more than an alley in a more modern city. Being able to open all the car doors meant parking in the middle of the road, which Sister Simonne did with zero compunction, setting the hand brake to keep the station wagon from rolling back down the hill.

Which pretty much reflected her attitude for the entire drive, as she'd woven between cars, careened down entire swaths of sidewalk when traffic became impenetrable, and blasted the horn at pedestrians flinging themselves out of her path. It was a good thing that the police were otherwise occupied.

It was also a good thing we hadn't blown ourselves up along the way.

I was pretty sure my heart had abandoned my body somewhere after the tenth jolt over something or other had rattled through the vehicle—and the bottles in the nuns' pockets. But we'd made it in one piece, and we were here now, and dear sweet Mary, where did we even begin?

The entire sky glowed ahead of us, and my jaw hung open as I stared up at the fiery roof of Notre Dame Cathedral. Orange and red flames roared up and outward, seemingly unaffected by the powerful streams of water aimed at them from countless fire hoses. The heat from them reached all the way to where we stood in appalled silence. At last, Sister Bernadette spoke.

"We'll get as close as we can," she said grimly, "and then decide where we go from there. Sister Colette, you're okay to walk?"

"Try and stop me," Sister Colette replied, her tone equally grim.

"Then let's go. And remember, the Mages could be anywhere, so stay alert, *mes amies*."

We set off up the remainder of the hill, with Sister Colette and her walker setting the pace. It was a mean one. She strode forward with fierce determination, slowing down for no one as she bellowed in both official languages for the gathered onlookers to get out of her way. They did so with an alacrity that I would have found amusing under other circumstances.

But not these ones.

Another barricade stretched across our path, holding back those who had come to watch—and some to grieve—the devastation taking place. A dozen fire trucks lined the street in front of and beside the cathedral. Half had their hoses aimed at the cathedral itself, the other half at the Christmas market across the street from the church and the shops perpendicular to it. They were fighting a losing battle.

For every fire in the market or a shop that they seemed to gain the upper hand over, another erupted—sometimes in a new place and sometimes in one that had already partially burned. No amount of water seemed to be enough.

And no wonder, because these were no ordinary fires. These were the horrid creatures that had attacked us on the train. They rained down from the sky over the entire block, exploding into fresh flames wherever they landed—

including atop one of the firetrucks. Hoses swiveled back and forth from one new blaze to another, and then another, and still the firebombs dropped.

"What *are* they?" Sister Lise murmured beside me.

I opened my mouth to tell her that I had no name for them, but a new sound cut across me and through the pandemonium—a kind of hissing screech that drew my gaze up to the bell tower brightly lit by the flames spilling from the cathedral roof. No, not one hissing screech. Many of them. Coming from many heads that sprouted from a huge serpentine body coiled around the tower. Human heads.

Human heads sprouting from a snake body, each with a mass of snakes sprouting from it in turn—like hair—and each writhing independently of its companions, with its mouth gaping wide. In an instant, everything happening on the ground became a mere blip on my mental screen of what-the-actual-fuckery.

Because what the actual fuck.

"*Tabernac,*" swore Sister Lise in French. Her gaze had followed mine, and her voice was soft, barely discernible through the chaos. But a thread of horrified awe underlying it echoed the one that would have been in my own voice—if I'd been able to find it.

Sister Bernadette grunted on my other side. "Guillaume's description was more accurate than I expected," she said. "That is indeed a many-human-headed serpent."

Indeed.

"What do we do?" Sister Colette asked. "If it comes down, there are too many people here for us to take it out, but I don't think I can throw one of these that far."

I was still trying to wrap my mind around an elderly nun using words like *take it out* when she let the coat she'd been holding fall open to expose the two Molotov cocktails tucked into the waistband of her skirt. Sister Simonne reacted the fastest, grabbing the garment's edges and pulling them shut again.

"Sister Colette!" she hissed, doing up two of the buttons. "Are you trying to get us arrested?"

The eldest of the Ursulines pushed her away irritably with one hand and grasped her walker with the other. "Do you really think anyone here is even going to notice us?" She snorted at the idea. "With that thing up on the roof, we could walk in the front door of that damned institution, and no one would see a thing. Not us, not our bottles—"

"You may be right, Sister Colette, but it's probably best to have more of a plan than that," Sister Bernadette interrupted. She looked at me. "Sister Monica? What would you like us to do?"

"They're coming," Methuselah had whispered. *"Run."*

I gulped back a giggle that the others might have thought was hysteria. It wasn't. Well, maybe it was, a little, because yes, running was absolutely what we should do, but—

But my urge to laugh subsided, swallowed by a growing determination … and a slow-burning fury. I'd told everyone tonight that I was done, but now I was done-done.

Done running. Done hiding. Done waiting.

The Mages had wanted to draw me out? Fine. I was out.

And I was going to be damned hard to put back into the proverbial bottle again.

My gaze dropped from the monster in the bell tower and settled on the open gates to our left, the ones that led to the university buildings that had once housed the boys' school and the massive square that they surrounded. The square that was still haunted by the weeping voices of too many little ones, too many vulnerable ones crying out to the parents they'd been taken from. A square that was currently deserted.

"There," I said, nodding my head. "We'll draw it down into that square." I held my hand out to Sister Colette, who had the biggest pockets and therefore the largest stash of Molotov cocktails, and wiggled my fingers. "Let's start by seeing who can throw the furthest," I said, "and see what happens."

With a gleeful cackle, the nun took a bottle from her pocket and slapped it into my hand. She'd been right. No one noticed.

CHAPTER 33

For a moment, I thought I'd made a mistake. From where we stood in the center of the paved square, we could see the flicker of flames from the cathedral above the rooftop of the building in front of it, but not the bell tower. And not the person-snake.

And if we couldn't see it, and it couldn't see us, then how—

"Sister Colette?" Sister Bernadette said.

I glanced over in time to see the eldest Ursuline stick two fingers in her mouth and draw a deep breath. Her colleagues clapped their hands over their ears, and Sister Lise started to say something to me, but it was lost in the shrillest, most piercing whistle I had ever been subjected to in my life.

Or perhaps *tortured by* was a better phrase.

Regardless, my eardrums retracted into my skull, my eyes watered, and my own hands found my ears in short order. I dropped them again when the nun took her fingers from her mouth, but the others did not, and a second later, I knew why.

Cupping her hands around her mouth, the inimitable nun bellowed, "Hey, asshole!"

I tilted my head away from her as the words reverberated around the enclosed square, bouncing off the buildings and my skull and making my eyes water a second time. Sister Colette's voice wasn't as shrill as her whistle had been, but it had been just about as loud—and as painful.

It hadn't, however, done what we needed it to do, I thought as I scanned the rooftops. There was no sign of—

"There," said Sister Simonne.

"Wh—"

I didn't finish. The massive serpent that had been on the bell tower a second before thudded to the pavement on the far side of the square, hiss-screeched, and began a slow coiling and uncoiling as it pushed its body—and its heads —toward us. Its many, open-mouthed heads, each of them —the mouths of the snake-hair included—equipped with curved, dripping fangs.

For an instant, sheer surprise held us immobile. Then Sister Collette screeched again—the woman really did sound like a banshee—and trundled her walker toward it with one hand as the other went to her coat pocket. The rest of us galvanized into action.

"Spread out," Sister Bernadette shouted. "Surround it, and don't throw unless you're sure you can hit near enough that the fire will coat it."

Sisters Lise and Simonne fanned out, one to each side of the serpent, and circled around behind it. The heads waved angrily, and the collective body's coiling and uncoiling slowed. Sister Bernadette gave me one of her bottles to go with the one I'd taken from Sister Colette, and I dodged around to the serpent's right while she went the opposite way. Across scales gleaming in the firelight from the cathedral behind me, I saw her throw the first cocktail.

I might never have heard of self-igniting Molotov cocktails before tonight, but I would never forget them after it, either. In a word, they were spectacular. In two words, they were also highly efficient. Sister Bernadette had a deadly aim, and as soon as her bottle hit the pavement and smashed, its contents spread in all directions, igniting instantly into a sheet of flame that spread to cover a section of the serpent.

The hiss-shrieks turned to squeals of pain as it writhed,

and my heart stalled as it lashed out in Sister Colette's direction. I needn't have worried. The nun had lined up all of her bottles on the seat of her walker within easy reach, and now she plucked them up, one after the other, and sent them sailing through the air with an aim that rivaled that of Sister Bernadette. Behind the serpent, sisters Lise and Simonne threw theirs, too.

Bottle after bottle smashed in front of the creature, and liquid flame covered half of its coils now. Greasy black smoke rose from the pavement where pieces of its skin had sloughed off, and the stench of roasting flesh filled the air. Its writhing turned wild. In less than a minute, all the bottles had been used except mine. I'd held back, waiting to see where they would be most needed—where they could inflict the final damage—and then I saw it.

The heads all moved independently, but there was a central one. One that moved with the snake rather than randomly like the others. That controlled the rest. That would be my target.

I hefted my first bottle, took aim, and executed the most perfect overhand throw I'd ever made in my entire life. The bottle arced high, dropped, smashed—and did nothing. I stared after it, blinking at the spread of liquid on the pavement, splashes of it gleaming on the serpent's skin. Had I done something wrong? Forgotten something?

I took an involuntary step back as a ribbon of light shafted across the courtyard between me and the fallen serpent, oddly familiar and near enough to the creature that the waving, screeching heads could reach out to touch it, if they stretched far enough. And they were certainly trying, but what—

Shit. I remembered. The goliath had stepped out of something just like that in the clearing where Eldon Rusk had captured me. Dear sweet Mary, was it *here*? I looked down at the last Molotov cocktail in my hand. My first hadn't exploded—even if this one found its mark and did what it was supposed to do, it would have no effect on a monster made of stone. We were done. Finished. The monsters had won.

I turned my attention back to the ribbon, helpless to do anything but wait and watch and—what the hell? One of the serpent's human heads had reached the light-ribbon, splitting it wide and making it brighten, and then it just disappeared. *They* disappeared. Light-ribbon and half-roasted serpent. Poof.

I gaped at the scorch marks on the pavement, trying to process the whole appearing/disappearing monsters thing. On the one hand, at least the goliath hadn't emerged, but on the other, *how?* Was it something the Mages had conjured? Like some kind of teleportation device? But if so, where were they? When the goliath had appeared in that clearing, Rusk had done something to summon the ribbon it had stepped out of. There *had* to be at least one Mage here somewhere.

"Sister Monica."

Sister Bernadette had come across the scorched pavement to join me. I looked at her, perplexity tugging at my eyebrows.

"Have you ever seen anything like that before?" I asked. "I have, but I have no idea—"

"I think we have a problem."

"A—wait. What problem?" I scanned the square quickly, making sure the others were okay. They seemed to be, except for the part where they had gathered in a cluster and were staring back toward the gate we'd come through with mixed expressions ranging from puzzlement to anger. I followed their gazes, at first seeing nothing. Well, not unless you counted the open-mouthed spectators who had gathered to photograph and video our battle with a monster. Was that what Sister Bernadette was worried about? Or was it—

My gaze stopped short on a woman's figure. Frail and thin, her back was turned to me and her shoulders hunched against the cold, but I would have known her anywhere. I blinked. Sister Margaret? But she was supposed to be looking after—

"Shit," I whispered. "Phoenix."

I started toward her, but Sister Bernadette caught hold of my arm before I'd taken more than a couple of steps. I tried to shake her off. "Let go," I told her, panic uncoiling in my belly. "Something's wrong at the monastery!"

Sister Bernadette held tighter as Sister Colette and her walker trundled up on my other side.

"Something's wrong, all right," the eldest Ursuline muttered. She jutted her chin toward the gate. "Look closer."

I stopped tugging at Sister Bernadette's hold and looked again at Sister Margaret. She still had her back to us. Why wasn't she looking our way? If something had happened, and she'd come to find us, to find me—

An invisible fist squeezed the air from my lungs as my gaze landed on the man she was talking to. A tall, thickly built man, his head bare despite the icy wind swirling around it, making his orangey-blond comb-over flop like a captive animal. Instantly recognizable even from where I stood as billionaire and political wannabe Ronald Drummond—and seemingly invisible to those standing all around him.

"Is that—" I croaked.

"Looks like it from here," Sister Lise agreed, joining us on Sister Colette's other side and lifting her glasses up to peer across the square. "The question is, why? Is he one of them, do you think? A Mage?"

"The consortium," I whispered. "He's one of the consortium." Because of course he was. Him, Eldon Rusk, and who knew how many others like them. And Sister Margaret was talking—

The fist around my lungs squeezed harder, and my vision blurred. This couldn't be right. Sister Margaret was our friend. She'd been injured by the Mages just as we had. She'd stepped into the breach with Phoenix when my own irritation had gotten in the way of our relationship, giving the young woman a much-needed shoulder to lean on and—

The train tickets.

Ice washed through me. Sister Margaret had been the one to get us bumped up to business class when our train had been delayed.

When our train had been delayed the very day after we'd had to flee from the cottage. The cottage we'd sheltered in without incident for weeks, despite being watched by the Mages' monster, as if someone had a schedule for us that we hadn't known about. A schedule that would put us here in Quebec when it suited *them* rather than us.

Sister Margaret had also been the one making dangerous forays away from the safety of the monastery, even if only "to the corner and back." And she hadn't just stepped into the breach between me and Phoenix, she'd nurtured that breach. Cultivated it. Deliberately, insidiously usurped my relationship with the young woman, gaining her trust and confidence so that …

Fuck, I thought.

"Fuck," I whispered as, across the square, Mage and betrayer turned and pushed through the crowd.

Sister Bernadette didn't ask questions. She pried the

last remaining Molotov cocktail from my clenched hand and pushed me. "Go," she said. "You can get there faster without us. We'll follow."

I didn't argue. I didn't hesitate. I just ran.

Phoenix, I thought. *Methuselah.*

Talia.

TALIA WAS SITTING WAITING FOR ME ON THE FLOOR OF THE front entry when I burst into the monastery. The handleless door was cracked open enough for me to wedge my fingers into the gap and pull it open; not enough for a neighbor to have noticed.

I dropped to my knees and skidded the last few inches to her side. She held a toque pressed to the side of her head. It was soaked with blood. I drew a sharp inhale.

"Holy Mother," I said. "Are you okay?"

She batted away my attempt to peek under the toque. "Don't. You'll start the bleeding again. And no, I'm not okay. I'm pissed. I can't believe I let her get the drop on me like that."

"She got the drop on all of us," I replied tightly, knowing she referred to Sister Margaret. "But I'll find her, I promise. I'll find them all, as soon as I call an ambulance."

"Do you really think I'd be sitting here if she'd taken them with her?"

Talia's voice stopped me halfway to my feet, and I dropped back to my knees as hope vaulted through my heart. "What do you mean? They're still here? Where?"

But she shook her head and immediately raised her

other hand to cover her eyes. "Jesus *Christ*, that hurts. No, they're not here. They took off out of here like goddamned rabbits—just bolted out the door without so much as a word. I yelled, but they didn't even slow down, so I turned to get my coat and boots, and *wham*. The last thing I remember was that *bitch* staring down at me and telling me she had no choice, and then she ran out the door, too, and then I was out." She peered at me from behind her fingers. "What the *hell*, Monica?"

"The Mages are here. We saw one of them talking to Sis—to Margaret," I said, leaving out the details. I'd tell her who later. Right now, Ronald Drummond's identity would just be a distraction—with good reason. "I don't think they were trying to draw me out so that they could follow me."

The blow to Talia's head hadn't affected her powers of deduction. "They wanted you out so that Margaret could give them Methuselah. Shit," she said. "Shit, shit, *shit*."

I would have seconded that, but my brain was racing. Phoenix had known about Margaret—but how? And where—

Run, said Methuselah in my memory. *They're coming*.

He'd told Phoenix. The idea—no, the certainty—jolted through me, driving me to my feet. He'd told Phoenix again after I'd left, and she'd realized that he wasn't talking about the attack at the cathedral but about something else, and—

"I promise I'll look after him while you're gone," Phoenix had said.

"Somewhere safe," I muttered. "She took him some-where safe. She had a—" I broke off and stared at Talia, who was still leaning against the wall, watching me. "I know where they went."

"What? But how?"

Her question floated after me as I pushed open the living room door and strode across to the bookcase hiding the cache. Like the front door, it was still part way open, and I seized it and pulled. Then I stared at the empty space that remained. The Ursulines had taken all their explosives with them. They might have others hidden away somewhere—given how precious their charge was, I wouldn't doubt it—but I had no idea where to even start looking. My fingers tightened on the wooden edge of a bookshelf. I was going to have to do this the hard way, and I had run out of time to pull those two ends of my rope of thoughts together.

"Monica! How do you know where they went?" Talia bellowed after me, then added, "Fuck, that hurts. Stop making me yell, goddamn it!"

"I'm coming," I called. I took a last glance at the cavity to be sure I hadn't missed anything, then straightened my shoulders and pushed the bookcase closed again. Returning to the hallway, I found Talia struggling to stand.

"Stop that," I told her, putting a hand on her shoulder to push her down. "The sisters are on their way back. They'll call an ambulance for you. Tell them Phoenix took Methuselah to the Citadelle, and that, if they have any of their cocktails left, I might need help."

"They worked? The Molotov cocktails?"

I picked up the mittens I'd cast aside when I ran into the monastery. "Be glad they don't have plans to rule the world," I said. And then, to be sure that she'd heard and would remember, "Now, where am I going?"

"The Citadelle," she snapped. "I got knocked on the head, Monica. I'm fine, my memory is fine, and I do not like you going up there alone."

"Then it's a good thing you can't stop me, isn't it?"

I closed the door, leaving a gap large enough for fingers

so that the nuns could open it the way I had when they got here. Then I turned and jogged across the courtyard, the hollow sound of my footsteps following me to the street as I turned my thoughts to my looming confrontation with the Mages, and then inward to the confrontation with myself.

Methuselah had been right about something coming, I thought. Maybe he would be right about me using the stone.

He'd damned well better be right.

CHAPTER 34

I knew only one route to the Citadelle that wouldn't get me lost. Unfortunately, it was the long, round-about route that Sister Simonne had taken me on that first night we'd gone out together. Fortunately, it was easy to find the beginning of the route from pretty much anywhere in the old city, because the towering Château Frontenac marked its beginning.

*Un*fortunately, it might also mark my personal end, because somehow, I'd forgotten about its three hundred and ten stairs and kilometer of boardwalk. And, this time, I was going to have to run.

Freaking hell, I'd be lucky to still be upright when I got to the Citadelle, never mind in any shape to fight off Mages. Which meant that I should get my ass in gear, get there, and find Phoenix and Methuselah before the Mages did so that I wouldn't *need* to fight.

If only it wasn't one of those *easier said than done* moments.

I put a booted foot on the first step, pushed my already-lagging body into a jog, and began the climb.

I'd endured a lot in my sixty-nine years. I'd taken up martial arts when I was fifty, and because I'd never been one to do anything in half measures, I'd started with muay Thai—also called Thai boxing. Calling the sport challenging was like calling a pissed-off grizzly bear "cute" as it chased you up a mountain—especially when sparring matches often pitted me against someone half my age.

But none of it—not the sparring, not the conditioning, not even the endless, brutal drills that I'd put myself through—had held a candle to how I felt by the time I climbed the last few stairs to the top of the cliff. I collapsed in a heap of oxygen-deprived, quivering, jelly-for-muscles, unable to move, unable to breathe, unable to function in any way at all through the fog that had descended over my brain.

I'd finally done it, I thought in mild astonishment. This was not something the stone could fix in me. I'd pushed myself too far, and I was going to die. Here, in the cold, on the top of a hill. I was going to die, and the Mages were going to find Methuselah, and everything I'd done—everything the sisterhood had done—would be for nothing.

Deep inside me, a small, quiet voice began the familiar prayer. *Hail Mary Magdalene, full of grace,* it whispered, *come and sit with me.* My hand, trapped between my chest and the frozen grass I'd fallen on, twitched. The voice continued, *Hail Mary Magdalene, sister to us all, come and pray for—*

A sudden cramp seized my right calf, and I bolted upright with a yelp to rub madly at it. Sweet Mother of All, that hurt! I cast a baleful look up at the fog-shrouded sky. Well, that was certainly one way to answer a prayer and yard me out of my little pity party, I thought as the cramp eased and I took stock of myself. My lungs still heaved like bellows, but maybe I was in better shape than I'd thought.

I cautiously climbed up onto wobbly legs. The right one promptly caved beneath me, but I caught myself and locked my knees to keep myself upright. Or maybe I wasn't in better shape, but at least I wasn't going to die of exertion, which meant I still had a chance of getting to Methuselah and Phoenix before the Mages did.

Lifting my head, I stared through the dark toward the lights that marked the Citadelle's expansive, star-shaped furrows in the earth and the many, many buildings contained within.

As soon as I figured out where they'd gone.

I'd caught my breath by the time I reached the trench that marked the outer edge of the fortification, but my muscles were still depressingly jelly-like. More so as I contemplated the twenty-foot drop I was about to make down onto pavement. I'd done jumps before, when I'd practiced my rolls, but none like this. None at this age, or from this height onto the most unforgiving surface possible, and none when I already didn't trust my legs to be where I needed them to be when I landed—such as absorbing the impact under me.

If this didn't go well, it was going to hurt like hell. It wouldn't kill me, but it would hurt like hell.

I patted my pocket. "You might want to get ready," I muttered to the stone in it. "Just in case."

Then, marking the spot below that I was aiming for, I shook out my arms and legs, let myself go as limp as I could manage, and pushed off with both feet into the air. For a heartbeat, panic seized me and my entire body tensed. Then focus and training kicked in again, bringing controlled relaxation with them—just in time for me to hit the ground.

I'd been right. The pavement was unforgiving—and it hurt like hell.

My left ankle snapped beneath me, throwing off my balance and my intended diagonal roll. Without the forward momentum I needed, my shoulder hit harder than it should have, too, and I ended up sprawled like a broken pretzel, gasping for air as I stared up through tears of agony at a security camera on the back of the building.

Shit, I thought distantly. I hadn't thought to check for those.

Whether it was because it had heard my heads-up or it was just getting used to me, the stone had already begun to work its magick. By the time I wondered whether the cameras were monitored around the clock—you know, this being a working military installation and all—and how long it would take someone to see me on them and come to arrest me, webs had spread through my body to my injuries and begun their work.

It was a weird sensation, feeling myself being knitted back together again. Weird being the understatement of the millennium—and the stuff of future nightmares, I suspected. But I shoved those thoughts aside as I gingerly tested my limbs and found them somewhat functional. More or less.

Well, enough that I could climb to my feet—albeit still painfully—and begin a slow limp toward the end of the long stone building. Enough to carry me around it and continue supporting me when I stopped to gaze in dismay at what was nothing more than the long, wide continuation of the trench I'd dropped into—and the building that I followed. Both went on seemingly forever, and the wide openings that I could make out in the wall on my left didn't exactly fill me with hope, because now I was remembering Sister Simonne's description of the fortification … and the photo that Phoenix had tried to show me that day on Sister Bernadette's computer.

Especially the part about the enormous double trench surrounding it, and the one about the only way inside the main fortification being on the inside of both of those trenches and closed to entry after museum hours. Even if Phoenix and Methuselah hadn't been able to get into the fortification proper and remained in the trenches—so to speak—with me, my search would be daunting.

And if they had found a way inside—and between them, it was entirely possible—it would take forever.

CHAPTER 35

I was halfway through my search of the second trench when the sound of my name stopped me in my tracks. That, and a sudden heat in the pocket carrying the stone and a stirring of webs at my core. My attention zeroed in on the latter. Was that what I thought it was?

You have got to be kidding me, I silently told the stone. *Now? Really?*

But the stone was not kidding.

The webs crawled to my surface as the quiet rasp of Sister Margaret's voice came again from deep in the shadows to my left and a little behind me, where a burned-out bulb on the back of the long stone building left a hollow in the night.

"Monica."

I felt her waiting for me to turn, the sound of her breathing shallow and labored. I closed my eyes and curled my hands into fists at my sides. With ever every fiber of my being, I wished that I could just walk away from her, but the weight of the stone held me in place.

I released a long, slow breath and looked back the way I'd come.

Her form was surprisingly easy to pick out against the stone wall where she sat with her legs outstretched. Sister Margaret—no. Not Sister. Not anymore. She had lost that privilege when she betrayed us. She was just Margaret now, I reminded myself, and it was a wonder I hadn't tripped over her when I'd walked past, hugging the shadows and trying to stay away from the cameras.

Although the fact that no one had come looking for me

yet made me think they weren't being monitored after all. Which meant I could afford a moment to ask Margaret some questions.

I backtracked a few steps and stood over her. My hand crept into my pocket and my fingers curled around the smooth edges of the stone there, willing it to quiet. Whatever it wanted from the woman on the ground, I wasn't interested.

"Phoenix?" I asked her.

"Here somewhere," Margaret said. "With Methuselah. The Mages are tracking them, but I don't know which direction they went. They … didn't need me anymore."

My eyes had adjusted to the dimmer light, and I could make out her features now. The hollow eyes, the wrinkled, grayish skin stretched over too-sharp cheekbones, the utter emptiness of her expression. She looked as near dead as she had done when she had come to the porch of the Mary Magdalene House for Women, when she had come to give me the stone and begin all of this. I tried to scrape up some of the horror I'd felt then—or the sympathy. I felt neither. The spiderwebs uncurled and spread beneath my skin, reaching for the stone in my pocket.

My fingers tightened on it. *No*, I told it. *I won't. I can't.*

"There was never any shed, you know," Margaret murmured.

The sudden change in topic threw me for a moment. "What?"

"When I told you they'd held me in a shed and starved me to get the stone? That didn't happen." She leaned her head back against the wall and exhaled a whisper of a sigh. "I touched it, Monica. When I took the stone from the cocooned disciple, I touched it. It was … hungry."

All right, so maybe I felt a little horror. Holding back the webs that tried to crawl from me, I stared down at her.

"I fought it for as long as I could," she continued, "but I wasn't as strong as you. I knew it would kill me. I could feel it. And the Mages were following me everywhere, waiting. It didn't matter where I went, they always found me."

Ice trickled down my spine. "So you brought it to me."

"I couldn't let them have it. I had just enough good left in me to know that."

"But not enough to think about what it might do to me."

"The stone wanted—it needed—" Margaret broke off and shook her head. "I did what I thought was best. It needed a keeper, and you had always been the strongest of us."

"I was never one of you at all," I reminded her in a low growl.

Paper-dry lips pulled back in a grimace that might or might not have been a smile. "And if you had known of our existence? If we had asked you to join us?"

Touché.

But I'd be damned if I'd give her the satisfaction of being right.

"And then?" I demanded. "What happened to you then, Margaret?"

Thin, frail shoulders shrugged. "And then I had nothing left in me. No good, no bad, only ..." She trailed off, frowning a little, then finished, "Only what remains where there is no light anymore. Except I didn't die. The Mages found me and kept me alive. They gave me a choice. They promised me that if I joined them, they would kill me once I'd found Methuselah for them."

"And if you didn't help them?"

"Nothingness is an awful thing," she whispered. "And it's an awful, awful place in which to exist."

Whatever she'd hoped to get from me by telling me

what she had, I couldn't give it. I had no forgiveness in me, no understanding, no words. What I did have was a growing sense of terror about my own fate, now that I was so thoroughly, irrevocably intertwined with the stone. But in this moment, I still controlled the role I played in that connection, and I had no time to dwell on—or panic about—what might or might not happen.

I had a frightened young woman and an unpredictable, potentially lethal old man to find before the Mages got to them first.

Against the wall, Margaret coughed weakly. "She's smart, your Phoenix. Sister Colette was right about the attack on the cathedral. It was a distraction to get you away from Methuselah. Talia was supposed to go with you, and I was supposed to stay at the monastery and let the Mages in to take him. But Phoenix guessed what I was, and she took Methuselah and ran, and I had no choice but to take care of Talia. Then the Mages arrived, and—"

"No," I said, my voice harsh. "The Mages didn't arrive. You went to them. We saw you near the gate beside the cathedral. *You went to them*, Margaret."

"I had no choice," she repeated, her voice quavering as bony fingers touched the wrist of the hand in which I held the stone.

I looked down at what remained of the woman I'd called sister, and at the gossamer-fine filaments creeping from my skin onto hers. I hesitated, knowing full well what it was doing, and what it wanted. I could stop it, I reminded myself. I still had time to walk away, to choose not to do this. I could choose to turn my back on her and—

"I'm sorry," she whispered. "Please."

Her plea, together with the whispered apology, was like a lance through my heart, and in a sudden moment of clarity, I saw the stone—the webs and what they did—as an act of mercy rather than retribution. I didn't want what the stone wanted, I reminded myself, and that changed things.

Lowering myself to the ground beside Margaret, I slid an arm around her shoulders. Yes, I could choose to turn my back, but leaving her to die alone, slowly and painfully, would be the coward's way. The dark way of the Mages. The stone might be devouring me, too, but it hadn't succeeded. Not yet.

In her final moments of good, the nun had come to me.

In the final days of mine, I would be here for her.

And then—

My thoughts tripped and fell over themselves. Wait. Her final moments of good … those had been then, not now. Now, she'd chosen the side of the Mages. She'd helped the Mages track us, plotted with them, helped them find Methuselah and Phoenix, and then—

The shell of Margaret laughed, a dry whisper of sound. "Too late," she murmured. "You're too late."

The flash of insight was almost blinding. Because no, she hadn't apologized. She had delayed me so that I couldn't get to Phoenix in time. And she'd lied about not knowing which way they'd gone. I practically threw her from me as I vaulted to my feet and began tearing at the webs binding us together—webs that had begun to cocoon her and drain the last of the life from her. She didn't deserve a quick end; she deserved to suffer for as long as it took.

Because fuck good. Fuck it to hell and back. I had an alien to find.

And Phoenix.

Chapter 36

I heard the commotion before I saw it. Then, when I burst out of the tunnel through the fortification's inner wall and *did* see it, it took me several precious seconds to make sense of it. I staggered to a halt and gaped at the battle raging before me.

At the purple and blue fireballs being lobbed—in opposite directions—by a dozen Mages on either side of the wide-open space that was the Citadelle's heart. At the goliath screaming at their center as it warded off the purple ones and advanced toward those conjuring them. My poor brain glitched at the scene, then glitched again at the implications.

Mages … at war with one another?

It really shouldn't have surprised me, given human history in general. Power inevitably wanted to be absolute, and it would have been more shocking if there *hadn't* been jockeying among the Mages. I'd just been so busy avoiding them in general that I hadn't stopped to consider the idea. Or what the consequences of such a struggle might be, where Methuselah and the stones were concerned. And I sure as hell didn't have time to ponder it now.

A movement to the right caught my eye. I turned toward it, then blinked and did a double take as I saw another dozen figures, these ones belonging to T-shirt clad, seemingly ordinary men who had formed a ring around a tall, fedora-topped figure and a second, shorter one with a shock of unmistakable pink hair. My heart skipped a beat, then two, then leapt into my throat.

Phoenix and Methuselah. They'd been captured. But—

My gaze flitted back to the fireball battle. The goliath was almost upon the Mages summoning the purple magick, and those with the blue were following in its tracks. But if those were the Mages, then who was holding Phoenix and Meth—

I turned back to the ring of half-dressed men, saw that one was actually a woman, and noted their weaponry. Their entirely inadequate weaponry. Two of the men brandished hockey sticks, the woman held what looked like a fireplace poker, and I caught glints of metal held in the others' hands—glints that hinted at knives.

I inhaled a sharp, quick breath. These weren't Mages at all. They were soldiers—the Van Doos—and Mother of All bless their heroic hearts and good intentions, they'd put themselves right in the middle of a magickal war.

Armed with what amounted to pea-shooters.

A shriek of agony pierced the general chaos, and I looked back to the battle in time to see a Mage go up in blue flames. The goliath responded with a roar that vibrated through the pavement at my feet and the building at my back, and the remaining purple-fire Mages fell back, leaving their companion screaming in a pillar of amethyst so bright that I had to shield my eyes. My heart plummeted. If their battle was ending, Phoenix, Methuselah, and the Van Doos would be next on their radar.

Ice crept through my veins, following in the path of the webs that had already spread through me, and my right hand clenched around the stone it held. It had taken me less than a minute to get here after I'd left Sis—Margaret, but I'd managed in that time to convince myself that Methuselah was right, that I *could* tap into the stone's power. I still believed that … probably … where *one* Mage was concerned.

Maybe even two.

Ahead of me, the purple-fire Mages turned tail and ran.

But multiple?

One of the blue-fire Mages bellowed words I couldn't make out through the pounding in my ears, and the goliath lumbered off in pursuit of those that had fled. That left—I did a quick count to be sure—yup. Six.

I didn't stand a chance.

The attention of the remaining Mages turned first to the grim-faced Van Doos surrounding Phoenix and Methuselah, then homed in on me. In my hand, the stone's heat flared to life as if in response.

I didn't stand a chance, but I had no choice but to try.

THE CHAOS BEFORE ME FADED AWAY, AS IF IT HAD MOVED TO the periphery of my mind. Sounds became muffled. Motion slowed. My focus narrowed to a pinpoint. I heard the breath entering my lungs and leaving again; the slow, certain beat of my heart; the muted rush of blood through my veins; the whisper of spiderwebs weaving them all together.

Turning my head to the right, I looked past the Van Doos standing shoulder to shoulder at Phoenix and Methuselah in their center. My gaze lingered for a brief, anguished moment on hers—frightened and so, so brave—before moving on to his. The galaxies were in his eyes again. I couldn't see them across the distance or in the dark, but I could *see* them. Their beauty, their infiniteness, their emptiness.

A distant part of me wondered if he would step in to

save me, to save us, but even as my mind posed the question, it answered it, too. He would not ... because he could not.

"I've become dangerous, haven't I?"

"Yes. I think you might have."

And then a sphere of blue smashed into my shoulder, making me stagger and setting my coat alight. I reached up with my stone-holding hand and snuffed out the flames, then knelt and placed the same hand on the ground. The stone's rage and my darkness meshed, melded, and surged outward. The two Mages coming toward me split away from one another. I chose the nearest as my first target.

The stone did everything that it was supposed to. Everything it could. Silver strands writhed away from it—from me—and across the pavement to wrap around the Mage as his fingers danced in another summoning of fire. He cried out as the webs wrapped around his ankles and began to encase his legs. Screamed as they climbed his body and forced themselves beneath his skin. Shrieked as the heat from my core turned to a fire that blasted outward from me and engulfed him. And then he fell silent, just in time for me to hear Phoenix cry my name.

Heavily, ponderously, I turned my head toward her, fighting the webs woven through me so densely that it felt like my joints had turned to concrete. The four blue Mages that weren't coming for me were going for the Van Doos. They weren't using their magick, presumably because they didn't want to chance damaging their prize at the center of the soldiers' circle, but they had weapons of another kind. A more real kind.

A kind that were a lot bigger than what the Van Doos had.

Swords? My brain, already glitchy with the goings-on, damned near gave up at that point. But another blue fireball splatted on the pavement in front of my face, sending a wash of flames toward me and galvanizing me back into action. I threw my free arm over my head to protect myself —my other was still glued to the ground by the stone and its webs.

The stone.

Oh sweet Mother of All, the stone.

It had taken over completely, now. Silver filaments crisscrossed my vision beneath my eyelids, searing with a heat that writhed through me and around me and *in* me until I wanted to shriek as the Mage had done. Panic filled my chest and clogged my throat. I was losing myself to it, I thought. It had turned on me as it had done to the others it had bound with, and it was devouring me. Devouring my darkness. Devouring me.

Deep, deep in my brain, a memory stirred.

"It likes your darkness," Methuselah's voice whispered. *"You know how to feed it."*

But I don't, my mind whispered back. *I don't know how.*

"You let it in," he reminded me, *"but you don't let it have all of you. You're still there, too. The others gave up too fast because they were frightened, and then it ran out of darkness to eat. You're not frightened."*

He was wrong. I was terrified. And I was losing.

"There is darkness in all of us, Sister Monica," Sister Bernadette's gentle voice chimed in. *"The stone did not bind to you because of that, but it can and will amplify that darkness, if you let it."*

I began to burn from the inside out, flames licking along the webs. It was too late to stop it. I was too late. With a soft, sad whimper of defeat, I began to slide beneath the surface of death. *Hail Mary Magdalene, full of grace, come and sit with me ...*

Yet another voice interrupted my final prayer and dragged me upward again. *"Don't let it win,"* urged Talia.

A tiny annoyance shafted through me. So many voices. So many memories. A choking half-sob, half-giggle tried to burble out of me. It was like a fucking cheering squad had taken up residence in my brain, and I couldn't even die in—

Cold clarity exploded through me. Those weren't just memories. Those were the voices of the people I needed to protect. People who counted on me. Who *still* counted on me. I couldn't die, because if I did, then they would die, too—and if the Obsidian Sisterhood was right about the stones and Methuselah, the entire world would follow suit.

"There is darkness in all of us."

"... don't let it have all of you."

"Sister Monica!"

Another voice, but this time, it was a scream, and it belonged to Phoenix. Real and immediate, it pierced the veil of webs that separated me from the now, from the good that I thought I'd left behind with Margaret. From me.

I sucked in a lungful of air and, only half-aware of the excruciating pain that accompanied the action, peeled my face off the pavement that it had been glued to by the stone's webs. The heat coursing through me surged for an instant, then subsided to only somewhat agonizing, as inch by arduous inch, I pulled myself up to my hands and knees, and then to a crouch with only my right hand still on the ground.

My right hand ... and the stone.

And then I saw why Phoenix had screamed.

The Mages had fought their way through to the center of the Van Doos, and two of them had seized Methuselah's arms. They were trying to drag him away as the soldiers valiantly—and understandably—rallied around Phoenix, who in turn tried to fight her way through them to the alien. All while the rotating blades of a helicopter—when in hell had *that* arrived?—in the far corner of the paved square sent wind and dust churning across the Citadelle's heart.

A little more of the web cleared from my mind—driven away by the adrenaline surging through me, no doubt—and my gaze darted over the unfolding chaos. My heart urged me to save Phoenix; my brain, to stop the Mages from getting Methuselah to the helicopter; the stone, to just succumb again to its webs and heat because I couldn't save both.

Grief and fury churned in my core. I'd never stood a chance. I saw that now. As powerful as the stone had made me, no matter how hard I fought to not let it devour me, it wasn't enough. *I* wasn't enough. Not alone. Not—

Over the shouts and the *whuppa whuppa* of the rotating helicopter blades came a new sound. Faint at first, then louder—and closer. And—

In the space of a heartbeat, I registered the sound as that of an engine, realized it was coming up behind me—quickly—and threw myself to one side as an ancient, battered van blasted through the tunnel, narrowly missing where I had just been. It skidded to a halt just short of the Van Doos and the Mages surrounding them, and I gaped as all of its doors flew open and the Ursulines—and was that *Louis*?—poured out of it.

Just like that, I was no longer alone.

CHAPTER 37

WHAT HAD BEEN JUST CHAOS BEFORE BECAME MAYHEM.

Before I could scrape myself off the ground for a second time, the first Molotov hit the pavement between the helicopter and the Mages towing the struggling Methuselah. A second landed between them and the two remaining Mages facing off against the Van Doos. Sheets of flame spread outwards from both, effectively cutting off the Methuselah pair, and with yelps of shock, they loosened their hold. Methuselah darted away, but as he ran through the flames, they caught the bottom edge of his long coat and set it on fire. Distantly, I heard Phoenix yell at him to roll on the ground, but he either didn't hear or was too panicked.

One of the figures darted away from the cluster at the front of the van and ran toward the alien—yup, that was my truck-driver friend Louis, all right—stripping off his jacket as he went. He tackled Methuselah, wrapping the jacket around him and carrying him to the ground with him in a tumble of arms and legs. I pulled my gaze away and turned to the rest of the fight being waged by the Ursulines.

Surprise had been on the nuns' side—and the Molotov cocktails had certainly helped with that—but the Mages were going to recover any second now, and then the women, as incredibly tough and brave as they were, would be in serious trou—

My thought was cut short as, beside the van, Sister Bernadette's arm curved up and over her head in a graceful overhand throw, Sister Colette's unendingly impressive voice bellowed, "Incoming!" and without hesitation, a dozen well-trained Van Doos dived to the ground, taking Phoenix with them.

Sister Bernadette had a mean arm on her—and an accurate one. The Molotov she threw this time easily cleared the Van Doos and landed smack at the feet of the Mages that Methuselah had gotten away from. Shrieks and bellows blended together, echoing across the square and drowning out the sound of the helicopter's rotors as clothing caught fire and Mages began to burn. The Mages who stood over the Van Doos hesitated, then ran toward their colleagues, trying to beat out the flames with their hands. In the far corner, the *whuppa whuppa* of rotor blades increased in speed and intensity.

The Mages had hesitated. I did not.

Even in the dark and the chaos, it hadn't escaped my notice that one face had been missing from the Mage numbers, and I was pretty sure I knew where that face was. Not the kind to get his own hands dirty, Ronald Drummond was the one responsible for the helicopter. He'd watched from it, waiting for Methuselah to be delivered to him, and now that his plan was disintegrating, he was abandoning it and minions alike.

I raced up the short slope, past the Van Doos and Phoenix, and stopped just short of the burning Mages. Crouching, I slammed my hand to the ground with the stone between me and the pavement. Webs reached again for me, and this time, I reached back. I knew not to let it have all of my darkness, but I would let it have enough. Silver filaments snaked outward from my hand, racing untouched through the flames and across the paved square toward the helicopter. Mages pulled their burning compatriots out of the fire and rolled them on the ground. The webs ignored them. The helicopter lifted from the pavement. The webs spread faster.

They were almost there. They stretched upward, reaching for the helicopter's landing skid. I felt their brush against it. Felt their retraction. Their resistance. I pushed, and they reached again, higher this time, seeking not a hold but a way past, a way through. Understanding dawned. The helicopter held no darkness and therefore nothing the stone could feed from—it, like me, wanted what the machine contained. We wanted Drummond.

And we were too late.

Once I'd felt the stone's irritation. Now, as I watched the helicopter lights rise higher into the night sky and then skew away, out over the river, I felt its fury. It took everything I possessed to hold myself away from the vortex that wanted to swallow me, but I did it. I held fast, held center, held me. Slowly, the stone's filaments retracted. Slowly, the heat that had accompanied them subsided.

WE WERE A RAGGED BUNCH AS WE GATHERED BESIDE THE van. Methuselah, with his long coat singed along the bottom and his fedora in need of reshaping—and the galaxies gone from his eyes; the Ursuline nuns gathered protectively around him as they fussed and clucked like a little brood of hens over a chick; Louis, his jacket back on and his chest puffed with pride as he beamed from ear to ear at me; and Phoenix, with her pink hair askew and one tearstained cheek scraped raw from when the soldiers had thrown her to the ground—and her eyes brimming with tears and more emotions than I could sort through.

More than the stone knew how to handle. I lifted the bottom of my coat, slipped the black square back into my jeans pocket, and let the coat drop back into place as one of the Van Doos separated from the others and advanced on us. His hands were clenched into fists at his sides, challenge underlined every forceful thud of boot against pavement, and ferocity was etched in the set of his shoulders and the scowl on his brow.

I didn't blame him for any of it.

"What in the actual—" he began, but his snarl was interrupted by a wizened hand on his arm as Sister Colette patted his bare, tattooed forearm—like the other soldiers, he wore a T-shirt and no coat—and beamed a gentle, beatific smile up at him.

"All in good time," she told him. "Wait your turn."

The soldier's mouth flapped soundlessly a few times as he appeared to struggle with—well, with everything, I supposed. With the mild censure coming from the old nun bent over a walker, who had nonetheless just pitched one of several Molotov cocktails into his fortification.

With the people she'd been aiming at, who had been throwing purple and blue fireballs at one another and then attacked his soldiers with swords.

With the mountain of a monster that had run off into the night after the ones who had fled.

I didn't even know where to begin explaining what he and his regiment had just witnessed. I didn't think I could. And so I focused on doing the next best thing—no, the very best thing.

The Van Doos had corralled the injured, beaten Mages and sat them in a row over which they stood watchful guard. Four of the original half-dozen purples that I'd counted when I arrived were in the row. The two who had caught fire lay to the side, unmoving casualties of the war they'd chosen to fight. I turned my back on all of them and pulled the tearstained Phoenix into my arms for a long, fierce hug.

"Thank you," I whispered in her ear. "Thank you for looking after Methuselah for me. For keeping him safe. You're an incredible young woman, Phoenix Rasmussen."

The young woman giggled tearfully against my shoulder. "I don't think you've ever called me by my full name," she said. "It's a good thing, right?"

"A very good thing." Reluctantly, and only because I had so many others to thank, I put her away from me with a promise to talk later, especially about …

"Her?" Phoenix's tone turned hard and bitter.

"Yes." I nodded. "Her."

Phoenix went to stand by Methuselah as I turned to the nuns next, hugging each of them in turn as I voiced my gratitude.

"We are the sisterhood, *ma belle*," Sister Bernadette reminded me with a little shrug when I got to her. "It is what we do."

It was Louis's turn, next. I stood in front of him, still not quite believing my eyes as I shrugged and spread my hands wide. "How?" I asked, looking to the nuns for an explanation.

"We couldn't get the car from where we'd parked it," Sister Simonne said. "Louis and his wife were in the city for the *Marché de Noël*, and he recognized us as *les Ursulines*. He stopped us to ask if you'd found us, and he offered us a ride back to the monastery when he heard about our car. Then he insisted on bringing us here when we found out where you'd gone."

"*Merci*," I told the beaming truck driver. My pronunciation still made it sound like *mercy*. It was still accurate.

Louis wrapped me in a bear hug that squeezed every

ounce of air from my body, but I didn't object. I just waited until his hold loosened and then inhaled deeply the scent that reminded me of the jacket he'd given me when he'd picked me up that night in Charny. The scent of kindness.

The trucker released me and launched into rapid-fire French. But before I could ask anyone to translate, a voice came from over by the Mages.

"Um, sarge?" it asked.

The soldier that Sister Colette had been holding back from asking questions looked over his shoulder. "Lachance?" he acknowledged.

"We were wondering ... did we just have our asses saved by a bunch of old ladies? With Molotov cocktails?"

A ripple of laughter went through the Van Doos, and even their sergeant's tightly compressed lips tilted a little at one corner as his gaze traveled our company.

"*Oui*, Lachance," he said. "I believe we did."

Sister Colette gave the forearm she'd been holding a comforting pat. "No one will hear it from us, *sergent*," she assured him, giving his title the French pronunciation. "What happens in the Citadelle stays in the Citadelle."

"Then how," he asked, pointing at the Mages sitting under the watchful eye of his soldiers, "do you suggest we explain them?"

Sister Lise snorted at my side. "*I* have a suggestion for how we *don't* have to explain," she muttered, pushing her glasses up on her nose. Sister Simonne shushed her, and she shrugged. "Well, it *would* save a lot of trouble."

She had a point. But when she looked at me for support, I shook my head too, and she heaved a disappointed sigh that made me raise my eyebrows. I was really beginning to wonder about the back stories of these Ursuline nuns with their self-igniting Molotov cocktails.

"Have it your way," she said. "But the sergeant is right. We'll need a story."

"Yes," agreed Sister Bernadette, "but not one that involves … well." She nodded at Phoenix and the somewhat scorched Methuselah in turn before her gaze settled on me. "Perhaps it would be best that you go back to the monastery," she said, "and leave us to—"

"What the *fuck!*" came a shout from over by the kneeling Mages.

As one, we whirled toward it in time to see a ribbon of light split the darkness horizontally, then expand to spit out the goliath. The soldiers scuttled backwards a few steps, then held their ground with makeshift weapons raised as the mountain tipped its head back and screamed into the night.

"Orders, sir!" one of men shouted over his shoulder.

I put a hasty hand on the sergeant's wrist before he could speak. "Leave it," I said. "I think it's here for them."

"We can't just let it—"

I didn't prevaricate. "I have no idea what it is," I said, "but I know that it will kill you—all of you, and probably us, too—if you get in its way. And that"—I waved my hand at the Mages and monster—"that part of it isn't your fight."

The goliath screamed again as the sergeant hesitated. Then, as if knowing—or assuming—that no one would interfere, it stalked past the stunned soldiers, plucked the Mages both sitting and dead from the ground as if they were so many rag dolls, wrapped them in its massive arms, and stepped back again. The instant its body touched the undulating ribbon, the light expanded to swallow all of them, flared bright red, and then winked out of existence.

"*Câlice,*" muttered the sergeant in French. Then,

remembering who stood by his side, he began an immediate apology for swearing. "*Je m'ex*—"

"*Tabarnak*," Sister Colette agreed, nodding her head and seeming unaware of the soldier's shock at her own language.

"*Merde,*" added Sister Lise, and the sergeant surveyed the little group of nuns in utter consternation before giving his head a shake as if nothing more could surprise him tonight. His gaze returned to me.

"You're the ringleader?" he asked, indicating our company.

I wouldn't have put it quite like that, but—

"I will answer your questions," Sister Bernadette interceded firmly. "Sister Monica has dealt with enough today."

A long silence ensued as his gaze traveled her length from head to toe, then mine, then turned to the cluster of soldiers who stood waiting for orders now that their captives had, for all intents and purposes, gone poof. He issued a directive in French, and they turned as one well-trained unit and fanned out across the damaged square. Turning back to us, he shook his head.

"*Honnêtement*," he muttered, "I wouldn't know what to ask, and I don't think I'd believe the answers."

"Probably not," Sister Bernadette agreed.

Sister Colette batted her eyes up at him from behind their thick lenses, clinging still to his tattooed forearm. "So … we can go?"

"Are you sure you will be safe? They—whoever they were—won't come back?"

"They won't come back tonight," Sister Colette assured him. "And we're as safe as we have been for the last few millennia." She cackled at his nonplussed look, gave his arm a final pat, and trundled around the van with her walker, telling the others over her shoulder, "I call shotgun!"

Sisters Lise and Simonne trotted after her, voicing objections since she'd apparently had the honor on the way here, and Louis followed, grumbling in French at the lot of them as he climbed into the driver's seat.

I hesitated for a moment, feeling as if I ought to say something to the Van Doos sergeant but not knowing where to even begin as I watched the soldiers stamping out the remaining fires that dotted the melted, smoking pavement pockmarked with fireball craters. *Sorry we ruined your Citadelle* seemed … inadequate.

I settled on, "Thank you. For looking after Phoenix and —" From the corner of my eye, I caught a tiny shake of Sister Bernadette's head and caught back Methuselah's name in favor of the nickname I remembered the Ursulines had given him. "Matt," I finished. "Thank you for keeping them safe."

Intelligent, assessing gray eyes met mine. Again, I saw the questions piling up behind them. "You're welcome," the sergeant finally said. "And now, you should probably go. We called 911 when the attack started. I'm not sure why the cops aren't already here."

"*You* called 911?" Sister Bernadette asked before I could, both her eyebrows rising behind her wire frames. "But you're the army."

"With hockey sticks as weapons," he pointed out dryly. "When there is a disturbance, we do what all citizens do. We call the police."

"But you came out to help anyway."

"This is still our home, and your people needed help." He shrugged, then cocked his head to one side. "Sirens. You should not be here when they arrive."

No, we should not. We should be back at the

monastery, checking on Talia's whereabouts—although she'd damned well better be in hospital with that lump on her head—and patching up whoever else needed to be patched up. I looked around to find Phoenix and Methuselah, but they were already at the van with the others. Phoenix was climbing into the rearmost seat, and Methuselah, squashed fedora on his head, stood waiting beside the vehicle. Leaving Sister Bernadette to say a final goodbye to the sergeant, I went to join him.

"You know how to feed it," the alien said as I stopped in front of him.

I looked up into his clear, grown-up eyes. "Not entirely," I replied. "But I'm learning."

He took his hand from his coat pocket and settled the palm against the coat covering my chest, just below my collarbone on the left, as if assessing my heartbeat. Or perhaps my heart. I waited for his verdict.

He nodded satisfaction. "You're not afraid of it anymore."

I thought about it for a moment. About how I'd almost succumbed, certain that the darkness had been more than I was, that it had been too much. Certain that the stone had swallowed me.

I knew better, now. I knew that it would always *want* to swallow me, but that I could choose not to let it. Choose to accept the darkness it fed from as part, but not all, of me. Choose not to let it win.

"No," I agreed, placing my hand over his and pressing his fingers. "I'm not afraid of the darkness anymore. Or the stone."

"Good," he said, and for an instant, the galaxies were back in his gaze. "Because now we must find the others."

Also By

The Obsidian Sisterhood

A Web of Obsidian

The Crone Wars

Becoming Crone

A Gathering of Crones

Game of Crones

Crone Unleashed

Rise of the Crones

The Grigori Legacy

Sins of the Angels (Grigori Legacy book 1)

Sins of the Son (Grigori Legacy book 2)

Sins of the Lost (Grigori Legacy book 3)

Sins of the Warrior (Grigori Legacy book 4)

Other Books by Linda Poitevin

<u>The Ever After Romance Collection</u>

Gwynneth Ever After

Forever After

Forever Grace

Always and Forever

Abigail Always

Shadow of Doubt

ACKNOWLEDGMENTS

ACKNOWLEDGEMENTS

This was the book that I honestly thought might do me in. The fact that I finished (and that I'm still standing) is due in no small part to the many amazing people who stuck by me, supported me, and cheered me on. Special thanks to my husband, Pat, who kindly (and wisely) listened to me whine while refraining from reminding me (too often) that I'd been down similar hard roads before and survived, and to my bestest writing friend ever, Marie Bilodeau, who sent me regular "I believe in you" and "You've got this!" messages when I hit my lowest points.

Huge thanks to Laura Paquet for her always stellar copy-editing skills. She is the reason the timeline in this book makes sense, people are seated in their proper places around the table, and the river is flowing in the right direction. (Yes, seriously.)

Thanks as well to Cat of Your Beta Reader for her helpful suggestions for tightening up the story, to Erica Ball for a fantastic proofread, to Deranged Doctor Design for another outstanding cover, and to AuthorTree Services for once again handling the layout. The book is a much better version of itself because of the team I have behind me.

Gratitude also goes to my fabulous agent Sara Megibow, audio publisher Insatiable Press, and narrator Senn Annis for their combined efforts in making sure that Sister Monica is brought to life in audiobook form. I'm beyond delighted that her story has been made more accessible.

Special thanks to Danielle Rae for her graciousness in educating me about keeping Phoenix healthy and cared for. Details matter, and I am wiser for knowing them.

And last but far from least, a huge thank you to Major Adam P.F. Strachan of the Royal Canadian Air Force for his assistance in setting up a very special meeting for me at the Quebec Citadelle—and to the Royal 22e Régiment stationed there for taking the time to give me a tour and answer my many questions about the Van Doos. It was an honour and a privilege.

About the Author

Lydia M. Hawke is a pseudonym used by me, Linda Poitevin, for my urban fantasy books. Together, we are the author of books that range from supernatural suspense thrillers to contemporary romances and romantic suspense.

Originally from beautiful British Columbia, I moved to Canada's capital region of Ottawa-Gatineau more than thirty years ago with the love of my life. Which means I've been married most of my life now, and I've spent most of it here. Wow. Anyway, when I'm not plotting the world's downfall or next great love story, I'm also a wife, mom, grandma, friend, walker of a Giant Dog, keeper of many cats, and an avid gardener and food preserver. My next great ambition in life (other than writing the next book, of course) is to have an urban chicken coop. Yes, seriously... because chickens.

You can find me hanging out on Facebook at facebook.com/LydiaMHawke, and on my website at LydiaHawkeBooks.com, where you can also join my newsletter for updates on new books (and a free story!)

I love to hear from readers and can be reached at lydia@lydiahawkebooks.com. And yes, I answer all my emails!